5 Star Publications

3383 Donnell Drive

Forestville, MD 20747

ISBN -13: 978-0-9843881-0-3

ISBN-10: 0-9843881-0-9

Library of Congress Control Number: 2010931539

First Printing: July 2010

Printed in the United States

www.icon5star.com

www.tljbookstore.com

www.daughterofthegame.net

Raves for KAI
And
Daughter Of The Game

"Kai makes you feel like you are a part of the story. *Daughter of the Game* is hot-drenching with intriguing pages from beginning to end."

—AAMBC

"There is a lot to like about *Daughter of the Game*. Newcomer Kai makes her mark with an impressive debut."

—OOSA Online Book Club

"This may sound like your typical street-lit novel but it is anything but...this is one of those books that will have you on the edge of your seat, trying to figure out where the story is going. *Daughter of the Game* is chock full of lies, deceit, betrayal and murder. I was hard pressed to put this novel down...that is just how good this book is. I was drawn to the story and the characters right from the start. I absolutely loved this book and eagerly anticipate the sequel!"

—Leona, APOOO BookClub

"*Daughter of the Game* is an entertaining street tale with a unique twist by Kai. It is full of murder, mayhem and street alliances that will keep readers turning the pages."

—Radiah Hubbert, Urban Reviews

"I was so blown away by this classic street novel. I could not put this book down because it touched on so many issues. The love in this story was overwhelming! I strongly believe that even those that don't like street lit can and will relate with this classy tale of love."
—Tina Brooks McKinney, author of *All That Drama, Lawd, Mo' Drama, Fool Stop Trippin', Dubious* and *Deep Deception*

"*Daughter of the Game* is packed with action. Characters indulge in a game of survival and demonstrate where their loyalties lie."

—Rawsistaz Reviewers

"Sketching a powerful portrayal of enflamed love, life's obligations and the streets, *Daughter of the Game* is a captivating and thought provoking novel. Newcomer Kai delivers a breathtaking story in unique fashion."

—Elissa Gabrielle, author of *Whisper to a Scream*

"In *Daughter of the Game*, Kai explores an all too familiar, yet rarely written about, dynamic of the smart girl's seemingly innate attraction to the street guy. The theme of the story is an urban one, but the style of writing is far from your typical Street Lit novel. Kai's words paint a vivid picture and capture not only the actions and emotions, but also the very essence of the characters. Kai takes a story that is unique to a particular demographic and makes it appealing to the masses."

—Monica Marie Jones, M.S.W, Author of *Floss and Swag*

"Kai has a smooth writing style that draws you deeper into the story with every page. *Daughter of the Game* has all the trimmings for a classic."

—Shani Greene-Dowdell, Author of *Secrets of a Kept Woman*

"This author's blazing pen is so descriptive that your mind and body will react as though you're in the middle of every scene. *Daughter of the Game* left me thirsty for more."

—Linda R. Herman, Author of *Consequences*

"Contrary to popular belief, the literary truth has arrived. There's a new pen in town and her name is Kai! *Daughter of the Game* is a perfect demonstration of just how sweet her pen game is."

—Kaiyos, Author

"Which comes first...loyalty or love? In this never-ending page-turner, *Daughter of the Game* captures everything that comes between. Kai has created a masterpiece."

—Kellie, *Dzine by Kellie*

Dedication

My life has one absolute purpose, one clear manifestation of God's grace:

My children.

For each of you, I am eternally grateful.

Grateful for your presence, your joy, your curiosity, your innocence, your love.

Grateful for the many generations you embody;

Grateful for the future generations that, from you, will spring forth

For your very existence, I am humbly thankful.

May God keep you covered and immersed in Him.

Love, Mommy

Acknowledgements

LaQuita Adams, 5 Star Publications, I love you, sis. You were the first to read this manuscript, and you immediately understood the book. You believed in this project and in me way back then.

Sarah Stephens, The Agency, for seeing more than just "another book." After reading the draft, you encouraged me to write this story to completion. Your outline brought clarity to my vision. I can never thank you enough.

Ann B. Wilson, even when the world seems so empty, I know that you are still there, reaching out a hand to hold me up. How can one understand mommy hood until they have lived it? I finally see. For your unbending hand and your unyielding principles, I thank you. You held me apart and shielded me from the world, which allowed me to be uniquely who I am. I love you.

Gerald Moore, thank you for listening to countless ideas and making time for me to write in all of the chaos.

Ian Bush, I love you, man, more than you know. And, to say I am proud of the man you are would be a simple understatement.

Idris Bey, I will always believe in you and I know your dreams will manifest into bountiful blessings.

Alden Burno, thank you for placing *The Coldest Winter Ever* in my hands, countering my discovery of *Flyy Girl* with a classic of your own.

To my internet family of authors and book lovers, who poured upon me continuous love throughout the years. Special thanks to Yasmin Coleman, APOOO Bookclub, Tee C. Royal, Rawsistaz Book Club, Rawsistaz Reviewers, Ella D. Curry, Terry Howcott, Peron Long, blog readers, Myspace and Facebook friends. To Onika Pascal, your poetry and artistic eye are phenomenal.

PROLOGUE

Eight Months Ago

Monique ran scalding water over the plate, turning it slowly to cleanse the suds without splashing her hands. Her eyes scanned the kitchen to make sure it was spotless as she dried the plate and placed it on the shelf. Monique didn't want to give her mother, Miriam, any excuse to keep her in tonight.

"What are you doing?" Miriam's warm voice flooded the kitchen as she entered it.

"Just cleaning up." Monique glanced at the clock on the microwave. Her boyfriend Armand was coming, he would probably be there in the next hour. She never knew the exact time he was going to show up, but she didn't test his patience by keeping him waiting.

"Why?" Miriam moved to the refrigerator as Monique dried the sink. "You have plans tonight?"

"Not really." The lie slid easily from Monique's tongue; she enforced it with a shrug. The lies used to hurt; they used to feel forced and uncomfortable coming from her mouth. Monique used to feel guilty. But she had trained herself to lie, to force the necessary words into the air to gain what she needed. Now the guilt was a distant memory. She could lie without blinking. "Just grabbing a bite. Maybe a movie."

"Hmmm."

Monique could feel her mother's eyes on the side of her face, waiting for more. The wait was futile. Monique wasn't going to explain that Armand, her drug-dealing boyfriend who had dropped out of school two years earlier, was escorting her to the senior winter dance. She wasn't going to admit that he had refused to attend any school events prior to this, so his acquiescence was a major coup, a chance for Monique to shine on his arm.

She wasn't going to justify the money she had spent on her outfit, hair and nails, intent on looking her best to match Armand's mandatory swag, his natural sexy, and his inherent manliness. And under no circumstance was she going to explain that she had no plans on returning home tonight because come hell or high water, she was spending the night wrapped within Armand's arms and legs.

Monique glanced at the microwave again. She needed to get upstairs.

"Who are you going with?" Miriam folded her arms across her breasts.

"Me and Army gonna meet up with Michelle and 'em." The words tumbled out as Monique moved around her mother and put the broom and dustpan back in the closet.

"Me and Army? Michelle and 'em?" Miriam pursed her lips.

Monique forced a cough. Her mother was always correcting her. It got on her nerves.

"Army and I are going to meet with Michelle and Raymond."

"Really."

It wasn't a question, but a sure statement of doubt.

Monique pushed forward anyway. "If it gets too late, I'll just—"

"Let me guess—" The sarcasm in Miriam's voice was thick, her face contorted with anger. "—if it gets too late, you'll just go to your father's house, right? Interesting how Pete's place is always your easy cover."

Monique didn't answer. She wasn't getting choked up on that hook no matter how blatant the bait. Instead she folded the dish towels, wondering how long it would take before Miriam walked away in disgust. Miriam sighed and stood in front of her. Monique kept her head lowered, her eyes on the towels.

"I hope you never have a daughter as secretive as you, Monique. But you will. One day...you will see what it's like and you'll be sorry." Miriam's voice was quiet. She walked away.

The curse splashed across Monique's mind like hand sanitizer, a painless sting for a single moment before evaporating. That was easier than she had thought. The mounting tension between she and Miriam made her sad for a second. But only a second. Monique listened to Miriam climb the steps and counted Miriam's footsteps down the hall to the master bedroom. When the door slammed, Monique exhaled. She was free. Once Miriam slammed the door, she didn't come out. Her attempt to hurt by ignoring suited Monique just fine.

Monique threw the towels in the drawer and ran to her room, taking the stairs two at a time. She snatched her dress from the back of the closet and quickly changed. The expensive wraparound dress clung to her body, stopping just above her knee. Monique searched under her bed until she found the stiletto boots that looked perfect with the dress. She thumbed through her jewelry case and selected a set of dangling earrings with a matching looping necklace that accented her brown skin. Monique smiled, but as she clipped the tags from the dress, she realized something else: she was out of spending money.

An easy fix. Monique flipped open her phone and pressed Talk. Her brother Ricardo answered on the second ring.

"Just about to call you, man." Ricardo's voice sounded strained and distant.

Monique instantly forgot her money request, worry tapping its way into her heart. "What's wrong?"

"Nothing really. Why you callin'?"

"No reason." Another lie. But a white one, at least.

Ricardo was Pete's eldest son, and Ricardo made it his business to look out for Monique, despite the fact that they had different mothers.

"What, you need cash?"

"Naw." Monique pushed her jewelry aside and glanced into the deep bottom of the case. The stack of cash in there was sufficient to dip into. She normally put aside a quarter of everything she received. Her "just in case" money. Tonight qualified as "just in case." She didn't want to add to Ricardo's aggravation. "I'm good."

"You sure?"

"I am going to be at Daddy's tomorrow. I'll get something from you then."

"Listen, Mo ..." His words trailed off into silence.

She waited patiently, tucking the phone between the crook of her neck and her shoulder. Sometimes Ricardo needed a minute to organize his thoughts, to straighten out his words. It was a nervous thing, something she believed their life had cursed him with.

"Monty quit yesterday. It was kind of ugly." Ricardo said, his words slow and deliberate.

"What?" Monique shifted the phone to her other ear.

Monty had been with the family since she was born, Pete's right-hand man.

"Why?" This Monique had to hear.

"Power move. He wants more. He's trying to take more."

"Shit." Monique rarely spoke business with Ricardo or Pete, but she knew how to read between the lines. In Pete's line of work, a person didn't just quit. A person didn't just request a promotion. The price was always blood.

"You gonna be alright?" Now she understood the strain in his voice.

"Yeah, listen. I'm getting my peeps together now. You and your moms should lay low. You heard?"

"Uh-huh." Monique's mind began spinning. She wasn't missing another event over Pete's bullshit. The decision to ignore Ricardo was made in the split second it took for her to shift the phone back to her other ear. Besides, Monique and her mother were so far removed from Pete's life, unlike Ricardo and her sister Michelle, that she had nothing to fear. "Yeah. I'll be alright," Monique said.

"No, Mo." Ricardo recognized her quick dismissal. "You need to tone it down for a sec. Stay in tonight. Come by tomorrow so I can square you away. I don't want to hear no bullshit."

"Yeah yeah yeah, Ricardo. Damn! You sound more and more like Pete each day."

His silence pained her.

In that instant she regretted her words. Words couldn't be taken back, the person couldn't unhear them. Monique bit her lip and pressed out a sincere apology anyway. "I didn't mean that, Ricardo. I'm sorry."

"Don't sweat it, Mo." He took a deep breath. "Tomorrow."

"Love you," Monique forced out before he hung up.

***

Armand was two hours later than she had expected. She knew how this was going to play out. They weren't going to the dance. Tension rattled up and down her spine, her mind developing scenarios about where he was, what he was doing, who he was doing. She imagined him standing her up completely and the devastation she would feel. Instead she wrapped her mind in anger, blocking out the weak feeling of vulnerability.

Ten minutes later, when she started taking off her jewelry, her phone vibrated.

Armand.

"Mom, I'm gone," Monique said as she slid into her coat.

Miriam didn't answer. Monique knew she wouldn't.

Monique walked down the steps and out the side door.

Armand was waiting for her, standing in front of the door, his deep brown Italian leather blazer rested over a striking light brown dress shirt, jeans and leather Ferrogamos. Monique's anger disappeared along with Ricardo's warning.

"I know you're mad, ma." The words flowed smoothly from Armand's mouth, a smile playing around his lips.

Monique loved the sound of his voice. She didn't answer, looking him up and down, noting how handsome he was. She tried not to smile, tried to hold on to her anger. Monique turned her back to him to lock the door. Warmth rushed her body as Armand pressed himself into her frame, hugging her from behind. The moan that escaped her should have been embarrassing, but it wasn't. Monique couldn't help herself, not when it came to Armand.

"I didn't mean to stall you," he whispered and his breath tickled her ear. Armand planted his lips on the back of her neck.

Monique closed her eyes and allowed the current of his magnetism to drown her.

"You look good tonight," he said.

He is pouring it on tonight. She didn't mind. Armand was a man of few words, so she appreciated the ones she received. "So do you."

He gently turned her around and stared into her eyes. Monique loved the pressure of his hands on her hips, inside of her coat and groping the small of her back. He kissed the tip of her nose, then her lips.

Armand pulled back just as she reached up to kiss him back. "You ready?"

She bit her lip. "Always."

X

Armand smiled at her and his intensity caused Monique's stomach to flutter. They weren't going to the dance, but she didn't care. She dropped her keys in her purse and followed Armand, her hand in his.

***

Two hours later, they finally exited the car, steam covering the back windows, their perfect outfits rumpled. Monique ran her hand through her hair and shook her head. *This is wild*. It was unfathomable how she couldn't stop herself, how she gave in to Armand anytime, anywhere.

"Where are we?"

"Charlies." Armand pointed to the sign above the restaurant as he reached in the car for his coat.

She nodded, feeling awkward in the aftermath of their heat. Monique didn't know the area well and glanced around the dark street, noting that they were on Goodman Ave. *Southeast side*. She had only been over here to go to basketball games at East High and then she always had a handful of girlfriends with her. This wasn't her side of town and something about it felt wrong. Armand wrapped an arm around her as they walked into the diner. When they entered, he nodded to a waitress, who greeted them and led Monique to a table in front of the huge picture window.

Armand placed his coat on the chair. "I'll be right back."

Monique nodded. She took in the humble restaurant. It was quaint but clean. Still, they were overdressed for a place like this and, after causing her to miss the dance, Armand should have taken her somewhere better. Monique watched him move through the restaurant, ease past the wait staff and walk into the kitchen. She had played herself.

Monique thought about her mother, about the disappointment that would flood Miriam's eyes if she knew her honor roll daughter was sexin' in someone's back seat. Shame swirled through Monique's mind. Since she was acting like a ho, wouldn't Armand start to treat her like one? Wasn't he already? Coming to her house late, sexing her in the car and bringing her here to eat, weren't those all the signs of disinterest setting in? She was already descending from wifey status to mere trick.

Monique stared out of the window into the cold night, her mind chewing on disappointment like a farm boy gnawing on a twig.

It took a moment before she noticed the figure walking directly toward her. His eyes were locked on her. He was a gauntly thin man whose desperation streamed from him like a trail of dust. His dark skin blurred with the night, making his large eyes seem wide and disembodied. He smiled as if he knew her. Monique could see his teeth against the dark night. Monique squinted; she didn't recognize him. The sneer on the man's face sent a spark of fear through her, which caused her to remember Ricardo, Pete, Monty, and the brewing street war. *Monty sent a hit man after me!*

Monique's body began moving before her senses could fall into place. The man's arm reached deep inside of his coat. Monique felt herself sliding backward. She forced her chair from the table. He stopped walking and gripped a flat, black object in his hand, which he pointed directly at the window. Her arm knocked over her glass and her heels slipped on the wooden floor as she screamed, scrambling away from the window.

Armand came out of nowhere. He was a few steps away from her, coming toward her with a look of complete confusion on his face. Armand reached for Monique, but she felt like she wasn't moving, like each step was taking a lifetime to complete. She felt helpless as she tried to propel her body forward.

Armand's eyes left hers and looked beyond her as the first bullet ripped through the picture window.

"Oh shit!" A waitress shrieked; the other handful of customers hit the floor.

Monique continued to run forward.

"Get down." Armand snatched her arm as she ran. He pulled her across his body and lowered her to the floor with one hand while his other hand reached under his dress shirt for his fire power. More dull sounds of bullets reached Monique's ears, but this time the glass shattered.

Armand fired. The gaunt man kept firing back. Random bullets poked holes in the diner. The phone on Monique's hip vibrated violently. Armand walked forward—unafraid—firing into the night.

His aim was more accurate. Within seconds the hit man lay flat on his back, his body riddled with bullets.

"Get up." Armand's voice was quiet and controlled. He lifted Monique, shoved their coats and her purse in her arms, and moved them quickly to his Lexus.

Armand was dead silent. She waited for shouting, questioning, some type of emotion. Instead his eyes remained steady, his lips clamped together, fury oozing from him like smoke.

"Mo, you gotta drive."

"What?"

He pulled the car over and stopped so fast that Monique bumped her head on the dashboard. Armand didn't seem to notice, perspiration lined his face as he pressed his clenched fist into the side of his thigh. "You drive."

She looked down at his leg and saw the blood for the first time. *Oh no, he's hit!* She swallowed the urge to scream. *How can this be happening?* "Where?" Tears flowed down her face.

"Over off of East Ave," he spoke through gritted teeth. "Just take Atlantic. You know how to get to there from here, right?"

She didn't answer. She had never driven on the southeast side; she hadn't even known there was a street named Atlantic. Armand called people on his cell phone and whispered directions at her as she sped across the city. She realized, listening to his broken conversations, that Armand assumed the gunman had been after him. She didn't correct him.

Ten minutes later, Monique sat in the doctor's basement, listening to Armand scream. *What if he dies because of me?*

"Mo, what happened?" Raymond, Armand's best friend, stood in front of her with his cousin Dut by his side.

She shrugged. She hadn't seen them come in.

"Who was it? Did you see anybody?"

Monique stared at Raymond. She wondered how he would react to the truth. Would he shoot her on the spot?

"I don't know. Just a man with a gun—"

"Yo, these south east bitches is playin' with me, son!" Raymond punched the air with his fist. "I'm about to clap at these fuckers right now, ya heard?"

Dut stared at Monique. She looked at the floor.

"Just wait, Ray. We don't even know who we going at." Dut bent over, his face directly in front of Monique. He was close enough to head-butt her and the expression on his face was ugly. "Cutie, you got to snap out of it and tell us something. Real talk."

Dut would do her harm. He seemed like the type to hurt a woman, just because. Armand wasn't there to protect her. She stuttered out the story just as it had happened. But she left out three vital facts: the shooter was a professional, not a street gunner on a mission; her father was Pete Waters, the underground gateway to Rochester's vice; and the hit man was specifically sent to eliminate her, Monique Waters, the daughter of the game.

Chapter One

Here and Now

The long, sheer curtains bloomed around the window as a breeze twirled through the open space. Armand smiled to himself as he lay flat on his back. He hoped the night breeze would seep through the open window and cool his damp skin. Monique didn't have him completely turned out. He would never let that happen, but he damn sure felt addicted.

He didn't spend much time in this high-end penthouse. The hustle kept him on the streets submerged in the pulse of the city and the struggle of the dope game. But this was the space he brought Monique to when he could separate himself from the underbelly of life and enjoy some of the benefits of his never-ending struggle.

This home was just a stepping stone, but it was also a reminder of how far he had come and how much he had already achieved. It was a hell of a lot more than the bedroom he had shared with his sister and mother in his grandmother's house most of his childhood. Just the thought of his family made his stomach knot, the pain swept upon him so quickly that it felt as though he had been punched. He shook his head to clear his mind, forcing his thoughts back to the present, to his wonderful penthouse, to his exhausted body and the lovely woman laying naked next to him.

Armand stared at the brass ceiling fan directly over the bed; its three blades resembled huge elephant ears. Neither he nor Monique had the energy to climb out of bed and turn the fan on.

Not yet.

Monique lay flat on her stomach with her head buried in a pillow. Armand glanced at the beads of perspiration trailing down her smooth back, leading a trail of moisture to her perfect behind. Armand

1

wanted to touch her. He wanted to lightly trace his fingers along the curves of her body and then firmly grip her mounds with both hands. He wanted to squeeze the back of her thighs as he slowly entered her. He wanted to let her never-ending tightness wrap itself around his center of mass.

But he didn't.

He wasn't ready to wake her up yet. Armand shifted in the bed, turning on his side so that he could study her face and take time to absorb every inch of her while she wasn't awake or aware of him. Monique was beautiful. Her raw sensuality surprised him whenever he took time to notice it; and sometimes, like tonight, it made him wonder about her.

Armand knew he had been her first lover over a year ago. Monique had been so tight that it took him forever to work his full girth into her. His groin was sore the next day. And she had been so nervous that he almost stopped, taken back by the quiet tears that slid from the corners of her eyes. Armand hadn't wanted to be the one to turn her out, to turn her on to sexing and then watch her play herself, giving her body to anyone who claimed love. It had happened before and with more than one. Monique said she wanted it, though, and made it clear that she wanted him. That night he had talked and kissed and rubbed her through the pain, gently rocking her into womanhood.

Now Monique was the one stroking out the loving and falling asleep while he lay awake thinking, desiring, craving for more. He couldn't get enough of her. Even now, moments after being submerged in her deepest pool, all he could think about was hitting it again. Getting one more taste, another touch, another deep thrust into her everlasting snug.

Damn.

Armand found Monique to be hypnotizing. She was simple in design, perfect in creation. He loved her round eyes, her full lips, and the sudden dimples that appeared when she smiled.

Monique sighed. Her deep breathing was temporarily interrupted by an angelic moan. Her thick, black hair was pushed back, wildly tumbling past her ear as wisps clung to her wet neck. She had made love to him in thick waves, her singular focus taking him past ecstasy in overlapping pleasure. Armand couldn't believe the depths he experienced with Monique, it was new to him—all of it. Love and continuous lovemaking were things he had never had time for before.

Apparently, Monique had never heard of straight fucking because every encounter with her was deep, quietly sensual, and dangerously erotic. Maybe it was too deep. Maybe he needed time to push back from it in order to save himself before he drowned, before his only fulfillment came from sucking on Monique's fullness.

Armand closed his eyes, exhaled, and focused on getting a grip. He needed to man up. They had been sexing, locked away from the world, for the past two days. He was losing his footing. The truth was that Monique's ass was far from perfect. First of all, she was too damn young. They were only a few years apart in age but miles apart in maturity. He had dropped out of school years ago and paved his way through the dense concrete forest, clearing out a green-lined path in the deceptive urban jungle. Monique had just graduated high school and finished some summer school college courses. Her life was about school, books, and spending her mother's money.

Second, she didn't know anything about the streets. She didn't know anyone in that life and couldn't possibly understand the long hours of hustle and crime, of dirt and filth, of life and death. Hell, between her school teacher mother and her neosoul-looking sister, life was simply an obstacle course of academics, social events, fundraisers, and Sunday morning sermons.

That was the reason he had wanted her; it was also the reason he tried to keep her separate from his life. He loved her sincerity and her immature ignorance. But she wasn't ready for what a life with him really meant. She didn't know anything real about him, nothing more than he allowed her to put together. The streets were the streets, and she knew he was in them. That was it. What more could she know about it than New Jack City hype and Tupac poeticism?

How would Monique react if she knew what it really meant to shed blood, sell demon dreams, and establish urban territory? Everyone who lived in the inner city thought they knew the struggle. They assumed that a city address alone gave them some type of hood credibility. Just pretenders. They all believed that seeing a fiend hustling on the corner, begging for a dollar, or stealing from his

3

mother somehow included them in the circle of urban ills. Monique was no different. She played ghetto girl now and then. Her tongue spilt raw rhetoric as she expressed anger when announcing that she wasn't scared of a fight, and when demonstrating her flavor with the requisite eye rolling and teeth sucking.

But that was all bullshit.

That wasn't the game. That wasn't the truth. It wasn't the deep layers of hell into which Armand sometimes had to reach into in order to pull out the cash. And the play-acting of inner-city glory didn't stick the pretenders with the feeling of filth. It didn't leave their souls weighted down and confused until they eventually became deadened to any sensitivity. Like he sometimes felt, especially when he was alone, when Monique wasn't there to jumpstart his emotion by infusing him with excitement where he had previously felt blank, when she wasn't pouring upon him unconditional love just when he had begun to believe himself a fucking monster.

That's why he needed her. Armand needed the lifeline her love extended him. But he also needed to keep her separate, to keep his mind clear and alert. Armand had seen the right women take down the most impenetrable men, and he wouldn't let that happen to him. He could feel for her but keep her distant. He didn't have a choice, his life depended on it.

"Baby."

Armand almost didn't hear her soft whisper muffled by the pillow. Monique turned toward him with her eyes still closed but her breathing light. She was definitely awake. He hadn't been hearing things.

"Yeah." Armand glanced around the foot of the bed for the sheet as a breeze swept across them. "Are you cold?"

Her soulful eyes cracked open and the corners of them slanted as a smile brightened her face. "No, I'm not cold. Are you?"

"No."

Monique slid her leg between his and shifted closer to him as she buried her head in his chest.

"See, you tryin' to start something," Armand said.

"Why not?"

"'Cause, you should have had enough."

Monique laughed and took the challenge just like he knew she would. She moved in closer and pressed her hips flat against him as she rubbed her fingertips across his chest. She softly planted her lips against his neck.

To Armand this shit was also dangerous. Monique was no longer the scared virgin, and her sexual curiosity made him wonder just how far she was willing to go. She obviously found power in their lovemaking and faced each hard-on like it was a personal challenge that she had to conquer. Sometimes he played along, letting her continue to outdo herself, and enjoying the euphoria her curiosity had caused. He would be damned if he let her have control over him in any way, definitely not sexually.

Armand's thoughts faded as Monique's tongue traced a slow trail up the length of his neck to his chin. She bit his chin softly, her hand moving to grip his wide shoulder blade.

"Monique."

"Yeah?"

"I'm thirsty." Armand wanted her to back up. He needed to separate from her for a little while, to start to prepare himself for the day and his reemergence to the streets in a few hours.

Monique bit his chin again and nibbled on his bottom lip.

"I got you," she said.

She slowly extracted herself from his warm body. Monique crawled over him, making her motions exaggerated for his attention. She smiled but Armand's facial expression didn't change. He simply watched her.

"What's wrong?" Monique sat at the edge of the bed before sliding down onto the plush carpet.

He didn't answer.

"Why you look at me like that?"

"Like what?"

"That cold look. Why are you looking like that?"

"How long you gonna take?"

"What?"

"I said I'm thirsty. You playin', crawlin' around and taking your time."

"Are you serious?" Monique studied Armand's face. "Why are you tripping?"

"I'm just saying." Armand purposely kept his facial expression blank. He knew she hated that and would react to it.

"Damn, Army." Monique placed her hands on her wide hips and narrowed her eyes.

Armand fought the urge to glance down at her shapely torso.

"Why you got to fuck up a perfectly good night?"

"You the one still standing here."

"Really?" Monique nodded her head and turned on her heels. "Well I got a solution for that." She headed for the bathroom.

Armand guessed he wasn't getting anything to drink. "Oh what, now you gonna leave?" He sat up, propping himself up on his elbows.

They had been here before.

"See, your spoiled ass is too sensitive. Want to play games and then get mad when you get called on that shit."

"Really?" Monique's voice rose as she called out from the bathroom. "Now you judging? I got to be a spoiled ass whenever you want something and don't get it immediately?"

Armand didn't answer.

"You the spoiled one. You can't wait a damn minute for something to drink. I hate when you do this. Ruin everything for nothing."

He knew she would keep talking if he didn't say anything. Armand didn't know why she was going through the drama of collecting things in the bathroom, slamming down the toilet seat and slapping his cabinets open and closed. She wasn't going any damn where. He wasn't going to let her leave and he knew that she knew it.

"Spoiled or not, you better not break my medicine cabinet again. You heard?"

He heard the cabinet slam loudly against the wall and flip back against itself.

"Monique, I ain't playing with your ass." Armand had already paid a grand to have the damn thing replaced before, the casualty of a previous argument. "Don't break my shit or you gonna pay for it."

"Pay for it? Whatever. I don't give a damn about paying for it. In fact—"

He listened as she ruffled through her large designer bag.

"—let me go ahead and pay for it now since that's all you care about any damn way, with your money-hungry self."

He heard the glass slam against the wall again and loudly flip itself closed. A rolled knot of cash flew through the bathroom door before she slammed the door shut.

Armand felt like choking her.

Armand slowly rolled off the bed and stepped into the long basketball shorts that were thrown over the chair. He bent over and picked up the wad of cash in the middle of the floor.

That was another thing about Monique that didn't make sense. She always had money. It was another reason that she was different from the other females in his life. While they were all about trying to hustle him for some cash, Monique had her own. Shit, tonight she had more than him. And the expensive handbag that Monique was still loudly digging through was new, as were the Manolo Blahnik shoes she was sporting when she arrived a couple of days ago.

While she was in high school, Armand had assumed that her mother just lavishly indulged her two daughters and spent her small teacher's salary on keeping them stylish. Monique's mother was nondescript and very humble in presentation. But once Monique was accepted to the University of Rochester with only a few scholarships, he knew her money would get tight. He was prepared to help her out, to step in and finally get to indulge her with his financial juice. Instead, she was still purchasing expensive digs and flinging around balls of cash without worry. Armand knew that her sister, Michelle, wasn't in the game, so the cash sometimes puzzled him.

Armand balled the cash in his hand and stood at the door. "Open the door."

"No."

"Monique, you starting to piss me off. Open the fucking door. You have until I count to five or I'm kicking it in." He started counting.

He heard the door unlock. She opened it slowly by the count of three.

"What's this?" Armand held up the money as his eyes locked on hers, daring her to lie.

She blinked, obviously not wanting to let go of the anger. She didn't answer.

7

"Answer me. Where you get all this cash from?"

"I'm spoiled, remember?" She jerked her neck with each word. She turned away from him, stepping back to the black, marble basin in the bathroom. The medicine cabinet just to the right of the framed mirror in front of the basin was cracked.

"Motherfucker," Armand said, his voice louder than he had expected.

He stared at Monique, wondering what he should do. He knew that he must have loved her because he would have body slammed any other female who had cracked his cabinet a second time. The fact that he was contemplating his options instead of reacting on pure emotion was a clear sign that he was in deeper than he'd realized. He gripped the wad of cash. She damn sure wasn't getting it back. He stared at her reflection in the mirror, looking into her eyes. Armand clenched his teeth and took a step back. His anger would hurt her right now. He didn't want to do that.

Armand turned and walked toward the double doors of his master suite. "You're spoiled ass just don't know." He tossed the words over his shoulder. "You better stay your spoiled self in that fucking bathroom and leave my motherfucking door open."

"Fuck you, Army." Monique's voice was low and quiet.

He almost didn't hear it through his anger, but the words tumbled softly into his sphere and nestled around his heart. That was a first. She had cursed at him before, but never a "fuck you." It took a moment before Armand noticed the irritated feeling lurking in his mind. He didn't like that shit. It wasn't the words themselves that bothered him. It was the fact that she had felt free enough to say it. Now she was challenging him.

She'd purposely broken his mirror, threw her money at him like he was some chump; and now, in his own home, had said "fuck you." When had she lost respect like that? Armand stepped into an elegant kitchen and put Monique's cash on the counter. It was probably some school loan money that she was carrying around. She didn't have it like that. There was no way she could, but he was damn sure going to keep it. It would teach her a lesson for being a smart ass.

Armand pulled open the refrigerator. He grabbed a bottle of water and slowly untwisted the cap. Most of his mind told him to let it go, but the small part told him to nip that shit in the bud. It was time to put Monique in her place. Like the lovemaking, she was getting more and more aggressive, more and more comfortable challenging and stretching her fit in his world. He poured the cold water down his throat as he strolled back to the master suite. He was going to choke the shit out of her. "What did you say?" Armand said.

He wanted to make sure he heard her correctly before he straightened her out. He needed to see whether she would be bold enough to say it again. Armand hadn't hit her before; he hadn't ever really been rough in any way. Something about Monique felt special and new. She wasn't ruined by other relationships and other men. He hadn't been able to bring himself to tamper with her in any way that might really hurt her spirit. But it was time to make sure that she recognized who and what he was.

"Yeah, I didn't see the message."

Armand stopped in front of the bathroom door to see Monique seated on the cold tile floor with her legs crossed, her cell phone flush against her head.

"Monique?" Armand's voice was quiet and deep.

She glanced up at him and frowned, shaking her head a little and placing a finger to her lips.

Armand felt his jaw drop. Had she just hushed him? He turned to glance at the digital display on his satellite box stationed just under his massive flat screen television. It was two o'clock in the morning. Who the hell was she talking to?

"Yeah, I know," Monique said into the phone and then glanced up at him again, obviously wanting him to move.

He didn't. Instead Armand walked into the bathroom and stood in front of her.

She lowered her head more, her voice soft and nervous. "Listen, can we just talk about this tomorrow?"

Armand started to yell, raise hell, pick up the phone and smash it with the steel bat he kept behind the towel rack. But he didn't. Something about her look, the nervous way she held her body, kept his mouth shut.

"My sister," she mouthed in response to the inflamed look that was absorbing his eyes.

9

"Why?" Armand mouthed the word.

Monique just shrugged and again put her finger to her lips. "I'm sorry. Just, just tell them I'm sorry. We can get it tomorrow. I know. Damn, is it really an issue? Yeah. Alright. Yeah. I'm good. Ok. Me too."

Armand noticed the code words immediately. "Them" was always a code word for the "him" that a woman was talking about. What was the "it" that she had to get and why was it so damn important? And "me too" was the tame response to an "I love you" thrown at an inopportune time.

She slapped the phone closed.

"What the fuck?" Armand said, his temper escaping him. "Who the fuck was that?"

"Michelle. Some shit is going on with her."

"Why the fuck would Michelle be calling you at two in the morning, Monique?"

"I just said. She had been calling all day; I just checked my phone and called her back. She is my sister, Army." Monique sighed, burying her face in her hands. "Damn, what the hell? Always some bullshit. And why did you go cold on me for no reason?"

He wanted to point out that the conversation hadn't been about Michelle, it had obviously been about Monique—she was the one apologizing—but that wasn't his style. He wasn't going to press the issue or even get into it with her. He would log this shit in his mind, though, add it in the "con" column that helped justify why, even after all they had been through, she couldn't be completely trusted. He tilted back his head, poured more water into his mouth, then stared at her as he swallowed it.

Monique kept her head down, her fingers wiping at her eyes.

"You good?"

"No." A tear tumbled down her cheek. "Sometimes they drive me crazy. And then I'm here with you and you just flip on me. I'm tired, man. I'm sick of everybody changing up, always putting some shit on me." She exhaled deeply.

Armand assumed "they" meant her mother and sister. They did seem clingy, blowing up her phone at odd times. And she was always hiding from them, eager to disappear into his world for a couple of days without telling anyone where she was. Maybe they were overwhelming her.

He held out his hand. "Come here."

Monique peeked through her fingers at his outstretched hand. After a second she grasped his hand, her fingers pressing firmly into his, and pulled herself up.

"People can only do to you what you let them." Armand felt the anger seeping from him. Monique had that effect on him. Sometime they were on some breakup to make-up shit. He wanted her more now than he had earlier while she was sleeping.

"True," she said.

They stared at each other.

"So, you can only be mean to me if I let you, huh?" Monique smiled.

"I wasn't mean to you." Armand took another drink of water.

"Yes you were. And I am thirsty, too. But you didn't get me shit to drink."

"I thought you were leaving."

"No you didn't." Monique smiled.

"I thought you wanted to leave."

"No"—Monique took a step closer—"you didn't."

"You said fuck me."

"I'm sorry."

He stared at her.

"I shouldn't have gone there. I won't go there again. I promise," Monique said, her eyes searching his, her voice soft. Monique lifted his hand to her lips and kissed his fingertips slowly, wrapping her lips around each one and lightly licking it with her tongue before planting an open lip kiss on it. "You forgive me?"

Armand kissed her forehead and then ran his finger along her cheek, wiping away the tears. He didn't like to see her cry.

"Can I have some?" Monique said.

"Some of ..." Armand's words trailed off. His eyebrows raised and a playful grin spread across his face

"Your water."

"Oh." Armand laughed. "Open your mouth."

"What?"

11

Armand put his finger under her chin and gently tilted her head back. "I said open your mouth." His voice was a deep whisper.

Monique opened her mouth and Armand lowered the bottle, pouring the water slowly into her mouth. She swallowed.

"More," she said, her voice husky with longing.

Armand stepped toward her body and slowly moved forward, while she stepped backward. They gingerly stepped into a shower stall that floated in the middle of the bathroom. Its circular shape could hold up to ten people. Its inner walls lined with ten different shower heads. He pressed her against its cold walls, enjoying the softness of her body against his. She grinned mischievously. Armand didn't smile. He just continued to stare at her, his longing energy invading his mind.

He poured the water into her mouth until it spilled past her full lips, down her neck, and tumbled across her luscious nipples that he loved to suck. He fingered the dial and the shower heads gently sprinkled water onto them, rinsing away her tears, his anger, her frustration, and their confusion. Armand slowly licked each drop from her moist skin, savoring the unique sweetness of his Monique.

Chapter Two

The beacon lights of a Monroe county police cruiser bounced around the interior of the sleek Hummer. If Monique were honest with herself, she could admit that she was in trouble.

Serious trouble.

Or at least she could acknowledge the twisting knot of pain pressed deep in her abdomen making her mouth feel dry and her throat constricted. But she couldn't cave in to her fear and weakness. She refused to let her inner turmoil show, but the police lights were making it difficult.

Monique had learned a long time ago that blanketing her fear with sarcasm and dry wit was the perfect cover; it had protected her, given her the appearance of an impenetrable shield, which gained the respect of her peers. The truth was none of them really knew her or anything about her. They didn't know how lonely she often felt; how she never felt comfortable with her friends or her family; how, despite having all the material things others desired: the designer crap, useless jewelry, overpriced bags, and ridiculously expensive shoes, she still felt empty.

Not even Armand, the only person she had allowed close to her soul and given full access to her body, knew the real Monique. But she trusted him most of all. But there was so much she couldn't tell him. Wouldn't tell him. So much that he never needed to know. Even he didn't realize that she was a good girl in camouflage, a nerd in hiding, and the seed of an urban throne.

Right now, the real Monique was shivering inside, terrified about her current predicament, but she wouldn't dare reveal it. Sitting in the back of the Hummer, pride wouldn't allow a tear to escape, and it refused to let her eyelids flutter. If she didn't think quickly, all aspects of her life would end within the next few minutes.

A second police car pulled up; its beacon lights ripping a hole in the black of the night. It parked directly in front of their Hummer. Monique glanced out of the rear window and saw the first policeman finally climbing out of the patrol car.

She had never envisioned that this was how her journey would end. Monique bit her lip, trying to calm the nauseous feeling that was surging forward, threatening to engage her gag reflexes. Inner-city glory or not, she had worked too hard to end up here. She had maintained straight A's in high school, taking all honors and advanced placement courses. There was nothing easy about working toward academic success while trying to hide her intelligence. It wasn't until she had graduated that her friends discovered her intelligence when she proudly sported her National Honors Society pin, her advanced placement and honors scarf, and received award after award, including an announcement of her academic scholarship to the prestigious University of Rochester. It was the only day she hadn't cared; the only day she had been herself in front of everybody.

And she had escaped. She had just completed the first session of summer school at the university a week ago. Living on campus gave her a freedom she had never experienced before, had saved her from the constant drowning obligation that she struggled with daily at home. It had saved her from the sadness of her mother's space and the crazy uncertainty of her father's life.

But she hadn't wanted to be rescued from Armand. Of him, she couldn't get enough, which was why she had been with him for the past two days instead of on campus where her parents thought she was, leading to her current situation: sitting in the back seat of a customized Hummer with two drug dealers and another girl, trapped between two cop cars.

Monique couldn't believe that this was how her life would end, how her dreams would evaporate. Like everything else, Monique kept her dreams and beliefs hidden deep in her heart and buried under her hard core shell. Watching her father had been all the proof she needed that dreams had to be protected just as much as her spirit and her mind. And now, it was all over.

"Monique." She barely heard Armand's deep voice, breaking into her thoughts. His breath felt hot against her skin.

She turned her head slowly to face him, to watch his lips as he spoke. He had been worth it. Even if this was how it ended, he had been worth every single moment and every single tear. Armand had been the first man in her life who felt solid. Steady. He didn't talk a lot, and she found comfort in his quiet, strength in his solitude. He understood her. He understood that sometimes words escaped her and emotions were wrapped so tight within her that she couldn't unravel them in time to express them properly. He never seemed to mind her inability to put emotions to words, feelings to sound.

They would sit together in silence for hours. Him rubbing her feet or her leaning within the crook of his narrow frame, gently resting her lips against his smooth skin. With Armand she didn't have to be the ghetto girl with flair. She didn't have to hide her love of literature and art. It didn't matter if she wore Chanel or Target, and it didn't matter if she still lived in the neighborhood or on a college campus. His love was always the same. Monique had never experienced that type of stability before, not even with her parents.

Armand spoke to her now in the same way he always did: a hushed voice accompanied with a direct gaze, making her feel like his words were only for her. Despite the doom that awaited them, he still made her feel like the center focus of his entire world. She stared at his lips. That was how she fell for him in the first place. She had avoided him, ignored him, and dismissed his advances until one day he had saved her life.

"Mo, just stay cool." He adjusted himself in the seat to get a better view of the cops. His lip quivered just a bit as he spoke.

For the first time Monique wondered whether he was scared. There was no reason to stay cool, but she could pretend. Pretend to be composed and cool despite the hysteria mounting in her brain. As Armand bent his head lower, casing the other cop, Monique realized he wasn't scared, just angry. Trapped in the back seat of this huge truck with the police on either side, his kingly exterior remained in place.

Armand had already taken a bullet for her eight months ago; she had no doubt that he wasn't afraid to die. In fact, he lived like each day was a challenge to death, a back-and-forth struggle of pushing the envelope and blurring the lines. He caught her eyes again, speaking a million thoughts without saying a word. Monique felt her breath leave her. The simple depth of his eyes said it all. He was telling her goodbye. That he was so prepared for the end should have unnerved her, but it didn't. She had seen it before with both her father and brother.

But Armand was different from them.

Monique did not like to group Armand with them in her mind. Them, she loved but feared; him, she couldn't bear to live without. Staring into his black eyes, Monique felt waves of love pour over her. She brushed his hairline with a fingertip, traced the deep scar above his eyebrow, and kissed the bridge of his nose.

"No," she whispered. "Baby, don't do this."

"I swear I ain't going back to jail, Mo. You already know. You will be alright. Just stay in the car."

"No," she whispered again. "You shoot at them and they will kill us all. You hear me? You know they will. Just chill a second. Just wait." Monique grabbed his hand and slid her tight grip up to his arm.

Her heart started to pray. Prayer was something else she never did in front of anyone other than her mother or the members of her church. Without moving her lips, desperation filled her spirit and surged forth, crying out for help. Any sort of help. She didn't want to go to jail, couldn't bear the thought of how her mother would react. Monique had read about a girl the same age as her older sister Michelle who was sentenced to over twenty years in prison for the drugs her boyfriend possessed. When she wouldn't give him up or turn informant, they had pinned the time on the girl. It struck Monique that she was a hypocrite. When the case was in the news, Monique shook her head in disgust at the stupid chick who had given up her life to protect her man. Now she and the stupid chick were the one and the same.

Monique's hand brushed against the side of Armand's Beretta lodged in its holster. He always carried two guns. He was the only other person she knew aside from her father who carried guns in holsters.

"Give them to me." She motioned for the Berettas.

He shook his head. "You ain't doin' a bid for me. Hell naw."

"Dammit, give them to me." Monique felt irritated, convinced that Armand was ready to get all of them killed.

They stared at each other; her fear screaming from her heart. She saw his resolution fade and noticed the shift of his chin as he considered her and the weight of her request.

"No," Armand said.

Raymond and Patrice sat there wide eyed and speechless. Monique was certain that they were scared.

To Monique's relief, he slid the guns out of the holster, laying them at his feet instead. Monique sighed as she glanced out of her window again. He had one more gun on him, the tiny one hidden against his ankle, but she wasn't going to push her luck. The cops were waiting for something, standing back from the Hummer and waiting. Monique realized that more police must be on the way.

Monique held her head down and closed her eyes. Her hand was on Armand's leg, this time not bothering to hide her fear as her soul pleaded for intervention. In seconds her entire life flashed before her eyes, all of the regret, all of the mistakes, all of the poor decisions.

Monique thought about how devastated her mother would be if her only child spent her life in jail. Life was bigger than her and Armand. Her obligations, her family ties, her loyalties required her to consider more than her love for Armand. If her father even got wind of this, she would be in serious trouble. If she got arrested or sent to jail, her father would make sure Armand's life would be short and his last breath would be a painful one.

She loved Armand, but there were other things she had to consider, other people she had to remember. A choice had already been made for her before she ever had a say, leaving a man in the game to ensure that she had a chance. Her mother had done it. Life had nothing to do with love. Love wasn't everything. In fact, it wasn't really anything but a wanting emotion. Love was not tangible, not something that Monique could run her hand against, hold close to her chest, or guarantee was hers.

Leaving Armand's love might be the sacrifice Monique would have to make. She didn't want to walk away; but, like so many other things, she knew she could. She had been trained to. If she got out of this situation alive and without being arrested, it was a clear sign that she needed to separate from Armand, to do what was best for both of them.

Chapter Three

The tension and uncertainty caused the inside of the Hummer to be unbelievably hot. With her eyes closed and her head down, it suddenly occurred to Monique how they must look sitting in the huge tank with black tinted windows shut tight. No wonder the police lingered around them waiting for backup. No fool would walk up on the menacing truck.

"Roll the windows down," Monique said to Raymond, the owner and reckless driver of their mini-armored tank.

"Hell no." Raymond finally found his voice, craning his neck from the driver's seat. "Fuck that. I ain't rolling down shit."

"Roll down the windows, Raymond. You're a damn jerk," Monique spat at him, leaning forward.

"Fuck y—" Raymond started but remembered Armand. His eyes flitted to the rearview mirror, meeting Armand's deadly glare. Police or not, Raymond knew that messing with Monique was a mistake. His man had let her closer than any other woman, and Raymond wasn't getting in between Armand and someone he held close.

"Just do it," Patrice said, finding her voice as well. Tears were streaming down her round face as she sat in the passenger's seat shaking her head. "Just do it, Ray. Shit. I shouldn't have gotten in the car with you tonight. I swear ... I could feel it. I knew something bad was going to happen."

Raymond sighed and pressed the button. All four windows lowered.

"Stay in the vehicle," a stricken voice called out. It was obvious that the cop was panicked.

"He's scared as shit." Armand shook his head. "Damn, we got a scared-ass cop."

19

"I would be scared, too, walking up on this big-ass armored truck in the middle of the night," Monique said, noticing how big Patrice's head was.

"Your ass didn't think it was an armored truck when you was rollin' in it." Raymond glanced at her through the rearview mirror. "You was the main one profiling."

"Whatever, Raymond. If you hadn't been speeding, we wouldn't be in this situation." Monique pulled the handle on her door, barely opening it. Her fingers scratched the handle as voices of panic poured upon her from every direction.

"Did you just open the door?" Raymond shouted.

"Mo, what is you doin'?" Patrice shrieked.

"Stay in the vehicle!" the white officer screamed. "Get back in the vehicle now."

Monique ignored Raymond and Patrice, addressing the cop instead. "I'm sorry, sir." She removed the throatiness from her voice as she pushed the door open.

"Close that door, dammit!" His face turned red.

Monique slammed the door closed then leaned out of the window. She called out to the officers in her most feminine and proper voice. Armand's hand was on her arm, gripping just above the elbow. It irked her, his grip on her while she was trying to focus. She snatched her arm away as she leaned through the window. A strange calm had invaded her; it was like she was on the outside watching herself role play. Monique felt like a chameleon, always turning into someone else to ease the situation, and she had to ease this situation and find a way out.

The screaming cop was kind of cute, under normal circumstances. His close-cropped brown hair led to a classic face with thin lips and high cheekbones. His skin was more olive than white. She figured he was Italian. His partner was black and stood back impatiently, eyeing them with malice. They were better off with the Italian cop. Monique knew that instinctively. Black cops were worse than the others, that's what her father always told her, that black cops had a bigger chip on their shoulder because they had so much more to prove.

"Sir." Monique's eyes traveled the length of his arm. She realized his hand rested on the handle of his department-issued piece. Her face suddenly matched his look of fear: her mouth fell open, her eyes widened. But Monique had perfected her look of stunned innocence and, as usual, it worked. She noticed the muscles in his face relaxing. "I'm sorry, officer, is something wrong?"

Monique prayed he would pay attention to her, focus on her and miss the guns on the floor of the car. That was the only way they could be safe, the only way they could all escape. She couldn't invoke her father's name. She didn't know these cops or whose side they were on. And her father, like so many other aspects of her life, was still someone she had never discussed with Armand.

But she certainly wasn't going to sit here and wait for more cops to show up, for an army of them to descend upon the truck and turn a bad situation into an unsolvable nightmare. The street was quiet; there would be no witnesses. The cops would have them trapped and would probably show off for each other, resulting in some torment. Monique could imagine the four of them turning up "mysteriously" dead because it was so easy to do and get away with.

The young cop held her eyes and lowered his hand past the handle of his gun. "Ma'am." His voice was calmer. More certain. "Sit back. Be quiet. Stay in the vehicle."

Ma'am? That was a good sign. She had a chance, especially if this cop saw past color lines or secretly liked a little cocoa in his milk. The cop took another step closer to the Hummer, drawing his flashlight and pointing the beam through the open window. His flashlight instead of his gun. Another good sign.

"Sir, is something wrong?" Monique kept her eyes locked on his, her mouth slightly open, her eyes wide. She licked her lips nervously. She watched his eyes follow her tongue. "My brother is taking me home, and I have to get there before curfew," she said innocently.

"Hold on one second, ma'am." He held a finger up. He ignored her and glanced at the others as his flashlight blinded them.

They squinted against the light.

"Patrice, pull yourself together," Monique whispered through clinched teeth when the cop moved to the other side of the car. "Stop crying like a damn fool."

Patrice wiped at her face just before the beam penetrated her space. While she didn't manage to look nonchalant, she also didn't look like a person with a handful of crack vials and white baggies at her feet.

The officer tucked his flashlight back into his belt and nodded at the second policeman. The black one eyed them again, pursing his lips together. He grudgingly nodded and climbed into his car. Monique watched him pick up the radio and felt relief surge through her. They were almost free.

"License and registration," the officer said, staring at Raymond.

Monique prayed his paperwork was in order. But she knew it wasn't. Nothing about Raymond was ever in order.

"I have to get it from the glove box." Raymond hesitated. "Can I?"

"Just get it." The officer sighed, lowering his flashlight and glancing around the neighborhood. "Were you aware you were doing fifty-five in a thirty?"

Raymond shook his head, his fingers fumbling around Patrice's knees as he grappled with the glove compartment.

They all flinched when the black officer suddenly jumped out of his car. "Aye," he yelled.

"Shit," Monique whispered, wondering whether he had run Raymond's license plate.

"There's a 187 on Wellington. One block away, our call. Units were diverted already. Make this bullshit quick," Black officer said, looking hateful as ever.

The young officer stared at Raymond as he fumbled through the glove compartment. "Hurry up." Then, he looked past Raymond's head and locked eyes with Monique.

She stared back, taking in his boyish face, the deep brown hair, and the light brown eyes. Since she had been at the university, more white boys had talked to her, laughed with her, and invited her to hang out. Monique had never considered them before. They weren't an option. Her world was what it was, and that didn't include white males. But her world had recently begun to change; and, sitting in this mess, she was realizing that she shouldn't shun all of her new options. Not immediately. She had to reevaluate her life and what she wanted it to be.

"Hurry up, Ray," Monique said in her annoyingly thin and proper voice. "Daddy is going to kill us for getting a ticket in his car."

Raymond pulled out an envelope with a clear cover and his license. As Ray handed them to the cop, the cop's eyes met Monique's again. She felt him take in her caramel streaked hair. She watched him follow the length of her thin neck to her cleavage.

"Lopreste, wrap it up," the other cop shouted, breaking Lopreste's lingering gaze.

"Listen, you got lucky tonight," Lopreste said to Raymond after a long pause, still looking at Monique, then finally glancing at the license. "Next time follow the limits. Consider this a warning."

The patrol car in front of the Hummer flashed his lights as he pulled off. Lopreste backed away slowly maintaining eye contact with Monique before turning around and jumping in his car. They sat still in the Hummer.

Monique watched him. She lowered her chin and kept her eyes locked on his car. He passed them slowly, meeting her eyes again. His expression changed just slightly, enough to let Monique know that she was the reason for their escape. She wasn't sure if he'd bought her act, found her attractive, or knew who she was. There was no doubt in her mind, though, that she would see this cop again. His eyes confirmed it; his lips curved into a small grin just before he sped off. Rochester, New York, was a medium-sized city and Monique wasn't hard to find. It was only a matter of time.

"Oh shit. Shit. Oh shit." Raymond bent over laughing. "I can't believe that shit. I ain't never in my life had that happen. The po-po just roll out? I can't believe that shit."

"Mo, you did the damn thing." Patrice sighed.

"Shit," Raymond said again, then opened the door and climbed out.

Monique watched him stretch out his long body before his head disappeared as he bent over.

"Get your ass back in this car." Patrice laughed, her fear evaporating.

"Man, my paperwork ain't straight on this ride. I bought this baby cash. And had he flashed that light down, son, do you know how fucked I was about to be? My piece was straight sitting by my feet. He was so busy looking at Mo he didn't even notice. Mo, you don't even understand how fucked I was about to be."

23

"Not to mention this." Patrice held up the small white bags between carefully manicured fingertips. "How you going to throw this shit on my side of the car? You thought I didn't catch that, huh? Going to set me up to do a bid for your punk ass? Naw, take my ass home."

"It wasn't like that," Raymond shouted through the open door, still bending over. "They wouldn't've searched your side."

"Fuck that. You was trying to set me up. I ain't lettin' that shit slide. Get your black ass back in the car." Patrice rolled her eyes, her hair weave shaking. "Take me the fuck home."

"I know that's right, Tricey. How the hell he going to throw that shit up under you?" Monique leaned forward, laughing. Her lungs loosened as the air made its way back into her chest. They had escaped. She couldn't believe it. "Raymond, what you doin'? You throwing up?"

Raymond didn't answer.

Monique began to chuckle, turning to Armand. "Army, this punk is ..." Her words caught in her throat.

Armand's black eyes stared coldly at her, a detached look that she hadn't seen before. It silenced her. It scared her. Of course Armand had a deadly side, he wouldn't have survived this long if he didn't. But he had never turned it on her. If she hadn't known better, she would have thought she had caught a glimpse of hate within his eyes. Without replying, he leaned down and picked up his guns and holster from the floor. Monique leaned back against the door, studying him, wondering how to move forward. She didn't have an answer, a role to slide into to make him smile. She didn't know what was wrong with him.

"Eh Raymond, let's roll out, man," Armand said quietly and stared out his window.

24

Chapter Four

Monique didn't speak for the rest of the ride. She couldn't believe Armand would sit there and turn cold on her for absolutely nothing. He wasn't the type who needed to shine or craved the spotlight. He obviously wanted to get them all killed so he could have some glory moment, become some stupid street legend. Her way was better and they all survived. Wasn't that all that mattered?

Monique stared at him. She ignored Patrice and Raymond in the front arguing about his trying to set her up. Raymond was Armand's friend and partner in crime. Patrice and Monique wouldn't call each other friends, but they knew each other from around the way.

Patrice and Raymond weren't what she and Armand were, or what she thought her and Armand were. With him sitting here pouting over nothing, she wondered what she was without Armand. In fact, in the thick of the tension, with the police threat looming, she had decided to leave him. Hadn't she? Hadn't that been clear and possible less than an hour ago?

Now she wondered whether it was possible for her to exist without Armand. It was times like this when she wished she could leave him alone. It would be easier; her entire life would be easier if she did. She needed to. It was the right thing to do. The best thing to do. But the pathetic truth was she couldn't. He was the sanity to her crazy world, the calm to her frantic pace. But she knew one thing: she wasn't going to stay in the back seat and be ignored by him for no reason.

"Raymond, take me home," Monique said evenly, breaking into his word tango with Patrice.

"Alright, Mo," Raymond said, turning up the volume on the music and swinging a U-turn. "Whatever you want, girl."

"Fuck that. She ain't going home," Armand said, still refusing to look at her as she stared at him. "Matter of fact, change of plans. Take us to the spot."

"Goddamn." Raymond shook his head and threw another U-turn. "Y'all gonna make up your minds."

"Raymond, I ain't even playin' with you. I want to go home. Take me home," Monique said.

Raymond slammed on the brakes. "Y'all decide. And, Patrice, I am taking your loud, nagging ass home. You don't have a choice."

"Boy, please. You take me where I say." Patrice folded her arms.

Monique studied her profile, taking in the huge earrings, the slicked-down home weave, and the tight purple dress. She liked Patrice more and more. Monique chuckled as she leaned back. She wasn't going to keep arguing with Armand. And she couldn't deny the small thrill that he had overruled her, had demanded she stay with him. Monique glanced back at Armand. He continued to stare out the window.

"Well," Raymond said, "ya'll make up your minds or what?"

"What I say, son?" Armand answered, the hissed command taking over the car like a loud echo.

The conversation was over.

Raymond continued down the street, shaking his head.

***

The apartment was at the end of a long and narrow hallway. It had a shabby, wooden door. Monique wondered how someone could have lived there. She glanced at the dirty cream walls and the ugly green floor tile. The hallway barely had any light. Monique prayed that no children lived in this filthy building. She stood behind Armand, careful to stay away from him. Normally she would have leaned into him, touching some small part of his body just to remind herself that he was near her. Not now. Now she was pissed off.

Armand hit the door once with the back of his hand.

"What's up?" a thick voice came from the other side of the shabby door.

"Three-two, son," Armand said in a low voice.

Monique listened to the sound of numerous locks turning and wood sliding across the door. She sighed, wishing she could press herself against Armand's wide back, but his stiff shoulders and the set position of his jaw let her know that her touch was unwelcome.

A short, chubby man opened the door. "Army, what's up?"

"Nothin', man." Armand nodded. "Absolutely nothing."

"Who this?" Chubby eyed Monique, slowly staring her up and down.

Monique looked at him blankly, ignoring his aggressive stare.

"She with me." Armand gave Chubby a sidelong glance.

"She strapped?" Chubby kept his eyes on her.

Armand smiled slightly. Monique raised her eyebrow, daring him to rise up from the chair and place a finger on her.

When neither of them responded, Chubby shrugged and gestured to Armand. "She's on you, Army."

Armand nodded and stepped deeper into the apartment, into another narrow hall. Armand walked quickly as Monique glanced around the apartment. She knew she should keep her eyes down, her father had taught her that much. Armand had never brought her inside his world like this. She wondered why tonight? What was he trying to prove?

Two women smoking marijuana sat on the couch. The flavored smoke filled the tight space. They were pretty. One had her hair smoothed back into a neat bun, a clingy summer dress wrapped around her body. The other had a head full of springy curls, smoke slowly oozed out of her lips as she watched Monique sashay by. Their legs were touching each other too intimately, and the curly haired one's arm relaxed in the other girl's lap.

Monique eyed them both, her lips tight and her expression fierce. She didn't recognize them and was glad for that. The cutest one nodded and Monique nodded back, refusing to acknowledge how their freedom unnerved and repulsed her. They shouldn't have been there, chilling, like they weren't in an apartment full of men, available to any of their desires. Like they weren't dependent on their sexuality for survival. Monique also knew that some sisters had to do what they had to do, though. Monique wouldn't let her face show judgment.

She kept on moving, walking past a television that blasted loudly. Three men sat around it, gun handles protruding from the waistline of their fitted jeans, smoke seeping from them like dust in the wind. The apartment was so smoky Monique fought the urge to fan the air. Armand walked past, nodding at the men, ignoring the women. All three men stared at her.

One winked at her, sat back in his chair, and puffed on his cigar. Monique felt her head getting light from all the smoke. She stared at the man who'd winked at her. He was light brown with magnetic, glowing eyes. She found him breathtaking. He looked familiar, but she couldn't remember where she knew him from. She didn't respond to his nod.

"Wade, you up on it, huh?" Armand's expression was blank, but Monique knew that Armand had seen the wink.

"Naw, partner." Wade looked away from them both, turning his focus back on the television. "Just handling mine."

"You do that." Armand disappeared behind a door and Monique followed him into a bedroom. The king-sized bed was pushed in the corner. There was barely any room between it and the walls on either side.

"This yours?" she said, giving the place the once-over.

"The place is, now. But I only use it when I want."

Monique nodded. She stood by the door.

"Move," he said, his voice barely above a whisper.

"Why?" Now she was getting frustrated.

He sat on the edge of the bed and turned on a flat screen television that sat on an old wooden dresser.

"I said move." Armand still would not look at her.

She moved, purposely standing directly in front of the television. "Better?"

"Yeah." He stared past her. "You don't stand with your back against any door in a trap house."

So this was one of his drug houses, a kind of storefront for the junkies. No wonder the chubby man had been guarding the door.

"Come here." He gestured with a finger.

"Nowhere to come. There's no space in this tight-ass room."

He stood up, closing the space between them with three steps. He grabbed her hand and she tried to pull away. She was pissed off and embarrassed. And hurt. He had acted like an ass for no reason. Monique had been proud of herself, proud of her game on the cops, and Armand had deflated her little accomplishment.

He chuckled a little and pulled at her hand again. She snatched it away.

"Now you mad?" Armand said, smiling for the first time.

"Armand, what the hell?"

He reached again, this time grabbing both of her wrists and pulling her into him. Despite the strappy heels she wore, she still only reached his chin and still had to look up at him. He leaned into her, burying his face into her neck, inhaling deeply, moaning softly. She wrapped her arms around him, loving the strong feel of his thin body against her. His tongue circled a spot on her neck. He kissed it, then bit it softly.

Monique moaned. She forgot where she was or how angry she was. This was the only space in time she wanted to be. He eased her to the bed, pushing one of her legs with his, physically guiding each step.

"I don't want to lie on this bed." Monique didn't know this place and didn't know who had been on this bed before her.

"You don't have to."

He lifted her, thrusting his tongue deep into her mouth. His tongue was so wide that it filled every inch of her mouth. She always felt an instant throbbing between her thighs when he kissed her. Tonight was no different. She didn't kiss back. She didn't have to. He gently licked the roof of her mouth. His tongue traced the ridge of her mouth, making it so sensitive to the touch that she shivered. He lifted her tongue with his, sucking her tongue deep into his mouth.

It was his mouth and tongue that had turned her out. These were the very moves that made her violate the one promise she had made to herself years ago after watching her father's life. She swore that she would never get involved with anybody even remotely tied into the game. One kiss from Armand and every barrier and self-promise had evaporated.

Monique didn't feel her legs wrap around his waist, nor did she notice he had turned around and sat on the edge of the bed. He continued to kiss her deeply as she straddled him, his tongue awakening every nerve ending up and down her spine.

Armand separated himself from the kiss and buried his head between her breasts, inhaling her deeply. Monique sighed in delight. She felt his warm tongue trace a path from the hollow of her breasts to the bottom of her chin to her lips. His lips against her. Those perfect lips.

Monique shuddered at the thought, feeling her silk flood her panties.

"Baby, stop." She gasped. "Baby, why were you tripping?"

"You love me?"

Love was a topic they didn't often discuss; he never directly said the words "I love you." She pulled back and stared at him.

Armand's hand slid slowly up her thigh, his thumb lightly tracing along the edge of her underwear. "Do you love me?" He pushed his thumb under the satin panties and traced the lips of her inner petals.

"You know I do, baby," she whispered into his ear as she clamped her eyes, clearing out all distraction and concentrating on the perfect pressure of his thumb. She leaned back, placing her hands just behind her on his knees, bracing herself for the fire of ecstasy that was guaranteed to follow his every touch.

"Tell me you love me."

His voice sounded so quiet and thick. She hadn't heard him sound like this before. While one hand pulled down the neckline of her tee and scooped her breasts, the other hand between her legs opened wide. His middle finger ran back and forth over her pleasure.

"I love you, Armand."

"Look at me."

She couldn't even close her mouth to catch her breath. How could she open her eyes to look at him? "Stop. Just stop for a second." *Then I can focus on you.*

Armand's finger pressed deeper into her. She jumped when she felt her clitoris expand, felt her silk spread over each intimate inch of her.

"Look at me," he demanded. His voice powerful, yet vulnerable.

Monique opened her eyes, feeling dizzy. She tried to focus on him, on the dim light, on the television glare reflecting in his black eyes. His hand pressed against her harder; his other hand massaged her breasts firmly. He bent down and captured her breast inside of his mouth. That wide tongue of his took over, making her cry out from its stimulation. When his tongue pressed against her breast, it rolled waves along her nipple. Monique fought the urge to close her eyes. She watched him take her entire breast into his perfect mouth.

The tremor that ripped through her radiated from the tip of his thumb, eased through her clit, evolving into an internal orgasmic eruption that shook Monique's entire body. She didn't want to scream, not with all those people just outside the door. She leaned into him and buried her open mouth on the top of his head, muting her anguish, releasing it into the soft spongy mass of his hair.

He wouldn't let her go that easy.

"Look at me, Mo."

She couldn't move, twisting her body from his hand, trying so hard to stop the continuous waves of euphoria that overtook her.

"Look at me." It was a harsh demand

Monique shook her head, snapped out of her daze for just a second and looked at him. If she didn't know better, she would have thought that his black eyes were wet, something close to tears within the lids clouding those big eyes.

"Don't ever do that again," he said.

Monique didn't know what he was talking about and she didn't care. She simply nodded and tried to resume her rhythm, hoping that he could take her over the top again before he even entered her.

"Mo, don't ever do that to me again," Armand said again. "Do you hear me?"

"Yeah, baby, I hear you."

He paused. She wanted the equivalent to his wide tongue, which was resting underneath the briefs and the jeans. His slender frame didn't reveal how well endowed he was, how thick and wide his center of mass could get. It was all she could think of right now, all she wanted. Monique longed to feel it pressing against her tightened cavity, shrinking in response to the delicious orgasm that had just rocked her core and its twin that was threatening to spill over.

"Monique, I swear," he whispered.

She unzipped his pants and reached in, smiling when her fingertips pressed against gold.

"I swear, girl."

He lifted her suddenly, holding her firmly by her behind before dropping her on the bed. Monique opened her eyes as he dropped his pants and climbed on top of her; his eyes locked on hers. She didn't want to lay on this nasty bed. She had told him that.

Monique started to protest, trying to shift quickly from under him, but he lifted her legs, throwing them over his shoulders as he grabbed her ass again. The first powerful thrust took her by surprise. Armand plunged deeply and without mercy instead of carefully pressing into her tight walls and working his length into her like he normally did. It hurt, but at the same time, it felt good to Monique. She wasn't used to him being so rough.

"Army ..." She met his eyes and noticed that they were squinted, focused completely on hers. His face was expressionless and Monique felt uncomfortable. She didn't recognize him.

He thrust into her again, holding her behind higher, moving faster, barely giving her time to recover before penetrating deeply again. Monique felt like he was beating against her insides, pounding at the bottom of her stomach. It almost made her feel sick, the raw sensation and pressure were overwhelming. It could have felt good if Armand wasn't so rough, so brutal with his delivery, so far removed from making love to her.

Monique tried to keep up with him, tried to slow him down. She couldn't. Armand bit his lip, his face contorted with anger. Armand hit her G-Spot; it was too much direct contact for her to enjoy it. Instead she whimpered. She tried to scoot back, but he pulled her forward and plunged into her again.

"Army," Monique said again. Her voice was a deep groan. Her eyes were wide with fear. "Army!"

He opened his eyes and looked at her. Armand stopped.

"What are you doing?" Monique heard the fear in her voice.

He stared at her, but Monique didn't recognize the look. He pushed himself back and looked lost for a moment. Monique watched him as she slid back, relieved that he was no longer pounding away at her insides, but terrified that he was capable of doing such. The vibe was different; she didn't feel like she could just get up and leave. She didn't know what to do. Monique didn't want Armand mad at her and she didn't want to feel the discomfort that overwhelmed her. Some part of her needed to please him, needed to make it all alright. She reached out to him, resting her hand on his chest.

"Mo ..."

Monique pressed her hands on either side of his face. He looked like a wounded animal. Her fear faded, lost in the stronger need to comfort him, to remove the look of confusion on his face. She climbed over him and lowered herself slowly onto him.

"Mo, I don't want to hurt you." His words were muffled as she held his pole and guided it into her.

"You can't hurt me, baby."

"No, Mo." He moved his hands to her thighs, keeping her still as he throbbed inside of her, not allowing her to raise her hips. His eyes looked like ice again.

For a second Monique felt scared. But just for a second.

"Don't ever look at another man like that. Not in front of me."

"What?" Despite being filled with him, thinking that her insides were going to explode with the throbbing feeling vibrating against the deepest parts of her well, making her stomach hurt, she finally understood. "The cop?"

He flinched. He couldn't bear to hear it. "Mo, don't ever do that again. Cop or not. You are mine."

"All yours, baby." Mo kissed him gently, sucking on his bottom lip. She kissed the tip of his nose and licked his lips again.

He finally let go and leaned back slightly, allowing her to rock gently up and down and drive them both into utopia.

Just before Monique fell asleep her mind replayed Armand's words, minus the lovemaking, and she finally understood the unspoken threat.

***

Monique swallowed as she glanced around the cramped room again. She wasn't going to spend the night in this place. She doubted that Armand ever really slept here. This place was obviously a hit-off spot, where the drug dealers distributed and the freaks knocked the hustlers off. Why had he brought her here? It didn't make sense. Everything Armand did had a meaning, some deeper purpose.

And he had threatened her. That was a first. A tangled, emotional threat that exposed his weakness. A threat he had mingled with her love and their lovemaking. Meaning that he had probably brought her to this place so that he could be in a street mindset. Here he could threaten her like she was a common hoe. Something she couldn't imagine him doing in the warmth of his sleek penthouse on the west side where she felt at home.

Despite breathing heavily, she lay there wide awake, thinking. Strategizing. Armand didn't know her as well as he thought if he assumed that she didn't understand what this meant. She had to be careful now. He had seen the side of her that could soothe a cop, or as he probably saw it, radiate lust for the enemy. And for a moment, he hated her. She had seen it. Then the tortured fervent lovemaking he had subjected her to, as if he were fighting himself between threatening her and loving her. Maybe he had been saying goodbye.

Monique's heart stopped. Had that been the real reason he brought her here? To kill her? Could he have done it, have knocked her off? Hell no, not over something like that. Monique sighed. She was changing. A few weeks away on the plush campus was making her paranoid and taking her out of her element.

The college students there lived so free. They seemed to worry about nothing except their grades and parental expectations, and they spent money like water. They had no idea that there was another type of life that thousands endured daily, one with real stress and strain. Monique was starting to feel like maybe she had a choice, maybe she really didn't have to lead a life like her family. She had never thought she had a choice before. Before, her world was what it was and she needed Armand to navigate it, needed his raw energy and his aggressive ability to keep her stable.

But she didn't need it in the same way now. Now she wanted him. She loved him, but she didn't need him. It was a realization that she wished she hadn't had. Her prayers and thoughts in the back of the Hummer had made that clear. She had looked at the cop and remembered those college students, thought of the easiness of submerging herself into that world. She had thought about her mother and how much she owed her to not stay in Armand's world. To steer clear of her father's kingdom.

Now she lay on the bed ashamed of herself for having had sex in this nasty apartment with strangers just outside the bedroom door. She was ashamed at herself for allowing Armand to test her in this way, to lower her standards and her highest idea of herself in both her eyes and his.

What was happening to them? What was happening to her?

Eight months ago, Armand still treated her like a queen. He was still proud then, still looked at her with warmth in his eyes. He would whisper in her ear that she was his college-bound beauty. Monique never questioned Armand's love for her before the police pulled them over a couple of hours ago. Now, laying in this cramped space, recalling his threatening words, she realized they were testing each other, unsure of each other, unsure of the new dynamic that her college education and experiences might bring into the fold. Armand bringing her here was the possible beginning to the end. She wasn't ready for that solid of a move no matter how self-assured she was feeling. She would have to be more careful.

Chapter Five

Monique felt Armand climb out of the bed and listened to him pull up his pants. She knew without looking that he still had on his guns. They never scared her; it was one thing he seemed to love about her. She listened as he paused, sure that he was staring at her. Then, she heard him unsnap his phone and begin texting. After a few minutes, he tapped her lightly on the shoulder, leaned over her lean frame with his long body and kissed her cheek.

"Mo, get up."

Monique pretended not to hear him. She was disgusted with herself for laying in this nasty bed, for allowing him to sex her and threaten her at the same time. She couldn't let her emotions show, though, couldn't let him know how upset she was. He had drawn the line in the sand, and she wasn't in a position to cross it. Not stuck in a slum in some part of the city she didn't recognize with his henchmen just outside the door. Anything that happened to her here could be covered.

She had to be smarter than that. She needed a moment to read Armand, to see how he continued to act. She had to figure out if he had closed his heart to her that quickly. For now it was better to reign in her attitude, retreat and return to the comfort of his quiet love than to experience whatever lay down the other path.

"Monique." Armand pulled at her arms and kissed the back of her neck.

She opened her eyes and looked at him, a feigned smile on her face as if all she could recall was their lovemaking, as if she were that simple.

"Come on." He stroked her face.

"Where are we going now?" Monique breathed.

"Home," he said simply and helped her to her feet. "I called Ray to come get us."

"I don't want to get back into that tank," Monique said, stepping into her panties. "I don't want to go near that thing."

"Trust. You will never see that shit again."

Monique took note of that, proof that he had agreed with her observation: a heavily tinted black truck in the middle of the night wouldn't lead to anything but trouble.

"He is going to grab Dut's Benz and scoop us."

Monique adjusted her clothes in the mirror, trying to pat down her hair. She pushed back the deep embarrassment. She knew that she would have to pass those men again and those two girls, and everyone would know that she had just been fucked.

Armand stepped closer to her, moving the hair out of her eyes. "I made them clear out. Ain't nobody here but us and Mike." He kissed her cheek and gazed at her.

It was a kind of apology, an acknowledgement of the situation he had put her in. She felt grateful, in some small way, that he was astute enough to know that he owed her an apology.

Monique nodded, deciding that keeping her mouth shut was her best bet. She really wanted to yell and scream, demand to know what he was thinking and why he was tripping. She wanted to ask whether he felt their love was changing, was stretching thin, and why. That would have gotten her nowhere with Armand and she knew it.

"You got class tomorrow?" he said, leading her from the bedroom into the now empty common area.

"No."

"You sure?" He raised a brow.

"Yes." Monique chuckled.

He always asked about her education and about her classes, making sure nothing interfered. Sometimes it irked her, like dealing with her father irked her. Both he and Armand were hypocrites like that, making sure she went to school while they pounded out a living on the streets. She knew she was the first college girl Armand had claimed so completely. Then again, she was one of the few folks from their hood who actually attended college.

"I'm sure," she said.

"Let's grab something to eat and go to my place and kick it tonight. Alright? Let me make love to you the right way," Armand whispered in her ear.

She giggled and leaned into his side as they entered the narrow hallway.

"Mike, what's up?" Armand gave him a head nod.

Mike nodded back. "Ray should be downstairs by now. I texted that fool and told him to come up when he get here. He shorted me and now he trying to talk his way around it."

Armand chuckled. "Y'all going to have to handle that shit some other time."

That was the last thing Monique heard before a cannon rang out, blasting a hole through the door.

Monique took a step back, staring at the back half of Mike's head splattered against the dingy wall. She couldn't believe that someone had shot right through the door. She wanted to scream but couldn't make the sound come out. Armand fell back into her for a second; his arms spread and his mouth opened wide. He pushed himself forward, regaining his footing and pulled both Beretta's from their holsters. Monique ran back into the common area of the apartment and crouched low. She didn't know whether they were ambushed or not, and was too terrified to look out the windows.

Armand unloaded his guns, bent over and scooped her up, and pulled her back into the bedroom. Monique shook her head in confusion; going back in there was a certain death trap. There was no way out. She could hear shouting and a few more shots rang out as someone kicked through what was left of the door.

How long could this last before someone called the police?

Armand reloaded his guns and fired again. Monique heard a dull thud as the bullet hit someone's flesh behind her. The person shouted. Whoever this was, they were already in the apartment, already prepared to kill her and Armand. Armand yanked harder and dragged her to the back of the bedroom. He headed for the closet. For the second time in one night, Monique prepared herself to die. They would surely shoot up the closet. Armand's viselike grip on her arm left her no choice. She stepped inside against her better judgment.

Armand kicked at a square panel on the inside of the closet behind a group of bags. The panel was a perfect square. Monique wondered whether they would fit through it. It finally gave and he pushed her into it. She scrambled to her knees and crawled behind raw pipes that were stuck between the walls of the two apartments. Monique's mind flashed quickly to the hall. There hadn't been an apartment next to this one. This must be the rear of the apartment across the hall. Were people in there?

She kept crawling until she came to another panel. Spinning onto her side, she used both legs to kick through and scoot out. Armand was right behind her. She was right. They were in an empty bathroom with rolls of toilet paper sitting on the commode. He pushed past her, running through the door, and Monique instantly understood that this was his place too. She entered the hall behind him. All of the rooms were empty of furniture except for the tables and chairs and drug paraphernalia: weights and scales, baggies and vials, baking soda and Pyrex ovenware.

Shaking her head, Monique tried to keep her eyes on the floor. She didn't want to know. She was seeing too much. First the trap house, now this: the center of drug production. This was too much information. This knowledge would make her life a gamble if she ever tried to leave him, if she ever had to respond to his threats again.

"Mo, come on," he said, disappearing into the common area.

Monique saw that the front door was barricaded with a heavy cabinet and wood planks were nailed across it. Armand yanked at the wood planks, and she heard the wood splinter under his hands. He didn't seem to notice the pain. He looked like a wolf on the hunt, operating on kill-only mode. He didn't even seem as unnerved as he had in the back of Raymond's tank.

"Help me push the damn cabinet," he said, putting his body weight against it.

She did. Her heels provided little support. They only got it a few inches from the wall, enough for him to ease out of the door.

"Stay here." His gaze was as serious as AIDS; his voice as cold as a blizzard.

"No. Hell no! I ain't sitting in here waiting to die."

"Stay here dammit. It's safer."

39

"Give me a gun." She held out a hand; her hip defiantly cocked.

"Hell no. You'll fuck around and shoot yourself by accident. Just hide in the kitchen and wait for me."

Monique continued to shake her head no, tears streaming down her face, but he disappeared into the dark hallway. The doorway to this apartment was directly across the hallway from the first apartment. She could see Mike's blood all over the hall and heard voices shouting. She wondered where Armand had gone.

Chapter Six

"Do you see that fool?" A male's voice rang out. It was higher than Armand's voice and strangely muffled.

The man who had been shot continued screaming until the muffled higher voice shouted, "It's just a flesh wound. Shit, shut the fuck up."

The screams temporarily subsided, switching to deep moans. Monique listened by the door, holding her breath.

"Naw, but he gotta be in here. He couldn't've got past me," another voice, deep and scratchy, said.

"Where he at then? He ain't back here. And he had some bitch with him. Where the fuck did they go?" High-Pitched said.

"If they got out," Scratchy said, "Les and them would've popped them on the street. Shit, they was on that car like lightning."

What was Armand doing? Monique moved away from the door. There were more of them on the street. She couldn't escape that way.

"Check everywhere," High-Pitched said. "There's no damn fire escape on this side of the building. I checked it all out. Look in closets, under beds, anywhere, son!"

"We ain't got much time," Scratchy said. "All that damn shootin'. Police will be here soon."

"We don't finish the job and it's us too, son. Believe that."

Monique headed back to the kitchen. She wasn't getting trapped staring down the barrel of a gun. If they were looking in closets, it was only a matter of seconds before they found the panel in the back of the apartment. For all she knew, Armand may have left the building or had run down to get Ray, leaving her alone. If so, he was a dead man. Scratchy had said others were in the car, meaning they had probably popped Ray. She and Armand were surrounded. Hell, *she* was surrounded.

41

Monique would be damned if she got killed waiting in the spot while Armand escaped. Monique knew Armand wasn't scared, but after how he had behaved over the past few hours, she didn't know what to think, what decision he had come to. Her life had taught her that love could disappear within the blink of an eye, that loyalty faltered in the face of jealousy and rage. Monique knew one thing for sure: she didn't hear any shooting, so this time Armand wasn't fighting for her.

She crept across the room and took a furtive look though the window, keeping her head low. High-Pitched had said "that side" of the building didn't have a fire escape, so there had to be one on this side. That was probably why Armand's crew cooked up the drugs in this apartment instead of the other; they could possibly escape from this side.

"Check it, man. It's a panel back here."

The speaker was too far away for Monique to tell who had said it. But that statement was all she needed to hear. Monique ran to each of the windows, praying for a fire escape. She saw the iron grate on the outside of the kitchen window. She heard the panel in the bathroom hit the floor with a raw thud. Where was Armand? Why didn't she hear shooting yet?

Monique scrambled to the kitchen, her heels giving her away. She heard the man hesitate in the hall, more than likely listening to the clacking of her heels. She pushed on the window but it wouldn't open. It was nailed shut. Desperately, Monique opened the cabinets above the sink. She was looking for something to pry the window open with, something to help her escape. She jerked open the last cabinet, then opened the cabinet under the sink. A sawed-off laid on the dusty shelf.

Monique didn't want that much of a gun; she knew the recoil would knock her off her feet. When she heard the attacker's cannon explode again, Monique screamed and picked up the sawed-off, cocked it like she had seen her father do, and fired toward the narrow hallway. It didn't knock her on her ass like she had assumed.

"Oh shit," Scratchy yelled.

Monique pointed the sawed-off at the window and pulled the trigger. She forced out the rest of the glass with the butt of the gun, raising it above her head as she ducked under the counter.

"Eh yo, I'm going to kill you, bitch," Scratchy shouted. "You got me with them buckshots."

Monique tried to hoist herself through the jagged window but her hand slipped, gashing her arm as she fell to the floor and bumped her head on the side of the counter. The gun laid next to her on the floor. Within a second, Scratchy was standing over her, his rifle pointed at her face, blood flowing down his arm.

"Where your man?" He poked her with the rifle.

Monique was trembling, too scared to respond.

He cocked his rifle. "Bitch, I said where is your man?"

"I, I don't know ... he went ..." Monique couldn't get the words out.

He poked her with the barrel again. "Who you?"

"Mo ... Monique. Nobody. I don't have nothing to do with nothing."

His eyes followed the length of her body and stopped at her neck. "Let me see that necklace?"

Monique couldn't believe he was going to rob her before killing her. Her hands were shaking too much to actually grip the small emblem on her chain. Blood poured rapidly from the gash just above her wrist. She scratched at her neck a couple of times before leaning forward and letting the necklace hang away from her neck on its own.

He snatched it off her neck, breaking the clasp. It pinched her skin as he yanked her neck forward. Her father had given her that necklace. The man examined it closely. She knew that he was checking whether the diamonds were real. She kept her eyes on his other finger, hoping he didn't pull the trigger by mistake and kill her.

She thought about the earlier prayer she had made, the desperate plea for intervention. Her heart sunk realizing that she hadn't kept her word. As soon as they were free she had completely forgotten her promise to herself, her promise to her soul. Now she was close to death and in no position to do anything. She couldn't ask for anything. She couldn't pray for anything. She still hoped an angel was standing somewhere near, though, ready and willing to intercede.

"Oh shit!" Scratchy said as he lowered his long cannon. "How you got that? What's your name?"

"I already said ... it's Mo," she stuttered.

"Wrong answer," he said with a scowl, his finger tracing the elegant shaped TW with a 2 weaved through it. "Eh yo, this bitch rocking the symbol, man," he called out to High-Pitched.

"What?" High-Pitched was getting nearer. "What you say?"

"I said this chick, she got the symbol on."

"Where y'all at?"

Monique watched as the big man ignored his partner, watched as he gripped his gun and raised it back to her face.

"Don't worry, bitch, I'mma return it to its rightful owner."

"Where you at?" High-Pitched's footsteps fell heavy in the back of the apartment. "Hold up, don't do nothing yet. Where you at?"

"Fuck that. This bitch got me with them buck shots." Scratchy's eyes were slanted and evil. His chin set and his teeth were clenched.

She was going to die.

His eyes told her that he would enjoy taking her life, would savor forcing the bullets through her brain. She prayed again hoping for forgiveness. She felt sad that she was going to lose her life. She felt sad that in the end, after all their love, Armand had left her.

Monique closed her eyes, prepared to die.

The whistling sounds of bullets filled the air again. The man in front of her jerked awkwardly as lead tore through his frame. Monique screamed and slid forward into his feet, trying to get under his gun in case he fired it anyway. It took a moment before she realized that the shots were coming from behind him, spraying across his side, into his back, arms, and thighs.

Monique didn't know who had fired and didn't care. As he leaned against the far counter, gasping for breath and trying to get a grip on his gun to fire back, Monique jumped up, slipping on all the blood, and slammed her body through the jagged windowpane. Shards of glass stung as they sliced through her skirt and tore at her hands and legs, but it didn't stop her.

She landed on the fire escape head first. She quickly shuffled down the ladder and took off running down the alley, staying close to the building and in the shadows. At the street she ran opposite the front entrance of the building. She took a left onto the main avenue, and then quickly crossed the street into another alley. She would rather take her chances against the streets than having to be questioned by the police if they somehow spotted her covered in blood.

Where the hell was Armand? Was he the person shooting? As her heels clicked against the pavement she thought about sending Armand a text. She decided not to in case his phone had fallen in the wrong hands. Instead she called her sister.

"What up, Mo?" Michelle said in her easy way.

"Listen, where you at?" Monique whispered, crossing another main street then darting back into the shadows. Her legs and arms stung. Her hands ached. She could hear police sirens.

Since she and Michelle had different mothers, "Where you at?" was synonymous with "Whose house are you at?"

"Daddy's." Michelle paused. "Why the hell are you whispering."

"Shit. You have to come get me, Michelle. But I don't know where the hell I am, and you can't tell Daddy."

"Yeah right. How is that supposed to work?"

"Please?"

"Do I hear sirens?" Michelle lowered her voice to a whisper. "Where you at, Mo? With Army?"

"I was. His place got shot up. I climbed out the window."

"Oh shit!"

Monique could imagine Michelle throwing on her Pastry kicks and searching her pockets for the car keys.

"I'm on my way. Wait, where are you?"

"I don't know, and I'm too scared to stop walking. I can't stand in any one place for too long."

"Look at the signs, heifer. At least I'll know the area. Then I'll call you back when I'm close."

"Hold on." Monique ran to the next corner. "Lyell and Lake. Do you know where that is?"

"Yep. Got some cousins over off Lyell. I'll be there in like ten minutes. Keep moving down Lyell, though. Lake is hot."

"Alright." Monique sighed, shaking her head and lowering her phone. How had she wound up in this mess? Her phone rang right back. She didn't look at it when she answered. "Yeah."

The phone disconnected; she stared at the caller ID. Someone had called her from Armand's phone. Monique slammed her body against the brick building she was next to and bent over. Had they gotten Armand? Why hadn't he shot them? Tears marched down her face, but she sobbed silently, forcing herself to keep walking.

Despite her anger at Armand and her suspicion about his inner turmoil, she loved him more than air. She loved his rugged street rawness that always had her back and always made her a little submissive. She could step over her other boyfriends, but Armand had called all the shots. She loved that about him, loved that he felt like what a man should be. Loneliness smothered her, making each step feel like she was pulling against gravity. If they had Armand's phone, then he was dead.

Chapter Seven

Pete looked out into the yard as the sun set and the evening sky glowed fantastic. He watched his son Ricardo palm some girl's ass. His son didn't take life serious enough, too busy playing gigolo. Pete had told Ricardo that some business needed handling. Now Pete had to run in behind Ricardo to get updates. Pete shook his head as his son all but fucked the girl on the front lawn. Sometimes he wondered whether his kids had it too good.

His girls were smart, though. For a second he had wondered about Michelle, his enigmatic Mikki. He wondered whether she had crossed over to the other team. Her ways were ugly, not feminine like her petite frame and pretty face. She was such an itty-bitty girl with the biggest street attitude ever.

No one would have ever known she had spent her life in private schools until she rebelled and her mother, Rebe, gave in and sent her to Edison Tech. Pete rubbed his head. In hind sight, he should have kicked Rebe's ass. He laughed at the thought. There was no touching Rebe, she would have whipped out a knife or a razor. He had made the mistake of laying his hands on her one time. She won his lifelong respect after that. He unconsciously rubbed the scar on his shoulder that Rebe had left behind.

But it aggravated him that Rebe had pocketed Mikki's tuition money for months before he found out. He had to wave it off. He realized that it was his fault for having a baby girl by a hustler. And he wasn't sure anymore, once she went to that wild-ass school, whether Mikki was straight or not. He didn't want that life for her, but it didn't change his love for her.

That was why Pete gave his children so much freedom. He allowed them to come and go as they pleased. He let them know they could always stay at his place no matter what. He wasn't a typical father, meaning he didn't breathe down their necks. He never had a parent, so he didn't know how to be one. All he knew how to do was care for his kids and raise them with knowledge of the game and knowledge of the empire they would inherit when he finally met his maker.

Monique was his other baby girl, his Mo, naïve as hell, beautiful and extremely feminine. Too much so. He started worrying about her as soon as he realized that she was becoming a woman. She had that thing about her that men liked, that needy thing that fooled them. She seemed soft, but he instinctively knew that she could also be hard as nails and stubborn beyond belief. Just like her mother.

Unlike Mikki, Mo had never tried to fit in with the streets. She had always just been herself: hanging out with Mikki and her mother's wild people or hanging out with her little honors classes friends. Pete saw her as the one with the strongest ability to adapt. She was the one he wanted to escape the game. She wouldn't need it. Mo made it to college. Pete breathed a sigh of relief daily that she, at least, was safely away from the streets.

Pete wondered how Mo was adjusting to the college boys. He knew that one of them would snap her up. Educated or not, all men loved a woman with some flair. Pete didn't know how to school her on dealing with black college boys, but at least he didn't have to worry about some thug stealing her heart and destroying her dreams. Pete had taught her everything she needed to know in order to stay clean and not let the game suck her in. Now that she had made it out, he knew that she could take care of herself.

Yeah his baby girls, Mikki and Mo, would be alright. It was this fool son of his that he had to get right.

"Ricardo," he said, "you better get your ass in this house."

He heard his son laugh a little. Ricardo and Mikki were never afraid of his gruffness. They had seen so much, had experienced so much pain, that they new his rough demeanor was only surface material. Only Mo seemed frightened by his anger, unsure of what to do whenever he opened his mouth. That was because her mother was always calm and patient. Mo's world had been kind and soft. He hoped like hell he could keep it that way.

Ricardo stepped through the screen door, turning his back on the little girl in the yard. Pete shook his head.

"Pops, you know what's up." Ricardo laughed.

"It's always pussy, huh?" Pete shook his head again. "But if you was player for real, you'd know pussy will always be there. You wouldn't have to chase it so hard."

That wiped the grin off Ricardo's face. "Man, whatever." Ricardo plopped in the chair.

"Whatever my ass. You ever see me chase tail? Ever?"

Ricardo looked in his father's eyes and grinned, shaking his head no.

"You ever seen me without what I want?" Pete gave him a hard look.

"Alright, Pops. Point taken." Ricardo sighed, leaning back in his chair.

Pete and Ricardo looked alike, although Ricardo was a little smaller and a little lighter than the six-foot-five Pete. Ricardo had wavy, black hair that he wore pulled back in a fluffy ponytail. Pete wanted him to cut it off. He was a damned "pretty boy." Pete smiled. He loved his kids.

The phone rang. Pete checked the caller ID, then clicked open the cheap prepaid phone. This was how he had stayed in the game so long, so deep that most of the hustlers didn't even know they worked for him. He was understated: a simple house in a quiet neighborhood in the city, a cheap phone, a simple life. No need to bling. He had everything a man could ever want. This was what he needed Ricardo to understand.

Pete put the phone to his ear. "Yeah."

"Missed opportunity." The message was plain and short. They couldn't say much more.

"How?"

"Fell off it."

"Why?"

The person didn't answer, just sat there breathing on the phone.

"Why goddammit?" Pete squinted and clenched his hands. This was his real anger; the side of him that only Ricardo had ever seen; and the part of him that kept his business straight whenever someone crossed him.

"TW2. On the girl."

Now it was Pete's turn to be quiet. He shut the phone and ran upstairs. Ricardo was right behind him. Was it possible? Was Mo up in that fool's trap house? She knew better. He had taught her better. She was still on campus, had decided to stay through until the fall semester. That's what her mother had said. His men had made some mistake.

He turned to Ricardo when they reached his attic bedroom, the only place he discussed business. "Where is your sister?"

"Which one?" Ricardo tried to read the expression on Pete's face.

"Mo."

Ricardo shrugged and shook his head. "I ain't seen her this week."

"You ain't called her?"

"Naw."

"What? Where is Mikki? She got to know."

"She in the kitchen." Ricardo headed back downstairs.

At that same moment Pete heard a car door slam and an engine start. He glanced out the window over the stairwell and saw Mikki's gold Malibu pulling out the yard.

"Ricardo, never mind," he yelled, feeling his heart stop.

There was only one place Mikki could be going in that much of a hurry without telling anyone she was leaving. Meaning Mo, his precious baby girl, was in the middle of some shit. The middle of *his* shit.

Ricardo's head appeared at the top of the stairs, breathing hard from running back and forth.

"Call Tony. Have him follow Mikki."

Ricardo nodded, whipping out his cell phone.

Pete dialed Mikki's cell and waited, shifting his large frame between either foot. He knew she wouldn't ignore his call. Out of them all, Mikki was always down for her pops. She picked up midway through the annoying ring tone that played in his ear.

"Yeah, Daddy."

"Where you going, Mikki?" he said quietly. He shouldn't have played it that way. They were two of a kind. She would know that he was hip to her just from his direct interrogatory.

She paused. He wondered whether she would lie.

"Uh ... Mo need me to pick her up."

"At one somethin' in the morning?" He deliberately tested her loyalty to both him and her sister.

"Yeah. She just called."

"What's up?"

"I don't know, she just called." Mikki's voice sounded shaky and uncertain.

At least she hadn't given Mo up easy. That pleased Pete a little. He expected her to stand up for her sister, even if it was against him. Although none of them had the same mother, they were tight as a fist. That was one thing he made sure of. Loyalty to the family first.

"Bring Mo back here when you pick her up." Pete hesitated, then spit out: "Tell her I want to know why the fuck she was up in a drug spot."

Mikki breathed heavy in the phone. "Okay, Daddy."

Chapter Eight

"Daddy already knows," Michelle said when Monique threw herself into the back seat of the Malibu.

"Shit! How?"

"Come on, Mo. How long you thought it'd before he got word that Army's place was shot up. Really?"

"How do you know?"

"He called me when he saw I had left. Asked where you were."

Monique held her breath. "What did you say?"

"Heifer, I ain't lying on this one. Hell no. He already knew. I told him I was coming to get you."

Monique's heart pounded furiously. She felt more scared than when she was in the apartment. "He still let you come?"

Michelle nodded. "You know he having me tailed. He think I don't know."

"What did he say?" Monique covered her face with her hands.

"Just said he want to know why you was up in a trap house. I said that you just asked me to come get you." Michelle shook her head as she sped down the street. "Sounded like he was about to lose his mind. Just so you know."

"So you did lie for me after all."

Michelle laughed. "A little something something. More like I gave him a shade of the truth. Shit, ain't that always the case with us anyway?" Michelle removed her long locks from swinging in her eyes as she looked at Monique. "But you and Army is finished. You know that, right? Daddy ain't having this, he gonna find out."

"It doesn't matter." Monique's eyes welled up. "I think Army is dead."

Michelle almost slammed into the car in front of them before hitting the brakes. "What? What you saw? Is that Army's blood all over you?"

"No. Someone called me from his phone and hung up. They didn't say anything." She wiped her tears. "Army wouldn't've done that."

"Oh word?" Michelle shook her head, a grim smirk on her face. "These fuckers must not know who we be."

"They knew TW2."

"Once Daddy gets in it, they gonna know." She hadn't heard a word Monique had said. "Especially with you lookin' like this. Trust. It's about to be some mess."

Monique sighed, covering her face with her hands. That's exactly what she didn't want, her father getting into it. But it was already too late.

Monique's phone buzzed violently in her hands. It was Ray's cell number, but she didn't answer it. For all she knew the killers had his phone too. Ignoring the call, she placed the phone in the cup holder next to Michelle's and watched it buzz and shake. Michelle glanced at it a few times, biting her lip. But Monique was too numb to think about any of that. All she wanted was to hold Armand in her arms, to look into his coal-black eyes, and to lick his chocolate skin one more time.

Michelle's phone began to buzz and she looked almost overjoyed. It occurred to Monique that if they had Armand's phone, they had Michelle's number, too. Hers was the only other number Monique had ever given him in case of an emergency.

Michelle plucked her phone from the cup holder. "You can ignore these fools if ya want, but I'm gonna see what the fuck they want. They don't scare me." She pulled the car over and pressed the flat screen. "Who this?"

Monique watched Michelle's eyes get wide as she shook her head, like the person calling could see her. "No, she alright, Army. She alright. Calm down. She right here. Hold on."

Monique snatched the phone. "Army?"

He let out a deep sigh, then was silent for a few moments.

"Hello, Army?"

"Damn, girl." His voice sounded like thick velvet against Monique's ears. "I thought we lost you, or they had someone else there who snatched you up and left." He was silent again. "Shit!" he screamed into the phone.

"I'm alright, baby," whined Monique. She hiccupped and began crying and her hands were shaking violently. "Don't be mad."

"I'm not mad. Where are you? Why wouldn't you answer the phone?"

"Someone called me from your phone and hung up."

"Don't worry. No numbers by name in that phone. They probably was pushing all my latest calls. My phone dropped off my hip when I was in there."

"Why didn't you do anything? How could you leave me in that apartment by myself? You left me!" The crying had released the fear, wild anger now followed. "Where the fuck were you while that idiot was pointing a rifle at my head?"

"A rifle?" Michelle screamed. "Who the fuck pointed a rifle at you?"

"I shot him, Mo. But I didn't know you was in there, too, and I didn't know he was down. He kept shooting and yelling out. Took a minute before I handled it. I looked around for you ... after. I tore both them fucking apartments up looking for you, but the po po got there. I didn't want to leave you, but I couldn't get got and shit!"

So Armand had killed him. And had searched for her. But he hadn't answered her question, though. What took so long? She wouldn't press it, not over the phone in front of Michelle.

"Where are you?" Monique said, eyeing Michelle.

"Raymond caught three. Dut was with him and fought them off. We're taking him to get some help now."

"Hospital?"

Armand didn't answer for a moment. "No."

"Oh."

"I need to see you." He took a deep breath. "I want to make sure you're good."

"Where you want me to come?" Monique asked.

"Naw naw. He is too hot right now. Hell no, you ain't going nowhere. Give me the phone." Michelle snatched the phone out of Monique's hands.

"Army, Monique got blood all over her. Her hands and legs and shit is all tore up. She looks a mess. I got to take her home." She hesitated, impatiently waving her hands in the air, speaking in complete exasperation. "I know, I know, I know. But that was your spot. So the cops gonna be looking for you. And you shouldn't have had my motherfuckin' sister in there in the first place." Again she stopped speaking, nodding her head and rolling her eyes. "Naw. I ain't doing it. To be honest, I don't know when you going to see her. My daddy wants her home and that's where I am taking her."

Silence.

Even Monique could hear the long drawn out silence. She took the phone back from Michelle. "Army."

"Where are you going?" he said.

"Home."

"I'll come by there."

"No. No, Army. Listen, just call me later, alright? Once you know what's up with Raymond." She glanced at the clock radio. It was two in the morning. "I'll call you after I talk with my dad."

"Hmph," Michelle muttered.

"Babe, call. You hear me?" Armand said, his tone questioning, searching, trying to put together the missing links.

"Army, who was that? Who were they?"

"I don't know yet, but I will soon."

Chapter Nine

Monique looked at the calm house with its tan exterior trimmed in white. It fit this quiet neighborhood perfectly. A heavy oak tree in the yard shaded across the wraparound porch. The house looked inviting, but Monique had no desire to enter it. The last person Monique wanted to talk to was her father.

She would have preferred dealing with her mother and all the drama that came along with her. At least her mother would feel sorry for her, worry about her safety, and check on her health. But Pete, Pete was the game. She knew that he was so high up and so deep into it that most of the street level cats didn't even know him. Armand didn't know him. They all answered to him, though, whether they knew it or not.

And Monique had been trained better and was still careless. She knew Pete would remind her.

When Michelle disappeared into the house, Monique waited in the car for a few seconds. She hoped Pete would be asleep but knew better. Most people didn't know anything about him. Even his children didn't really know what made him tick. It was easy to live with him. If they stayed out of his way, he stayed out of theirs. There were no rules. No parental barriers. His house was a playground as long as his things were respected, as long as no heat was brought to his house.

Monique had stayed there for weeks at a time without ever seeing her father. He would leave money on her dresser and keep it moving. He didn't call her much, didn't require anything of her academically or socially, and didn't invade her space or ask personal questions.

When they did spend time together, he would talk about his life, about situations she might encounter and how she should handle them. He would tell her about his tours of duty in Vietnam, how he had studied people, how their true nature showed. Pete was so raw, his life so real and razor sharp that Monique dreaded those talks, but she always listened. Carefully. Pete was not one to waste his time, and she wouldn't disrespect him by not listening. His lessons were never preachy, just short, simple, and real.

No matter how long she lived in his parent-free zone, she eventually missed the stability of a regular home, of an active parent who vocalized how much she cared. So Monique never stayed longer than a month before she went back to her mother. At least that's how it was before she moved into the dorm on campus. Now she rarely stayed more than a weekend.

Her brother Ricardo stepped onto the front porch. "Mo."

She slowly got out of the car and watched his eyes widen with each step she took.

"Mo, who did this to you?"

There was no answer to give Ricardo, because she didn't know. Ricardo was a miniature Pete—just as crazy too—so she couldn't tell him about Armand, either. The last thing she wanted was for either of them to declare war against Armand. She stopped in front of him and he leaned into her, resting his lips against her forehead. He still kissed her in a childlike greeting. He still saw her as a child. They all did.

"Come inside," Ricardo said quietly. His eyes scanned the street; his hand moving to his waist.

"I'm alright." She eased past him.

He peered down at her and shook his head in disgust. "What the fuck were you doing up in some idiot's crackhouse?"

"I don't know."

"What you mean you don't know?" Pete's deep voice ruptured the air.

Monique realized her father was standing just inside the door. "I don't know why we were there."

Her father stared at her without blinking.

She hated talking to him sometime. She always remembered how crazy he was once it was too late, and she was already stuck under the unrelenting beam of his eyes. "I went for a ride with some folks, then we went there."

"Why did you go inside? Why didn't you go home?" Pete spoke softly, but his fierce expression terrified her.

Monique shrugged. She didn't have an answer for that, either. Not one that she was willing to share. Ricardo stepped into the room behind her. He pulled his cell phone out and started text messaging. He eyed their father for a moment. Pete nodded and Ricardo sent another message.

"What's going on?" Monique said, looking from Ricardo to Pete and back again.

"I'm going to deal with this shit. Why was you up in there? You know this boy Armand?" Pete pressed.

"Yeah."

They stood in silence. Then Pete grabbed her arms suddenly, looking up and down them for tracks. She yanked her arms away and stepped back.

"You sucking that glass dick?" Pete said, scaring her with his intensity and crassness.

"No."

"Then you poppin' that heroine," he said definitely. His eyes hard as nails.

"Hell no!"

"Daddy, it ain't like that," Michelle called from the kitchen. "Stop scaring the shit out of her."

"Somebody better fucking tell me something." Pete's gaze narrowed; his jaw bones throbbed.

Monique flinched. Her eyes filled with tears as she cowered down. The truth was that she was terrified of Pete. She never really knew what he was capable of, and his instability scared her. "I ... I was messin' with this boy, Daddy. He went up in there."

"You fuckin' with a fiend? My college-student daughter runnin' behind a damn fiend?"

"No." She didn't want to say it, but she didn't have a choice. "No, uh, it was his spot."

The room became so silent that all Monique could hear was Michelle in the kitchen moving around dishes, trying not to seem like she was listening. After a second, even the kitchen became quiet.

Pete blinked and shook his head while Ricardo stepped closer to her, peering in her face.

"What?" Pete said.

Monique wasn't foolish enough to say it again. She thought Ricardo was going to hit her for a second. But she would have jumped on him. She wasn't afraid to fight him, but she knew he would never hurt her anyway. She wasn't going to just stand there and absorb an attack, though, she had had enough abuse tonight to last a lifetime.

Then it dawned on Ricardo. "You fucking with Armand, Mo? Oh shit."

"You fucking with Armand?" Pete began to laugh, a quiet chuckle.

Monique hated him at that moment.

"And while you were chasing dick, you followed this thug up into his trap house."

Monique didn't answer. She didn't know what to say. She was starting to feel exposed and naked under their inquisition. She wished Michelle would come out from hiding and help her. That was too much to ask of anybody. It was better that she didn't. The last thing she wanted was for them to question Michelle on whether or not she knew about Armand, and more details about their relationship. Michelle knew it all and she wouldn't outright lie to Pete.

"You his jump-off?" Ricardo's nose flared, anger building in the deep wells of his eyes.

"No. Of course not."

"Why would he take you to a trap house, Mo, if you was really his girl and not his jump-off?" Ricardo said.

"It's the first time he ever did."

"How long you been messing with him?" Ricardo said.

Monique shrugged. There was no way she was going to answer that question.

"So you let this hustler get you dirty." Pete shook his head and lowered it as if he didn't want to look at her.

"No, I don't use that shit." Monique was getting pissed.

"You being stupid," Pete shouted. "His spot is hot, Mo. Now they got you going in a goddamn trap house. You don't know who fuckin'watching, whether the police sitting on it. You don't know who spotted you. You in the game now, at least to whoever was watching. You dirty. You supposed to be at college and, instead, you fuckin' dirty."

59

Pete had never spoken to her that way. Ricardo looked at the floor. She heard Michelle drop a glass in the kitchen; it exploded. Monique could hear Michelle shuffling around. She wondered whether Michelle had shattered it on purpose, shattered it just to fill the thick tension with some type of sound. Monique stood in silence, listening to the glass splinter, feeling her heart pumping in her chest. Out of all of them, Monique rarely heard her father talk raw because she spent the least amount of time with him. Out of all of them, Monique couldn't take it and felt whips across her body with each harsh word.

"Armand wouldn't do that to me." The words sounded foolish falling from her tongue. Monique dropped her gaze to the floor. She knew they were right; her instinct had warned her that Armand had an ulterior motive. But he loved her too, that much she was sure of.

"What the hell is wrong with you?" Pete slammed his fists into the coffee table.

Monique flinched as if he had hit her. Michelle was in the kitchen fussing and talking loudly over the hum of a small vacuum sucking up the broken glass.

"No need to be up in here yelling," Michelle called out from the kitchen.

Pete turned toward the kitchen. "Mikki, get your ass out here. If you going to be a part of the conversation then be in here."

Monique watched Michelle enter the room. She looked over Michelle's head and focused on the swinging kitchen door as tears streamed down her face. Being under this type of spotlight in front of the two people she loved more than any other in the world, and the one she feared most of all, was embarrassing.

Pete turned back to her. "Why? Why are you messin' with this cat?"

"He took a bullet for me."

"That don't mean shit, Mo," Ricardo said. "He probably took a bullet for the game and you were just in the wrong place at the wrong time."

"He took the bullet when Monty's man came at me." This time she didn't flinch. She had never told the entire truth about that night before. She had spun it as she always did. She had said that someone attacked her and had gotten away. She hadn't been able to explain how the hit man had died or even verified that he had died at all. It hadn't mattered anyway. Monty's wife became a widow within four hours of her telling Ricardo about the attack, holes in her story and all.

Ricardo's mouth fell open.

"Mo, I gave you everything you needed so you wouldn't have to be with a hustler. Now your prints are all in his spot in the midst of a crime scene. Why would you let that happen?" Pete pressed, accepting Ricardo's dismissal of her statement.

Monique was afraid to shrug again. Pete looked like he was one second from throwing her against the wall. He had never put his hands on her, but living in his house she had seen what he was capable of. She never knew what trigger could cause him to cross the line. She just stood there.

Ricardo's phone buzzed. He flipped it open, looked at the incoming message and stood up. Pete met Ricardo's eyes and Ricardo headed for the door.

"Where are you going?" Monique said, watching Ricardo.

"He is going to handle this shit." Pete's voice sounded low.

"You going after Army?" Monique's voice shook.

"Mo, this is about more than just you," Michelle said.

Everyone looked at Michelle.

"So now what? Ricardo, what are you going to do?" Monique searched for her brother's eyes, but he wouldn't connect.

Ricardo walked out the door without answering. She turned to look at Pete; he shook his head slowly.

"Leave it alone. And be here when I get back," he said in a low whisper then he followed his son out into the dark night.

Monique stared at Michelle, who shrugged and slowly shook her head. There was nothing left to say.

Chapter Ten

"It don't make sense," Armand said around the joint in his mouth, sitting on the sofa in the basement apartment of a large Victorian house near downtown. "I keep replaying it over and over in my head."

They were at the house of a surgeon who worked off the record. The same surgeon Armand had visited less than a year ago. The same surgeon that everyone who was a part of Titan's family used free of cost. That was one of the benefits of working for Titan, one of the perks that less ambitious idiots didn't seem to recognize. Armand and his crew didn't get strung up in hospitals, fingerprinted and identified while under anesthesia. Instead, all medical needs went through Dr. Robinson. Titan was forward thinking like that. He was the only person higher up in the game who Armand actually respected.

Doctor Robinson assured them that Raymond was going to be fine. Now Armand and Dut sat waiting for Raymond to be stitched up, exhausted from reliving the attack, but strategizing all the same.

"It just don't make sense," Armand said for the hundredth time.

Dut sighed. "I know, man."

"Who the fuck? What the fuck? Why?"

Dut shrugged. "The why is obvious."

"Hell no it ain't. Those wasn't the normal folks, man. Not just some robbing fools. They was fully loaded and came at us professional style."

Armand took a long drag on the joint. He needed something to mellow him out and take off the edge. He wanted to kill somebody, but he knew this was the time to be smart, not just react. That knowledge didn't calm down his basic yearning for retribution.

"I had Mo with me, man."

"Yeah?" Dut's brows pointed inward. "How she got out?"

"Player, she must have threw herself through the window and onto the fire escape." Armand chuckled to himself, still amazed at Monique's survival skills. "That shit is damn funny when you think about it."

Dut chuckled. "That shit ain't funny, fool. Damn, Army. Think about that."

They both chuckled some more.

"You right," Army said. "I just can't imagine her doing that, though. There was blood everyway, glass all over the place. She must look a mess."

"I bet."

Armand wasn't much of a talker so Dut didn't tell him to shut up and to let him enjoy the buzz, which is what Dut really wanted to say.

"She talking about I left her. I had to get all that shit hid. I wasn't leaving all that shit there for them to take."

"That's fucked up." Dut gave him the once-over. "You left her ass under attack and went to hide the stash."

Armand glanced at him, fury radiating from his eyes. "I told her ass to be still. If she had been still, they wouldn't have found her. Even I could her hear her shuffling around in the other apartment."

That wasn't true, but what else could he say? He loved her, but he had to stash some things away rather than leave them to the robbers or, later on, the police. For all he knew, they were rogue cops. Either way, the product had to be protected or destroyed. That came first. He wasn't going to survive that break-in just to get killed by the mafia when he came up short with their money and couldn't cover the reup he already had in the works.

He had counted on Monique taking care of herself. Hadn't she proved able to do that when she sat up there and flirted with the cop in front of everybody?

What would he have done if she had been popped? Armand shook his head. It wasn't a possibility. He wouldn't have let that happen. He didn't let it happen. When he heard her heels click clacking on the floor, he had stuffed the money in the bathroom ceiling stash, replaced the panel, and rushed in to kill that fool. Armand had to admit his heart had stopped when he first heard the explosion from the sawed-off. Of course he had thought Monique was dead. How could someone her size handle a sawed-off, having never fired a gun before?

He remembered that she had asked for a gun, but a good college girl like her couldn't possibly know what to do with it. Or so he had thought. After the explosion made him stop in his tracks, thinking she was dead, he heard the man yell out that she had caught him with buckshots.

The whole night had shown him a Monique he hadn't seen the entire year and a half prior. The way she spoke to the cop pissed him off and turned him on at the same time. He didn't think she had game like that. That's why he had gotten with her because she was safe. The young girl who was so naïve to the game. He had wanted someone pure at heart who didn't know anything about the streets, someone who would see him as their everything.

Monique had been that up until tonight. Up until she used her wide-eyed, innocent expression to game the cop. He had to wonder if she had gamed him as well. Now she had somehow used the sawed-off and clawed her way out of an impossible situation. Case in point: how was she so calm on the phone after having just escaped the shoot-out? She should have been hysterical, calling everyone she knew and trying to get help. Yet, he was the one calling her phone over and over again—like a little bitch—while she was in the car with her sister, chilling.

Armand was more pissed at Monique than anybody, but he couldn't put his finger on the reason why. Even the way she had freaked him at the trap house pissed him off in hindsight. Their lovemaking was always intense; in fact, she had him turned out sometimes. He had expected her to get pissed off that he would try to get some pussy in that situation. He thought she would have raised hell, demand respect and privacy, and argue with him. He had been hoping for it actually. He wanted to put her ass back in her place, to slap the shit out of her for the first time in that hole-in-the-wall apartment to remind her that she was with a true hustler who was not to be disrespected even for the cops.

But she had gamed him again, rolling with whatever he wanted and loving him like a champion. He thought about how she had straddled him with her heels on, skirt pushed up to her waist, velvet wet and smooth before he ever touched her. She had been wet for that cop. He knew it. He saw when it had happened; when she went from acting to actually considering; when she looked out the window and caught the cop's eye before he pulled off, all while she sat right next to him.

Was he getting played? Monique was gaming him!

He shook his head to clear his mind. He was high and paranoid. That's what it was, and he was obviously tripping. He remembered how Monique had cried hysterically on the phone, asking why he had left her. She had relied on him. She had waited on him. Monique could have squeezed through the door out to the hall, which would have been certain death, but she didn't. She had waited for him until she couldn't wait any longer.

When he shot that big 'bama, he hadn't realized that Monique was on the floor, although he had heard her shrieks. After he hit the man, he heard footsteps behind him. Armand had turned and fired as the other person dipped out of sight. It was hunt or be hunted from that point on, until the person managed to disappear. Armand had popped the wounded one, determined that anyone found in his spot would die.

When Armand had finally went back to the kitchen, stepping over the dead body to look under the cabinets, he found Monique's necklace in the dead man's hand and the sawed-off laid against the wall under the fire escape window.

It had made Armand mad that the dead man had the nerve to hold Monique's necklace. It was odd. In the middle of a clear killing spree, the fool had taken the time to snatch a chain from Monique's neck. Why? Armand had tugged it out of the dead hand, tucked it into his pants as he leaned over the windowsill, and looked at the trail of blood that snaked its way down the fire escape. It had clearly been Monique's way out. Armand followed suit.

After following Monique's trail of blood down the fire escape, he had run down the street until Dut sped past him. They spotted each other in the same second and Dut slammed on the brakes. Armand threw himself through the open front window, hopping in as smoothly as Bo and Luke of the Dukes of Hazzard, as Dut mashed the accelerator. He glanced around to check the damage. Dut wasn't shot, but Raymond lay groaning in the back seat with bullets in his arm and chest.

Armand punched the dashboard and scowled at Dut. "Why didn't you go straight to the doc?"

"Ray insisted, man." Dut felt Armand's cold gaze. "We weren't going to leave you in a war zone. We were going to circle one more time."

"Damn." Armand tapped Dut on the shoulder. He didn't have any words for that type of loyalty. Armand loved Dut and Raymond like brothers. Only a true brother wouldn't flee a gun fight trying to help him escape. "I'm glad y'all made it out."

"Don't know how," Dut said, shaking his head.

Armand glanced down and noticed how tightly Dut gripped the steering wheel, how his fingers shivered as if they were sitting directly on a running engine.

"One of them walked right up to the car, man." Dut swallowed. "We were finished. Then, instead of firing, they all just walked away."

"What?"

"Yeah, man. Just when I was out of bullets. I … I couldn't believe it." Dut shook his head harder this time, indicating that there was nothing left to say.

Armand didn't know what to make of it. They had been under attack for a long time. The shooters certainly weren't afraid of the police or of finishing the job. Why had the one Armand chased fled instead of firing back? Why had the others walked away without finishing off Raymond and Dut? Were they mere pawns on someone's chessboard?

***

Now, the question still lingered about the necklace. Armand dug into his pants and took out the blood stained necklace. He never knew why Monique wore the symbol TW2 around her neck. She always wore it. The *T* and *W* looked like delicate diamond snakes with the number two weaved through them.

Very nice. Armand dangled it in front if his face as he lay back on the couch. He would make sure his future wifey got her necklace back when he went to check on her. He needed to make sure Raymond was straight first. He knew that he should lay low, but he had to at least check on Monique and make sure she was good. He was glad she was with Michelle because Michelle could hold her own, but Monique was his responsibility and he would make things right.

Armand took a deep, slow drag on the joint pinched between his lips and twirled the necklace again, watching the diamonds sparkle against the soft light of the waiting area. Now that he thought about it, Michelle wore one of these necklaces too. He wondered what it meant. They both wore these odd necklaces without explanation. It was probably because Michelle and Monique were very close. Armand shrugged as he tucked the stained necklace back into his pocket.

The smoke swam before his eyes like twirling swirls of ribbons. Michelle had mentioned their father tonight. He had never ever heard either of them say anything about him before. There weren't any pictures of him at their house. He had assumed Monique didn't have a functional father. Not one word, ever. And then, tonight, Michelle mentioned him like he was second nature, like they were close to him. Monique had a father who she answered to that she had never mentioned?

It was too much. All of it. Big Mike dead, Raymond shot, cops pulling them over, Monique being the queen of the sawed-off, and now her having a father that he never knew about. Someone whom she had failed to mention in a year and a half. The flavored smoke wasn't making him high enough. He needed something else to dull the confusion until he could make sense of it. He glanced around the large room, wondering where Dr. Robinson kept his alcohol. It had to be there somewhere. *All doctors drink, don't they?*

"So," Dut said, interrupting Armand's thoughts. "What are we going to do?"

"Retaliate, man. What other options we got?" Armand went toward the cabinets at the far corner of the room.

"Retaliate against who?" Dut wondered what in the hell Armand was doing.

That was the big question. Who had funded this type of operation and didn't think anything of lingering around that long to take them out? Armand rubbed his hand repeatedly over his head as he opened the cabinets. There was no alcohol, just stacks and stacks of folders. Armand pivoted in a circle in the middle of the room. Of course there was no alcohol in there. He slammed the cabinet doors closed, wishing Dut would shut up. He didn't have any answers. The last thing he needed was more questions being tossed his way.

"We're going to know who soon. Trust." Armand sounded stronger than he felt. The truth was he had no idea of where to start. Raymond handled all of his street communications. Without Raymond, Armand felt lost. Armand threw his body back on the couch and closed his eyes. What had saved their lives? He pulled Monique's necklace from his pocket, trying to figure out what to do next.

"Army?" Dut said.

"Yeah."

"I think you got to go underground for a while, dog."

"Yeah." Armand nodded while studying Monique's necklace.

"Damn straight. And you might have to take your girl with you, son. They know who she is now."

Armand hadn't thought of that. He wondered why. Why would the realization that he needed to protect Monique come to Dut but not come to him at all? He should have had the foresight to make sure Monique was taken care of. He didn't have a cell phone and there was no telling where he had lain Raymond's phone. He was going to call Monique again to make sure she was straight. Armand began to search the room for the phone. "You seen the phone?"

"Yeah, on the edge of the table."

Armand ran his hand across the empty table, then he bent down to run his hand in the space between the coffee table and the couch. As Armand grabbed the phone, Dr. Robinson came out of his private room. His light brown skin was flushed and damp. He rubbed a hand over his face, coughed and then met Armand's eyes.

Armand stood up. "Is he all good? Can he leave with us?"

Dr. Robinson sighed and blinked. For a second he almost looked fearful. The moment quickly vanished, however, and Armand saw a rare glimpse of kindness. Normally older black folks avoided his eyes or glanced at him in rage. It was nice, the momentary acknowledgement. But then Dr. Robinson ran both of his hands over his salt-and-pepper hair and leveled his chin.

He looked straight into Armand's eyes. "I'm sorry, son. He didn't make it."

Chapter Eleven

Armand was operating in zombie mode. He turned toward the door and walked out of the doctor's house.

And just like that, the plan changed.

Raymond's death changed everything. Fuck going underground. Fuck playing it safe. Armand's lifelong best friend was dead. His lung had collapsed from the bullet's implosion. The one least deserving of death was dead.

Armand had been prepared to die. He knew that Dut was too. Armand figured that Big Mike had weighed the risk and led the life that he had to lead in order to get by. Big Mike was a warrior and guarding the trap house was a relief from the streets. Armand had given Big Mike that job as a promotion after endless years on his grind. Armand figured he owed Big Mike a seat and a steady pay. Big Mike had always been prepared to die, had always lived as if it were his last day.

Raymond was different. Raymond never thought more than three steps ahead; he didn't have to because he had Armand. Likewise, Armand had Raymond, who reminded him of youth and having a good time, his brother in spirit.

Armand didn't remember the rest of what the doctor had said. He didn't recall Dut shouting his name as he turned on his heels and slowly walked from the house. His mind was on autopilot, putting together clues and links that would give him the identity of his attackers so he could take them out one by one. Every single shooter that had been at the spot would die. For Raymond.

It wasn't until he got to the car that he realized he didn't have the keys. He never drove anymore. Armand kicked a dent in the door of the Benz; its silver color pissed him off. He leaned on the hood of the car with his head hung low. The bile climbed up the back of his throat, threatening to spill over. Armand clutched his stomach, fighting back the wave of nausea. The only family he knew was dead.

Armand leaned forward and placed his forehead against the roof of the car. The neighborhood was so quiet and peaceful. Every house was an old Victorian mansion, and each plot was surrounded by manicured lawns. Space, grass, and fresh air. That's what came with being a doctor. That's what being a teacher's daughter would get Monique. She, her mother, and Michelle lived in their sterile little world of nice smaller homes, oblivious to the pain that others faced, the choices that they made.

Armand raised his head slowly. He hadn't been born to this world. Neither had Raymond. They hadn't had a chance to see what this type of life would be with the neat, manicured yards and the perfect married couples. How could life be so random, picking and choosing who had a chance at an easy existence? He had landed the crapshoot of a life, trying to build a dynasty that would take care of him and his boys out of absolutely nothing.

That was the lot he had drawn in this life, always pulling the shortest stick.

It took a second for Armand to notice them. His overwhelming grief had dulled him and the tranquil morning air had offered him a soft reprieve. He hadn't noticed the black Impala parked half a block away, but he saw a head move when he raised his hand to wipe away the lone tear that had managed to escape his soul. His heart stopped. How long had they been there watching the doctor's house?

Armand took a step back, maintaining his calm, refusing to look directly at them. He counted two heads now. One bent lower. Both were watching him. They had come to him. They were still hunting him. Even here at the doctor's neutral territory, while he was trying to get help for Raymond, they had followed.

Something in Armand snapped. He felt when it happened, when pain and emotion and anguish disappeared and everything just flipped to rage. Armand slowly moved back toward the front door and stepped through the threshold. Instead of joining Dut and the doctor, he ran past the winding stairwell through the wide hallway, through the two-story family room and through the sliding glass door. Stepping onto the deck, Armand hopped the fence into the next door neighbor's yard. He ran across six more backyards while estimating where the Impala was parked.

He came up behind them quietly with both Beretta's drawn. They had the rear windows open. He could pop them both at the same time. He rethought his strategy. If he killed them both he wouldn't know who they were or why they were hunting him. Armand pressed his back against a tree and glanced around. People were at work earning the buckets of cash necessary to pay the bills on these huge houses. The street was deserted. Even still, he had to be quick to do this unnoticed.

Armand dashed from behind the tree to the rear passenger door. He stuck both guns in the car and unloaded one bullet into the back of the head in the passenger's seat, then threw his body through the back window, landing on his back on the seat.

"Oh shit!" The driver covered his face with his hands as blood and brain matter splattered across the windshield. He shook his head and stuck his finger in his ear. "I can't fucking hear."

Armand lodged both guns into the back of his neck, his body stretched across the back seat. "Drive, fool." Armand didn't want to shoot again. One gunshot might be mistaken as a car backfiring if they were driving. Two could be trouble. Plus, he couldn't get far with blood all over the windshield.

The driver shook his head no.

Armand put the lips of one Beretta into the driver's rib cage. "Drive now," he said, no longer shouting.

Armand's sudden eerie calm must have triggered the driver's common sense. He pressed the pedal and they sped off. Armand saw Dut running out of the doctor's house from the corner of his eye, but he never turned his head. Armand knew that he was solely responsible for Raymond losing his life and he would pay this debt alone.

***

Like every city, the old mansions were only blocks away from the city park. They pulled into Cobbs Hill park and drove deep into the lush wildlife before Armand signaled for the driver to turn the car off. It was time to get some answers. Armand hopped out of the car and

71

dragged the driver out. He popped the trunk and found cord, plastic bags, and a shovel of all things.

"What you thought you was fixin' to do with this, huh?" Armand spat on the ground. He jammed his gun into the man's side. "Get to the ground."

Armand hog tied the driver, looping the cord around his hands and ankles and connecting the two with a length of cord along his back. "Son of a bitch, what you thought you was about to do? Huh?"

The driver kept his mouth shut, straining his neck to keep his face from the moist grass. Armand kicked him as hard as he had kicked the Benz.

"Who you with?" Armand said.

"Nobody," the driver spoke through clenched teeth.

Armand had already hammered him over the head with the butt of the gun hard enough for the driver to possibly hope death was imminent.

"What's your name?"

"Why?" the driver said.

Armand shrugged and unloaded the shovel from the trunk of the car. He walked toward the driver with the shovel against his shoulder, his hands gripping it like a baseball bat.

"Tony," the driver said, eyeing the heavily rusted shovel.

Armand poked him with the shovel's tip. "Tony, who you with?"

"Nobody," Tony said again. This time his eyes roamed past Armand, searching the trees for the hope of another person.

"Son, don't play with me." Armand shook his head. "Y'all blow up my spot then wait for me at the medical? That's neutral territory and you know it."

"That's why we just sat on it. Why we ain't do nothing."

Armand considered shooting him through the gap in his big ugly teeth for that statement. Instead, he leaned forward. "I don't even know you, so why you after me?"

The driver shrugged.

Armand popped him with the shovel. The driver shouted and spat blood. Armand leaned down and spoke next to the man's ear. "This how you want to die, son?"

The driver shook his head.

"I might let you go. A messenger. That's what I need. Someone to let them know that I'm coming for them, but I got to know who I'm going after first." Armand doubted this soldier would take the bait.

The driver shook his head again. Armand realized that he would have to do some maniacal stuff to make this man talk and that wasn't him. Not yet, anyway. He snatched out the man's wallet, but it contained a fake license. He had already pocketed the dead man's cell phone. Armand leveled his Beretta between the man's eyes.

The driver lowered his head and closed his eyes. Armand pulled the trigger without blinking. The bullet dug into the man's chest. He gasped for air; his body jerked and twisted. Armand dug in his pocket and his finger scraped the tip of Monique's chain as he pulled out his lighter. The cigarettes had belonged to the driver. Armand was sure the dead man didn't care whether he smoked one or not.

He pulled slowly on the cigarette and squinted as he pondered on why murder was getting easier and easier. He used to avoid it, abhor it, certain that for each life he took he would suffer some horrific punishment. Some eternal damnation. One day it suddenly occurred to him that his life was already hell, that he was daily paying dues, and it hadn't felt impossible to pull the trigger.

Looking at the blood pouring out of the dead man's head, Armand realized that some part of his soul had died. It had to for death to no longer mean anything, for him to stand here smoking over a dead body and feel nothing. He turned from the body and walked away. Armand heard the other dead man's cell phone ring. Armand purposely waited until the third ring before he answered. "Who this?"

73

Chapter Twelve

Ricardo stood in the dining room in complete confusion. He stared at his phone and shook his head. What the hell was going on? It was easy to figure out where Armand would be to finish the job. With the ammunition and manpower he had sent after Armand, someone in his crew would need a doctor. There were only a few doctors that worked for the underground, loyal to the different families.

Armand worked for Titan's crew. Titan's one up-and-coming superstar. Titan had the west side of the city on lock. Pete had told him that he could operate it without a battle if he stayed within his boundaries. Lately Titan had started pushing, opening a bar within another hustler's area, letting his men kill some women who were getting protection from another family. Pete had gotten tired of facilitating meetings and negotiating truces that Titan and his people repeatedly disregarded.

Pete had repeatedly warned Titan to end the disrespect. If Pete couldn't enforce his word, then nobody could trust the forum they had working, which was the family network that allowed them to all get part of the wealth. That lack of trust would weaken Pete's position and start an all-out war across the city, something Pete wasn't going to deal with again. He had seen the results of that in the '90s when the crack game brought in a new type of hustler: the foolish players who were willing to sell their own momma for the paper. The bloodshed had been remarkable and devastating. He wouldn't engage in that again, not when he could nip it in the bud in advance.

The last straw was when Titan's people had robbed and shot Lyons over in the northwest corridor. They had no business over there, and Lyons was well respected. Lyons had been in the game a long time and his family upheld the same beliefs as Pete. It was a mistake that left Pete with little options. If Titan couldn't control his people, Pete would, and he would start by taking out Titan's highest earner and most well-known young gun, Armand.

The entire operation should have been quick and simple. Instead, Armand had gotten away, Monique had been in the mix, and now Ricardo's latest instructions to finish the job were failing. His men had sat on Titan's doctor's house for hours. They hadn't called with updates. They weren't returning his calls. The doctor's spot was always neutral in these matters; it was one of the benefits of the forum. Ricardo couldn't figure out why his people weren't responding. They were not supposed to engage Armand until he was away from the doctor's house. They should have called to update Ricardo when they were.

"What's good?" Pete's deep voice shattered the silence. Pete had been a First Lieutenant in the Army and his authoritative tone issued an unspoken command.

Ricardo knew that his question was a signal for him to get on his men and get a status report.

"Nothing," Ricardo mumbled, wishing his father would leave well enough alone.

Ricardo dialed Steelo, his right-hand man. Steelo handled his street operations, making sure that the teams carried out orders as instructed. Ricardo had decided a while back that he wasn't going to be a foot soldier pounding it out on the street, despite Pete's insistence that he personally handle every aspect of their business. He had too much to do. Too much to learn. A dynasty to prepare for.

"What's up, playa?" Steelo answered the phone on the first ring.

"What's good?" Ricardo exhaled.

"Ain't heard nothing."

"I need someone on it. It's almost noon. Shouldn't go this long without someone touching base."

"I'm one step ahead of you," Steelo said. "Me and Rock heading that way now."

"Holla back."

"No doubt."

Ricardo hitched his phone to his hip and went into the family room. This shit was going to turn into a war. He could feel it. He had warned Pete months ago, told him to just handle Titan when he was exposed. Titan came to them so often lately that it would have been easy to set that up. But who was this kid Armand? No one knew

75

anything about him. To tell the truth, they didn't even know what he looked like until they decided to go after him to hurt Titan. That's when Steelo managed to get a snapshot.

Ricardo had heard about his success but nothing more. Armand never accompanied Titan anywhere and didn't affiliate with anyone else in the game. Going after Armand had been a bold move, the louder statement. It was also a much bigger risk. Having gambled and lost meant there would be tremendous bloodshed.

Ricardo glanced at Monique. She sat on the couch in the family room, staring at the television. The set was off. He shook his head while watching his baby sister sitting there staring at a blank screen. That, in and of itself, was a bad sign. Ricardo couldn't believe that Monique was messing with this Armand cat, that her nose could be so wide open for someone that wasn't even on his radar. How had this character infiltrated his home and consumed his baby sister and all he had was a snapshot to identify this guy? Ricardo felt vulnerable and it was a feeling he abhorred.

The entire scenario was playing out like some terrible movie in which the bad guys lose and the good guys prevail. Ricardo was sure that, in the scheme of things, he and Pete were more bad guys than good.

"Mo." Ricardo went to his baby sister, the baby of the family. "Mo."

She looked at him, her eyes glossy and unseeing.

"Mo. You talked to Armand?"

"No," she said and returned her gaze to the blank set.

"Did he call you?" Ricardo pressed her because he was under pressure.

Pete sat quietly in the other room, thinking and strategizing. Ricardo knew that this situation was under his control, and his father's future reliance on him would rest on this issue.

"No," she said just above a whisper.

"So you haven't talked to him in all this time?"

"No." Monique looked at him and her eyes seemed blank.

"Then, Mo, maybe he ain't your man like you thought," Ricardo said softly.

He needed her to get her head off of this fool. Armand was a dead man and the harder Monique's heart was against him, the easier she could dismiss his death and the role Ricardo and Pete would play in it.

"No, that isn't it," she said simply, her facial expression never changing.

"You need to tell me when he calls then."

Monique shrugged, hugging the large sofa pillow.

"I ain't askin' you, Mo, I'm telling you."

Monique simply stared at him. He recognized the fight in her. He knew that she was the last person to obey a forced command. He knew that he would have to fight her to get any information. Maybe it was time to fight her, to show her that they weren't children playing tug of war anymore. This was life. Maybe it was time to teach her a lesson. He decided to force the issue.

"Give me your phone."

"What?" Monique said. That jump-started her.

Ricardo almost laughed at her response. Even in her anger, her normal fire and attitude were cute.

"I said give me your phone."

"Ricky, you must be trippin' off something. You better not touch my phone."

"If he call, you better let me or Daddy know."

Monique didn't respond. She just raised her eyebrows to the challenge.

His cell phone rang.

"Yeah," Ricardo answered, sounding pressed.

"Car is gone." Steelo sounded breathless. "We don't see no one."

"The others still in the house?"

"I don't think so," Steelo said. "No cars."

"Drive around. Get back at me." Ricardo closed his phone.

He couldn't figure out what was going on. Maybe his men were following Armand, trailing him, and had simply forgotten to touch base. If so, he would blow them up for making him worry like this. He decided to try them one more time.

Ricardo flipped though his phone and found the latest number for Tony, the driver. Music filled his ears and then someone answered.

"Who this?" Armand answered the dead man's phone on the third ring.

"Where you fools at?" Ricardo yelled. "Y'all trailing that motherfucker or what? And why you ain't picking up when I call?"

The second of silence immediately let Ricardo know that something was wrong.

"Your boys trailed me. And both got got. Now I got their phones, their wallets, and your info." There was a pause. "Ricardo."

Ricardo pressed his palm flat against his forehead while staring at the caller ID. Dumb-ass Tony must have stored Ricardo's number under his actual name. He couldn't believe it. Ricardo held his tongue and waited. There was only one person that this could be. It was Armand. Ricardo had Armand on the phone and had absolutely nothing to say.

"You know me?" Armand said. His voice was simple and calm.

Fear spread through Ricardo's chest. "No."

"Then why you after me?"

"I ain't," Ricardo said, his voice strained.

Monique looked at him through squinted eyes and suddenly sat straight up. Pete quietly moved into the room.

"Then who is?"

"Nobody. You Titan's man. Titan got some business he needed to handle. He didn't and now his people are getting got."

"Really?" Armand laughed.

Monique must have heard Armand's soothing laughter because she jumped off the couch and moved quickly to Ricardo.

"You got the wrong one, son," Armand said. "This wasn't my fight, but now it is. I got two at the spot; two more just now. I am going to get each one of you, a life for every drop of blood spilt. You heard?"

"It ain't going down like that, player." Ricardo's anger finally replaced shock and fear. "You don't want to threaten me, son."

"Do the body count. See if this is an empty threat." Armand laughed.

"Army?" Monique said loudly. "Army, where you—"

Ricardo shoved Monique back and she stumbled into the couch. Panic spread through Ricardo as he realized that Armand might hear his baby sister, might come after her to do her harm. Of course he would. Monique was the sure-fire way to hurt Pete. Ricardo had to shut Monique up, do something sudden to silence her.

Ricardo pointed an authoritative finger at her. She sucked her teeth and immediately jumped up, about to lunge at Ricardo when Pete moved in front of her. One look into Pete's eyes and Monique fell silent.

"Was that Monique?" Armand screamed into the phone. "What the fuck? You got my girl?"

Ricardo didn't answer as Pete turned to face him. He couldn't tell Armand that Monique was his baby sister because he couldn't risk revealing his identity. More important, he couldn't reveal Pete to anyone but the major players, the ones deep in the game. Pete had spent a lifetime disappearing and Ricardo wouldn't expose him, but something in Armand's voice let Ricardo know that he and Monique were a real thing, much more than Monique simply hooking up with some boy like she had said earlier.

"Bitch, is that my girl I just heard? Put her on the phone!" Armand's cool demeanor evaporated and his voice sounded like a crazed man.

"No."

"Fool, you got my girl? You just moved up on my death chart. I'm coming for you next."

"You don't want to do that. What you need to do is lay low. Stop going after my men. Then the girl goes safely and we are even."

"I don't make deals with the devil. You better not touch her or when I get to you, you going to wish you had never fucked with mine."

The line went dead.

Pete turned toward Ricardo. As soon as his eyes were off Monique, she ran and tackled Ricardo with all her might, jumping on his chest. He was so unprepared that the phone went flying as he reached out to brace himself for the fall. Monique pounced on the phone and picked it up, trying desperately to recall the number.

The sudden pain across the side of her face was so sharp that Monique lost her breath as she fell to the floor. Her face was numb. Dropping the phone, she sat there holding her cheek, wondering what had just happened. When she could finally locate her senses enough to look up, her eyes met Pete's. The look he gave her froze the blood in her veins. Monique felt her chest heaving in and out as she tried to catch her breath.

"What the fuck is wrong with you?" Pete said. The question was loaded with a million things never said between the two of them.

"What is wrong with me? Why the hell would you hit me? What—"

"This is family." Pete motioned to Ricardo and then himself. "Right here. Not some gunner running the street. He ain't your goddamn fam."

"Fuck you." Monique pushed herself up on her elbows. "He's more to me than you—"

"Fuck me?" Pete stepped forward, his frosty stare turning into a look of wild bewilderment. "What did you just say to me?"

"Aw shit." Ricardo stepped in front of Pete, who pushed him out of the way. "Mo, just shut the fuck up."

"I said fuck you," Monique screamed over Ricardo. "You don't put your hands on me. Don't no man put his goddamn hands on me!" Monique voice cracked as her screams ripped from her body. She scrambled backwards toward the wall and inched up it, instinct replacing civility. Her eyes scanned the room for something— anything—to attack Pete with. "That's the last motherfucking time you put your hands on me, I know that much." Monique felt like her head was going to explode. Nothing made sense but the clear desire to hurt Pete.

"Mo, calm down." Ricardo stood in front of her, his hand gripping her arm.

"You threatening me? In my own home, you threatening *me*?" Pete's incredulous expression was covered with a wide smile.

Monique knew that smile well. It was the smile he wore when he decapitated his enemies, when he disarmed the ones foolish enough to misread the smile right before he put a dagger to them. She had seen it often when she was a child, when someone would mouth off and Pete would slide over to crazy without missing a blink, putting his pistol against the person's temple before telling her and Michelle it was time for them to leave the room. Pete's voice was always calm and quiet. And Monique's stomach always twisted with fear at how cruel Pete could be, how he never thought about the pain he caused.

She had seen the result of that look ripple waves of pain across a person's entire family.

And now that insidious grin was aimed at her. Monique would have to kill him or leave.

"Mo, take your ass upstairs," Ricardo whispered, as he released his grip on her and moved toward his father, trying to intercept the unthinkable events that were bound to take place.

None of the Water's children had ever raised up against Pete before.

"Just go," Ricardo said.

She didn't move, tears running down her face, her jaw trembling.

"You saying fuck me for some little street buster?" Pete shook his head. "I trained you better."

"Pops, she don't mean it." Ricardo stepped in front of Pete again but his father's massive hand pushed him away.

Pete's eyes never left Monique, the smile faded. "Dammit, you know better." Pete took another step toward Monique. "I created an empire for my children. For you!" His voice rebounded off the wall and shook Monique's heart. She had never heard him yell like this before.

"My seed! TW2 is infinite! Forever! Everything that you need!" Pete said.

Monique felt the tears running down her face, but in her anger, she didn't care. She wanted to put a dent in the side of his head with the vase on the fireplace mantle. She wanted to spit at him. Something to hurt him. But she didn't dare. That smile and its implications had her frozen. Her anger was stifled by one very real thing—fear.

"Pops, she just twisted up over this young gun." Ricardo moved back in front of his father. "Just—"

Pete ignored Ricardo. "You are my child. Mine. I ain't losing you to these streets, not giving you to this little bastard. No daughter of mine will be turning tricks, sliding down nobody's pole, icing up their veins with that blow."

Monique opened her mouth to defend herself, but quickly shut it. Pete was past angry. He was past the rage that she was experiencing. Ricardo floated between them.

81

"I don't give a fuck who or what you think I am, Monique. You better know this: I'll scratch my own seed off the face of this earth before I let the streets gobble them up. "

The crazy look that filled his eyes reminded Monique of the distant look he got when reminiscing on the Vietnam War. Or that far distant look he had when he sat in the front of the fireplace and stared into its flames for hours, mesmerized.

He stood just in front of her. His voice was a hot whisper pressing against her skin, burning into her eyelids. "Don't you ever in your life disrespect me again."

She tried to look down, but Pete gripped her chin, turned her head upward toward his, gripping her face.

"Don't ever disrespect TW2 again. Not for nobody else."

Monique wanted to snatch her head away, but she didn't dare. In a few seconds, everything changed. Her father had just labeled her expendable as far as she was concerned, someone who could also be made to disappear. It was a threat she didn't take lightly, and it made Pete her deepest enemy. Father or not.

"Pops," Ricardo's voice was throaty, as if it was dragged over coals. He tugged at Pete's hand, trying to loosen the grip from his sister's face. "Pops, she got the point. Let her be, man. Just let her be."

Monique met Pete's eyes. She refused to blink, refused to back down. She wanted to let him see the rage that broiled inside of her, that foamed over the lid and ran down her soul like the tears across her face. *Fuck you*. She wouldn't say the words, knew better than to voice the emotion, but she knew her eyes spoke volumes.

"Get the fuck out of my face." Pete looked at her with a cold and detached frustration. He released her face and she ran up the steps.

Chapter Thirteen

Oddly enough it was Dut who returned Armand to normal. He had tried to follow the Impala, thinking whomever had shot them up earlier had managed to get Armand. So Dut trailed far behind, watching the car turn into the park. When the car pulled onto a narrow trail, Dut parked his Benz on the side of a tree-lined avenue and ran up a hill that overlooked the spot.

That was when he realized Armand had taken the driver hostage. He watched Armand, noticed how his black eyes shined with hate. His ruthless demeanor was scary, even Dut had to admit it. Dut wondered whether Armand would even recognize him in his current state of mind. Dut knew better than to surprise him.

Instead, Dut returned to his car and drove to the edge of the trail and waited. When Armand finally broke through the hedges, he didn't seem to notice Dut, didn't seem to see anything in front of him. Armand simply walked straight with the gun in his hand and the cigarette resting on his lips.

"Army." Dut hoped this didn't turn out bad.

Armand looked up, squinting as he focused on Dut's round face and thick locks. "Why you here? Did you take care of the doctor?"

"I'm going to get it taken care of." Dut spat at the ground. "Why you left me?"

"This ain't your fight. I owe Raymond. I got to do this for Ray." Armand looked past Dut into the trees. He dropped the cigarette and stubbed it out.

"You can't go underground alone. You'll be an easy target with no ear to the streets and no finger on the pulse. Can't be done. You'll be dead within two days."

Armand stared at Dut. He wasn't used to being told what he couldn't do and it irritated him. "You get the stash to the other spot.

Make sure the doctor is paid up and Ray's family don't have to pay for shit, you heard?"

"No. You ain't doin' this." Dut leaned against his Benz again, wondering whether Armand would shoot him. Dut didn't put anything past Armand when he was like this. "Not without me."

Armand kept walking.

"Fuck you!" Dut screamed.

Armand stopped and slowly looked back at him.

"Yeah, I said it. Fuck you, Army. Raymond was my cousin. My blood. You hear me? I had him waiting with a bullet in his chest while I circled the building for you. He told me not to leave you. I did that. I delayed him and now he dead. That's on me, too. So fuck that. Get your ass in this car."

Armand turned slowly. He stared at Dut, at the Benz, at the ground. Then he lowered his head and finally cried. Not a sobbing cry, but he actually released a few tears. When he composed himself, he walked over to Dut, who stood with his head in his hands. Both men pounded a fist with one hand and embraced in a loose half-hug with the other arm.

It was all they would do. That was all the emotion either of them knew to express. The three of them had been friends since elementary school. There was nothing left to say.

Armand walked around to the passenger's side of the car, and they both slid into the leather seats.

"You figure out who they are?" Dut said.

"Naw. Some cat named Ricardo. He named Titan on it, though, making me think Titan got me implicated in some shit."

"Ricardo." Dut shook his head as he pulled through the narrow park avenue. "There was a Ricardo over on the northeast side. But he was a black Puerto Rican or some shit. He couldn't have nothing to do with the game."

"He called his man's phone," Armand said. "That's the name that came up on the caller ID. I don't know many northeast cats. Gots some people over that way, but—"

"I'll make some calls."

"First thing is to get a safe house. Next, set up a meet with Titan. They used to talking to Ray. I don't know."

"It ain't no thing, Army. I know how to get to them."

"Shit, he should be contacting me. The streets should know about my spot by now. He should be looking me up."

"True."

"And we got to go by Mo's. Let's do that first."

"She all good?" Dut studied Armand from the corner of an eye.

"I got to check. They could've just been fucking with me. It sounded like they had Mo."

"Shit, Army, why you ain't say that from the jump?" Dut said, pressing down on the accelerator.

Armand shrugged and stared out the window. He hadn't said it, because he didn't know how to say it. He couldn't wrap his lips around the words. He couldn't admit that he had first left Monique in an apartment to die while he collected cash and demon dreams. Now, she was kidnapped and he had no idea of how to save her. He couldn't admit that he didn't even know who had her, that he couldn't imagine living with her death on his hands, that his own death would be better, easier to swallow. What words did anyone have for his current situation? Every single person between he and Monique would have to suffer, and whatever it was about him that kept letting her down would have to be killed as well.

She wasn't part of the game and could easily have a life without him. She didn't ask him for anything and refused any money he offered. Monique would shrug and kiss his lips, saying his love was all she wanted. She just wanted him.

The truth was her love repelled him. Why would she want him when he wasn't shit? What was wrong with her that she would leave the comfort of her clean dorm to sit in a smoky trap house, sexing on the edge of a raggedy bed? He kept trying to show her what he really was, to get her to leave him. He wanted to prove to himself that in the end she was simply another gold digger who had bailed when she couldn't get what she wanted. But Monique was nothing near that, and she met every challenge defiantly, proving that she wanted him in spite of all the bullshit he put her through.

"Fuck." Armand ran his hand across his head. He could only imagine what they were doing to her right now, the nasty thoughts running through the mind of whatever low-level idiot set to watch over her. He had to find her. He had to make things right. He had to be whatever she needed him to be. It just occurred to him that he couldn't really live without her.

They exited the expressway and combed through the gridded city streets. Armand spotted his crews on the corner and they nodded at the car as they passed.

"It's good we rolling through. Let them know we still alive." Dut tapped the horn twice.

Armand hadn't thought about that.

A youngster ran up to the window while they were at a stoplight. Armand had one hand on his Beretta as Dut rolled down the window.

"This my young gun, Army." Dut turned down the music and leaned over. "What's up, Michael?" Dut said.

"You, from what I hear," the small voice squeaked back.

Armand was surprised that someone so small had such quick wits about himself. Armand didn't like using children in the game. Dut would have to get rid of him.

The small boy reached into the window and dropped a key onto Dut's outstretched hand. "It's all good," he said and quickly walked away from the car.

"Who was that?" Armand said as the car slid through the intersection.

"Triana's lil' boy, Michael."

"Oh, your son."

"Whatever, man." Dut shook his head. "Before you say anything, I don't have him in the game. I can see it on your face. Although, I sure as hell want to. I trust him more than them other ones, that's for sure. He just makes my connects for me. This is the key to our spot." Dut put the key in the console.

Armand shook his head. "That's crazy, man."

"It is what it is."

"I still got to hit Mo's before I go there. I got to know that she is alright first."

"Call her. You can't go up to her mom's spot like that."

Armand glanced down at his filthy wife beater, noticing the blood stains across his clothes. He shook his head. What was he thinking to even be on the street in these clothes? Each speck of blood linked him back to the people he had killed.

He nodded, relenting to Dut's advice and leaning back against the leather seat with his eyes closed.

***

The house was on a quiet street off of Jefferson Ave, on Heisle alley, a couple of blocks from Bronson Ave. Armand glanced around, surprised that he had never been on this street before and hadn't even known it existed. He hadn't thought there was a street in his section of the city that was hidden from him. The spot was perfect.

Dut made a call as they pulled into a long driveway that ended in a narrow backyard. As Armand opened the door, Dut dropped the phone, reaching across the seat and pulling him back into the car.

"What is wrong with you, son?" Dut looked at Armand as if he had lost his fucking mind. "Wait for some clearance. Damn!"

Armand shook his head. He was used to rolling with Raymond and moving with freedom. Had he not been so shaken up, he would have laughed at Dut. "Clearance, huh?" He would have to get this situation handled and quickly. The entire thing was testing his patience.

Armand watched a shadow move across the rear porch door, then Chew opened the door and nodded. Armand hadn't seen Chew in a few days. He was one of their foot soldiers who ran the corners near Genessee Park. Armand and Dut climbed out and quickly made their way inside the house. It was a long and narrow house. Armand glanced around the pantry. He noticed that it was stocked with supplies then walked into the kitchen.

"What's up, man? You good?" Chew shook his head in disbelief. "I don't know how y'all made it outta there. The place is destroyed."

"You went up there?" Armand said.

"Huh?" Chew blinked in surprise.

Armand noted his response, wondering what was going on with him.

"Hell naw." Chew laughed.

Armand turned his back on him, seemingly dismissing him, and slapped hands with Mike's baby brother, Andre, who stood against the far wall.

87

"I don't even know what to say, man," Armand said to Andre, who nodded his head. "I can't even—"

"I know, Army," Andre said, wiping his face on his shirt and stepping back into the shadows.

"You ain't got to be here," Armand said, meeting his eyes. "You need to be with your family."

"Naw, I'm good. I can only take so much of them right now. I'll go back later. I just wanted to make sure y'all was straight."

"Everything is taken care of, you know, with Mike's arrangements, money for your peoples, you know." Armand looked at Andre, wishing he wasn't there. Armand hadn't wanted to face him just yet. "I'mma take care of all that."

"It's all good, son," Andre said, once again wiping at his face.

Armand thought about the driver he had killed earlier that day, about his family and the people who would be affected by his death. A circle of chaos. There was no other rhyme or reason. Mike was dead for doing a simple job. The men this morning were dead for doing the same. All because of some shit that didn't have anything to do with any of them. All because bigger men with deeper pockets were playing them like pawns on a chessboard, waging a stupid war that wouldn't directly affect themselves. Armand wasn't going to keep being a pawn; it was time to start sliding diagonally across life's board. He was promoting himself in the scheme of things.

"Dut, get a hold of Titan. Tell him I want to meet now. Ain't time for no official setup."

Dut nodded as Andre lead Armand upstairs to the middle bedroom. A pile of his clothes sat on the bed, and his personal things rested on the dresser in the far corner.

"Y'all went by my spot?"

"Yeah, right after it happened. Dut called and told Chew to get some of your things. We both went in case there was a trap up there." Andre rubbed his hand across his bald head. "Wasn't no trap, but some chick was there in the lobby, crying, talking about she couldn't get in touch with you and was worried."

"What? Who? Monique?"

"I don't know. I don't think so. Chew said she wasn't nobody, but I thought you should know."

The information should have come from Chew. Armand noticed that Andre had said it suspiciously as if he didn't trust Chew to relay the message. He couldn't address that right now. There was no telling what silly beef Chew and Andre had going on.

Armand nodded his head and exchanged a pound with Andre. "Good lookin' out."

"No doubt." Andre headed out the bedroom. "Holla if you need something."

Armand wondered who the girl was. He hoped it wasn't a blast from his past, some stupid chick stirring up trouble. Whomever she was, she was irrelevant to the shit he had going on now. He took a long shower and then lay across the bed in his towel. He hadn't slept in two days, and his energy was all over the place. Sleep wasn't going to come to him. Plus, there was too much to do. He needed to get to Titan and figure out who these folks were and why they were after him. He needed to ascertain whether Titan had sold him out. Then he was going to track his attackers and take each one of them out. There would be time for sleep later.

And Mo. Sitting up, he realized that he had forgotten about Monique again. Shit. He fished in his pocket for Raymond's cell phone and then decided against using it. He couldn't hold it without seeing his man. Instead, he shouted out for Dut's phone. Andre brought it upstairs and Armand snatched it, furiously dialing the number to Monique's cell phone.

What the hell was wrong with him? How had she slipped his mind again? He needed to get dressed and get to her mom's spot in the 19th Ward to make sure it was really her that he had heard when he was on the phone with Ricardo. He also wanted to check to make sure they didn't have Michelle, too.

Armand's heart was beating frantically. The phone rang twice before someone answered. A man's voice, muffled and low.

"Who this?" It was Ricardo again.

"You again, fool?" Armand felt his blood boil.

"It's simple. End it."

"Where is Mo?"

"She's safe."

"Put her on."

"No."

It was stupid of Armand to call and make demands when he didn't have a power position. He hadn't expected them to answer her phone, but of course they would. That much should have been obvious.

"End it and the girl goes," Ricardo said.

"For all I know she is already dead. And that is the assumption I am operating on until I hear from her. So consider yourself marked, ya heard?" Armand hung up and called Michelle's phone. It rang but she didn't answer. He threw on some clothes and ran downstairs. Dut was asleep on the couch, so Armand told Chew to come with him. Then, he sent Andre home.

Chew glanced outside for a few seconds and led Armand to the yard. They both jumped in Chew's Accord and pulled slowly into the alley.

"We going to Mo's house," Armand said.

"Cool." Chew turned on the system. The mellow beat of *Day-n-Nite* by Kid Cudi flowed through the car. "Yo, this my shit, son." Chew cranked the sounds.

Armand leaned back in the seat, closed his eyes, nodded his head, and listened to the words. He wondered how such a simple song could capture his vibe.

Chapter Fourteen

"Michelle, get up," Monique whispered. She had crept into Michelle's room late in the afternoon, her worry driving her into a state of panic.

Michelle didn't respond. She was sound asleep on her stomach.

"Get up, Michelle. Come on."

Michelle rolled over onto her back. Keeping her eyes closed, she yawned loudly.

"Come on, Michelle, get up." Monique shook her some more.

"Why? What's up?"

"I need a ride," Monique said.

"Uh-uh." Michelle shook her head. "Daddy said you got to stay here until everything blows over."

"He can't keep me here. He can't stop my comings and goings."

"Why can't he?" Michelle blinked Monique into focus. "You are so blind sometimes, Mo."

"Why you say that?" Monique felt offended.

"You are in the middle of a mess. What you mean Daddy can't tell you where to go?"

"This is his and Ricardo's mess." Monique was on the verge of tears.

"I don't know about all that." Michelle's long locks fell across her face. "I just know Daddy said you need to stay here."

"I'm not. I am going to find Army."

"Why?" Michelle sat up, fully awake. "You and him are finished, Mo. You better deal with it."

Monique turned to look at her.

"What happened to your face?" Michelle gasped.

Monique tenderly touched her cheek, feeling it swollen under her touch.

"Your face is black and blue. What happened?"

91

"Your father slapped me," Monique said bitterly. She glanced down at her taped-up hands and felt the burn from her scratched legs under the cool linen pants she had changed into. Even her arms were scratched, which was why she wore the sleeveless tank top, and now she had a black-and-blue cheek. This thing between Pete, Ricardo, and Armand was damaging her more than anybody else. She bore the pain across her body.

Nothing hurt worse than the realization that Pete had slapped her, threatened her and dismissed her. Monique had always been loyal to her father and had kept the few family secrets she knew. But deep down she always felt scared of Pete, sure that he was unstable in some unforeseen way that nobody suspected. Monique had always known deep down that if he ever flipped on one of his children, it would be her. She wasn't like the others, didn't have their easiness with his wildness, didn't understand the unspoken rhythm of his life like Michelle and Ricardo did.

Tonight he had proven her right and verified that her fear was well founded. She didn't have to stay here, and she wouldn't stay where any man who had put his hands on her lived.

"I'm leaving, Michelle. Are you going to take me?"

"Hell no. I love you, baby girl, but I ain't about to deal with Ricardo and Daddy on this."

"Fine." Monique shrugged, heading for the door, snatching Michelle's keys off the dresser.

"Mo, don't do this."

"Michelle, it's already done." Monique walked out the room.

***

Monique could hear Pete and Ricardo talking downstairs in the family room. There was no way around them. She took a deep breath and ran down the stairs. Ricardo looked up, spotted her cheek, and quickly looked away, shame dotting his face. Pete stared at her blankly before turning away. Monique knew he didn't feel any remorse, which made leaving all the easier.

Monique searched the couch and the family room for her cell phone. She moved the pillows out of her way, running her hands along the seams of the couch.

Ricardo finally spoke: "Mo, what you looking for?"

She ignored him, standing in the middle of the room trying to figure out where she had left it.

"Mo?"

"What?" Monique snapped, staring at her brother with the same look of contempt that Pete had held for her.

"What you looking for?" Ricardo repeated.

At that instant she knew he had her phone. She knew that he and Pete had probably gone through her information to search out Armand. She wasn't going to play this game with either of them. There was no reason to waste anymore breath on the situation. Instead, Monique went out to the front stoop.

She waited for a moment, knowing that both Pete and Ricardo were listening to her, trying to figure out whether she was lingering on the porch or intended to go somewhere. The smell of Pete's flavored smoke filled the air. He was the only father Monique knew who smoked ganja in front of his kids, with his kids. It had all seemed cool before, having a father who demanded nothing and operated on a real basis. Now, the other side had proven that limits were necessary. He gave too much freedom, and he took too many liberties. Monique would be damned if he touched her again. It was better for her to leave now than to burn the entire house down in an effort to kill him.

She stepped quickly into the yard, lingering for a moment. The potent smell floated to her nose as their murmured discussion tingled in her ears. Monique quickly jumped into Michelle's car. When the engine started, Monique prayed it was quiet enough that they wouldn't notice.

It wasn't.

Ricardo stepped onto the porch, staring at her in disbelief. He shook his head at her. His eyes pleaded for her not to leave, not to cross the invisible line, not to invoke her father's wrath.

Monique tried to shift the car into gear. Michelle had insisted on buying a stick shift, true to her nature of taking the cheap way out and pocketing the remaining cash. And of course, Monique barely knew how to drive a stick.

The car bucked forward. Then the engine roared as Monique fed it too much gas but didn't release the clutch.

"Shit!"

"Mo, get back in the house." Ricardo moved toward the car.

Monique gritted her teeth and set her chin. That wasn't an option. If she went back in there she would force Pete's hand. She couldn't help it. She couldn't stay there and be quiet, not after what he had said and done. She balanced her feet against the gears, finally managing to get the car into Reverse. The car rolled down the driveway.

"Mo, you don't know him." Ricardo jumped off the porch and ran toward the car. "Come on, baby girl, please. Mo, don't fucking do this."

"He slapped me, Ricardo," she yelled out the window. "Fuck that. Fuck him." She fidgeted with the car while trying to shift out of Reverse. "What grown-ass man puts his hand on his daughter? Huh?"

"You pushin' too hard, Mo." Ricardo reached the window and leaned his body in. "You ain't seen the shit I seen him do, Mo. You don't want to do this, baby girl."

The look in Ricardo's eyes scared her. Ricardo knew more than both she and Michelle. And whatever it was that Ricardo did know, he carried it with him like a burden, trying desperately to protect his family.

"He can't do shit to me, Ricardo. I ain't like y'all. I don't need him." Monique's lip quivered, but she refused to breakdown. She was tired of crying.

The car jerked in the street as she tried to put it in Drive. Ricardo continued to trot next to her, his arms reaching into the car, grabbing at the keys. She swatted his hands away with one hand, her other glued to the stick shift.

"My car!" Michelle's high voice pierced the air as she pushed through the screen door, her eyes wide and her locks flapping behind her.

Monique had the crazy desire to laugh.

Michelle jumped off the porch and ran toward them. Monique popped Ricardo's hand and shifted the clutch. The car jerked forward.

"Mo, you better not fuck up my car. What is you doin'?" Michelle stopped at the curb, shouting at them with her arms raised in the air.

As Monique looked at her, Ricardo threw his narrow frame through the window, his body pressed between hers and the steering wheel as he reached in for the keys.

Monique punched at him, hitting the top of his head as he went for the keys. The car rolled forward and swung dangerously close to Ricardo's Escalade, parked on the street.

"Ricardo, get out the way!" Monique pressed the window control, trying to pin his torso in the window frame. The car rolled toward the other side of the street.

"Goddammit!" Ricardo yanked himself out of the window, but trotted next to the car trying to reach in as Monique rolled up the window.

"Let her go," Pete yelled from the porch, a thick blunt clenched between his teeth. "She's willing to get herself killed and try to kill both y'all in the process. Fuck it. Let her go. She gonna see."

Monique slammed on the brake and looked at her mountainous father. Ricardo stopped running. Michelle remained still. His command ended their sibling chaos and reminded them of the gravity of Monique's move.

Monique snatched the clutch hard and the grinding sound reverberated down the quiet street. She flooded the gas and jerked forward, speeding away.

She glanced back in the rearview mirror. Ricardo stood there with his arms in the air, pressed against his head like he was catching his breath. She couldn't see Michelle. She didn't want to see Pete.

At the corner, she turned right onto Dewey and coasted past Bishop Kearney High School, headed toward Ridgeway. She wasn't Michelle or Ricardo. For them, their father was a safer option than their mothers. Their father offered them a safe haven from the chaos of their other siblings and large families. Michelle's mother had seven brothers and sisters, and they all had at least four kids, including Michelle's mother Rebe.

So every moment at Rebe's place was loud and noise filled because of sibling rivalry and family battles. Michelle helped her mother when she could but then escaped to Pete's for a reprieve. Plus, Michelle couldn't tell Rebe about her life. About her attraction to women and how she felt safer with them. Less threatened.

Monique couldn't blame her. Not considering the things Michelle's male cousin had done to her when they were kids. Things Michelle had never told anyone other than Monique. Things that Pete couldn't know because murder would surely follow.

Michelle knew that Pete wouldn't say anything about her female lovers, and probably wouldn't blink an eye. Rebe would surely raise hell, though. Monique shook her head, imagining how quickly Michelle's mother would throw Bible verses at her daughter, cussing and crying and condemning her to hell.

And Ricardo hadn't even bothered to go back home a few years ago. His mother, Lesley, was addicted to the game and anyone in it. She had turned into a dope man's groupie, sinking lower and lower, eventually winding up with a pimp. After the pimp tricked her out, she escaped with Pete's help, but she couldn't kick the drugs.

Monique remembered seeing Ricardo at school. His clothes were filthy and he had not eaten. Monique was still so young, she really didn't understand. She knew, however, that her older brother and his sisters were walking around school looking horrible. Ricardo hadn't wanted Pete to know and since he was older than her, he threatened her not to tell. She didn't care about Ricardo's threats. One thing Monique always knew in her heart was that Ricardo would never hurt her. Even tonight had proved that. He hadn't stood up to Pete for her, but he had tried to negotiate a peace. It just hadn't worked.

After months of giving Ricardo her lunch money and trying to keep his secret, Monique told her mother, who called Pete, who went to Ricardo's house and found his son living in unimaginable filth. His mother was geeking up in the bedroom. Pete had taken Ricardo, but Ricardo went back, afraid to leave his other sisters there alone. One day after school, Ricardo returned home to find two men beating his mother as if she were a grown man. Her clothes were gone and from the blood trickling down her legs, he guessed that she had been raped.

Before Ricardo could react, they had pointed a gun at him. Monique remembered how Ricardo had cried, retelling how they put the gun in his mouth and how he knew he was going to die. The only thing that stopped his certain death was the shooter had noticed Ricardo's necklace. The same chain all of Pete's children wore all the time; Ricardo's was thicker and more masculine.

Instead of recognizing it, like Monique's would-be killer had, Ricardo's assaulters had snatched it off his neck, claiming it might start to repay Lesley's debt. They laughed at Ricardo and told him that he needed to drop out of school and find a hustle because they were coming back for their next payment within a week, so they let him live. Within the hour, the idiots had tried to pawn the necklace at a pawn shop owned by Pete.

Monique ran her hand across her chest. Her neck felt bare without the delicately woven emblem. It had saved her life. It had saved Ricardo's life. It was Pete. His mark under which those whom he loved were protected. But now she didn't have it. Instead, it had been replaced by a black-and-blue cheek, a wounded spirit, and a scared soul. Life outside of Pete's protection.

For a moment she hesitated. Her heart faltered. Maybe she wasn't so different from Ricardo and Michelle after all. She didn't have the unstable family life that they had; but, just the opposite, she and her mother didn't have anybody. Was she willing to live outside of Pete's radar? Was Armand worth forfeiting the security that came under her father's armor? Of course not. No man was, but this wasn't about Armand. This was about her and the things her father had said and hadn't said. The accusation in his eyes and the disdain in his voice. It was about being treated like she was less than all of his other children, although she had been the only one to graduate with honors. She was the only one to go to college. And, obviously, she was the only one that Pete considered weak.

Pushing away the tears that tumbled down her face, Monique sped down the street, heading toward the harbor. She was going to Armand's penthouse first. If he wasn't there, then she would look for Raymond or Dut or someone who could tell her something.

Chapter Fifteen

When the black Honda Accord turned into her driveway, Miriam sighed. She enjoyed sitting on her sun porch and relaxing. The dark screen and tinted windows gave her optimum privacy. She could watch someone approach her home without them ever being aware that she was sitting right there.

After thirty-five years of teaching public middle and high school, Miriam knew just about every family on the west side. Chances were she had taught at least one child in that family, had tried to get them to see a life broader than the one an economically depressed Rochester could demonstrate. Miriam knew that this particular Honda Accord belonged to the oldest boy in the Taylor family. The Taylor child she had taught in seventh grade when Monique attended the same school she taught at. Despite Pete's money, Miriam always insisted that Monique attend public school. What would it say about her if she taught in a school district that she didn't believe would properly educate her own child?

It hadn't been easy, though. Monique was one of a few black kids in the "smart classes," meaning all white classes, in a majority black school. She had watched her daughter struggle with trying to fit in. Miriam had been proud at how Monique had formed herself into a happy medium, able to socialize with a variety of different people from different backgrounds.

And then the boys.

Miriam shook her head remembering how many of the little boys were after Monique. This one, Anthony Taylor, had been a major pursuer for the longest time. Chew. Another silly nickname given to a child who was never told that he was a king. Miriam shook her head. In all these years, she had never uttered the nickname out loud. She had adamantly refused to call him something so meaningless. A man was as good as his name, but it wasn't Miriam's place to remind him of that. Instead, she always smiled warmly and called him Anthony. He and Monique were on and off again for years. There was no doubt in

Miriam's mind that Anthony was the first little love of her daughter's life.

Miriam wondered what he wanted now. It was no secret that he had dropped out of high school and had followed a career she'd lost the majority of her students to: the streets. Even still, he had always been a respectful young man. Patting her hair down, she watched as Chew exited his car, furtively glancing around. That wasn't a good sign. Who was he on the lookout for? Then the passenger's door was opened and out climbed Armand.

Armand. Miriam nodded. Her poor daughter. She sympathized with Monique because she knew what attracted her daughter to this raw young man. His energy was thick and unwavering, an alpha male through and through. Miriam had met him several times. She noticed that he always looked in her eyes when he spoke and used his words sparingly and carefully. Armand loved Monique, although Miriam doubted whether he knew yet that he was in love.

It was her fault, really, for having ever gotten caught up with a man like Pete. What else could Monique look for in a man, find satisfying in a man if he didn't at least match up to Pete? This Armand fellow had the same fervor Pete had when Miriam met him. Pete had been no good for her just like Armand was no good for Monique. What could she say? How could she explain to Monique that the game would always come first, that Armand's love for her could never dominate? How could Miriam make clear that his lifestyle would always make Monique a victim to chaos?

Miriam only hoped that Monique would realize it for herself before she was tied in with a child, with a secret marriage, with a love so desperate for a hustler that she would have to deny herself a normal life. Miriam never wanted Monique to wind up like she had.

Armand tapped lightly at her screen door with Chew just behind him.

Miriam leaned forward. "Come in," she called out.

Armand pushed open the screen, squinting as he stepped into the dim light. Chew jumped a little, obviously startled that she was sitting there.

"Hi there," Miriam said with a smile.

"Hi, Ms. Rodgers," Chew said.

"Anthony." Miriam smiled warmly. She noticed that Armand looked back and forth between she and Chew with a confused expression.

"Sorry to interrupt you, Ms. Rodgers," Armand started, his voice sounding strained.

She looked deep into his eyes, which reminded her of black coal. Something was wrong. Years of dealing with Pete had taught her how to read body language, to prepare herself for any circumstance. "No interruption." Miriam sipped her tea. "Monique isn't here. Would you like something to drink or eat? I can give her a call."

"No ... no, that's ok." Chew scanned the block again.

"I thought she was home," Armand said.

Miriam could tell that Armand had just lied to her by how he looked away from her when he spoke. *Maybe Monique and Armand had an argument or were on the outs. If so, today was a great day indeed.* Not that Miriam had anything against Armand, but she wanted more for her daughter, more than the life she currently led. "No. I think she is at her father's place. That or the dorm." She noticed Armand's confused expression again.

"Well, is Michelle here?" Armand pressed.

"Michelle?" Miriam's forehead creased.

They stared at each other for a full minute while Miriam's mind surfed through all of the Michelle's that she knew.

"Michelle ... oh, Mikki? Monique's sister. No, sweetheart, Michelle doesn't live here."

Armand clenched his teeth; his body language was tense with confusion.

Miriam coolly explained: "Michelle has a different mother. Same father as Monique. You know how these things go."

Armand nodded, but his eyes seemed darker. He hadn't known they were half sisters, that much Miriam could tell. Most likely, he didn't know anything about Pete.

"Anthony, how have you been?" Miriam said. "Your mother?"

"All good, Ms. Rodgers."

"Good." Miriam looked at Armand, watching the conflict pass like a shadow over his face.

He didn't know anything about Monique. Smart girl. It was a relief to know that Monique hadn't spread out all of her family secrets when she poured her love on this young man. Maybe some of what she taught had actually stuck to her daughter.

"Armand, I can give Monique a call for you." Miriam moved toward the front door of the house.

"No, no, Ms. Rodgers, it's all good," he said, taking a step back and squinting his eyes. "Can you just let Mo, Monique, know I came by when you see her?"

"Most certainly." Miriam smiled. She leaned in and gave Armand a light hug, then hugged Chew.

Her heart said a prayer for both of them. The chance that either would be alive in five years was slim to none. She had watched this merry-go-round for the last thirty-five years. Pete was the only one she knew to separate himself from the chaos of the game. And at any given time, even Pete was only a day away from disaster.

"You be safe," Miriam said quietly to their backs as they exited through the screen door.

She sat back in her chair. She watched Armand glance up at the house with a puzzled look on his face. She also watched Chew shrug before lowering his tall body into the Accord. Within a minute, they were gone, leaving Miriam to ponder why they had actually come by and what was going on with her daughter.

Chapter Sixteen

Pete stood in the doorway and watched his baby girl drive away. One thing was for sure, he shouldn't have hit her. Pete chuckled to himself as he shook his head. Monique had a fire about herself that none of his other children had. He hadn't thought about it at the time. He had been so pissed off that she had opened her mouth while Ricardo was on the phone with Armand and put her own life at risk.

What was it with women and love? Why did they think that emotions somehow put them in a position of power over common sense or just plain good business sense? He and Ricardo were responsible for blowing up one of Titan's most lucrative trap houses in the lower west side. Not only that, they had also gone for Armand's life without hesitation, thinking they had the element of surprise on their side. And his daughter was still calling to the boy, wanting to be by his side.

Pete didn't understand it. He couldn't see what Monique saw. Anybody in their right mind would see that Monique was the easiest target. The baby daughter of the man who had just ordered a hit on his life? How much easier could it be for Armand to hurt Pete but through Monique? Just because she had slept with him, Monique now thought that somehow she wouldn't be on the receiving end of Armand's bullets once he put two and two together. What was she thinking?

It was like he hadn't spent years talking to her and preparing her for the ruthlessness of street reality. She had no future with Armand. She shouldn't have been with him in the first place. What was all Pete's money going to that college for if Monique was still tying herself to the streets? Now he and Ricardo had a damn mess on their hands. Armand was out of pocket. Monique was not only out of pocket, but she was probably out searching for Armand. The streets were always watching, always taking note of each miscalculation that methodically eroded Pete's authority and respect.

He would have to take the situation out of Ricardo's hands. That much was obvious, but it wasn't Ricardo's fault. If anything Monique was at fault. She should have never let herself be connected to the game in such a visible way. Armand had to die. There was no two ways about it. Four of Pete's men were dead. Four. Pete hadn't lost that many men in years, and Armand had disrespected Ricardo.

Pete needed to flush Armand out and put an end to this debacle. He had resources; his money ran deep. He didn't want to involve the police, but they would have access to more snitches than his people, have access to more folks who might have heard rumors about where Armand was hiding out.

It was a simple solution.

He needed Monique's prints to be removed from the crime scene at Armand's trap house. He couldn't have his baby girl tied to anything related to Armand, not for her safety or for her future endeavors. Involving the police was the only prudent move to make that situation disappear and to give him some freedom to track down Armand and complete the job.

It was going to cost him, though. He shook his head and thought about how to proceed. Even Ricardo didn't know his police contacts. Pete would have to handle that himself. The cell phone on the table rang, a classical tone that irritated him. Monique's phone. He had demanded Ricardo leave it on the table so that he could have the next conversation with Armand and explain to the boy how things were going to go down.

Pete steadied himself, lowering his blunt onto the small saucer and exhaling the pungent smoke. He snapped the phone open. "Yeah?"

"Hello?"

Miriam's light voice shocked him.

"Who is this?" she said.

Pete sighed, feeling the dull throb of a headache coming on. "It's Pete."

"Pete, where is Monique?" she said, suspicion making her voice rise.

"She's upstairs. Had a late night I think 'cause she's taking a nap."

"Oh," Miriam replied.

He could feel her tension slowly releasing itself. Pete didn't normally lie. He hadn't found himself in a situation where he needed to in years, but this situation was testing all his boundaries.

"Why do you have her phone?" Miriam pressed.

"Huh?" The women in his life didn't question him, but then again, Miriam was never like the other women in his life.

"I said," she repeated with an edge on her proper voice, "why are you answering Monique's phone?"

"I saw your name on the caller ID. Wanted to make sure you knew she was here."

Miriam accepted that. He could tell by her silence.

"Yeah, she was going to stop by today."

"She probably still will," he said through gritted teeth, knowing that he would have to eventually answer to Miriam for these lies; it was something she wouldn't tolerate.

Miriam was still his queen, the one who had left him to make a quiet and safe life for their daughter. Miriam still had his heart completely, although she didn't know it.

She sighed again. "Well, I was just sitting on the sun porch and her little boyfriend came by. I wanted to let her know."

Pete felt his heart stop. Of course Armand knew where Miriam lived. Everyone on the west side thought that was Monique's only house. How could he have been so careless to leave her so exposed? "What boyfriend?"

"Huh?" she responded, being funny now. She never wanted to tell him who Monique was seeing, teasing that she didn't want the boy to disappear.

"Miriam," he said slowly.

"Oh alright. This boy named Armand. He is one of the young men who grew up around this way. He and my former student Anthony came by."

"Are they still there?" Pete lost his breath. He wondered whether they had been listening to the conversation, preparing to harm Monique's mother as a response to him.

"No. They left. Just tell her they came by. I'll call her later."

Pete coughed. He needed to move faster than he thought. Monique was going to Armand, and Miriam had opened her house to Armand. Those two lives were worth more than any he had taken from Armand or any Armand had taken from him. Pete now had no doubt that Armand knew the connection between he and Monique. It had only been a matter of time. Time was up. Armand had the power and he was letting them know.

Pete knew it was time to fess up. It was a conversation he had never had before. He didn't quite know what to say. "Miriam, I'm coming to get you."

"What?"

"I will be there in thirty minutes. I'll explain then. Get some things packed." He stubbed out the remains of his blunt and tucked a gun in the small of his back. He searched the kitchen counter for his car keys.

"Pete, no. I have a meeting with my pastor in a couple of hours. We are trying to get an early start on next winter's Angel Tree program. I am not waiting until November to get it together, and we are dealing with more prisons than just Attica, so—"

"Now!" he shouted into the phone and headed toward the door. "Get your things together now." He tried being calmer this time, forcing the words through clenched teeth. Miriam knew how this life worked, he thought. She should remember how everything stopped at the drop of a dime. The last thing he wanted to hear about was some damn prison-gift program. "Lock the front porch and wait by the basement door."

"What's going on, Pete?" she whispered.

He hadn't shouted at her in fifteen years. The last time was when he demanded she stay or at least leave his baby girl with him. When she was his woman but was still insistent on leaving him because of the game. He didn't answer. The memory momentarily stopped him in his tracks.

"Pete?"

He could hear her crying, her sniffles invading the air. She was remembering how this went down. It pained Pete that this was the situation he brought to the calm life she had built.

"Ok. Listen," she said. "One question. Is Monique alright?"

"Miriam, honest to God," he finally answered, stepping through his front door, "I really don't know."

Chapter Seventeen

Titan couldn't believe the old man had actually tried to make a move against him, against his main moneymaker, Armand. He laughed, shaking his head in disgust. Pete and Ricardo. Who the fuck did they think they were? Titan ruled the west side, and he didn't need their permission. He didn't need them at all. He had simply been playing the role to keep the peace. It had seemed easiest.

The problem with the old heads was they always wanted the younger guys to pay homage, to worship them for having survived the game. To hell with that. Titan didn't have to kiss Pete's ass, and he sure as hell had no intention on being ruled or monitored by Ricardo. It had never occurred to Titan that they would have the nerve to go after Armand. He couldn't believe it. Even now, standing in the shadows of the surrounding buildings, watching the police and forensics teams scouring the building that contained Armand's center of operations, Titan found himself stunned.

Pete and Ricardo had stepped outside of the lines. What was the point of a family forum if Pete could just order a hit on one of his major spots? Why was Pete the leader of the forum any damn way? Titan glanced around the crowd gathered on the corner. He wanted to make sure that no one had noticed him before he stepped back into the trees. He walked easily between the buildings and pushed his way down the alley toward his car. His man, Wade, walked just behind him, keeping his space but also keeping his eyes peeled for trouble.

Titan glanced back. "You think they gonna try for me?"

"Don't think so." Wade spat through clenched teeth. "They can't now even if they want to. All eyes are on us now."

"Yeah, but a message has to be sent."

Titan couldn't let his number-one earner get attacked without retaliation. He had enough juice to mount a solid attack against Pete and Ricardo, but Titan knew he couldn't go against the entire forum. It would take a day or two to find out which families were with him and who he could rely on. No doubt the Tyson family would support him. They covered the entire south quadrant of the city. Between just his family and the Tysons, he might be able to pull off an attack.

Titan pushed himself into a black Escalade.

Wade jumped in the driver's seat. "Can't find Army," Wade said once they pulled off. "Been calling him all day. His crew has circled the wagons."

"Damn straight. He is underground for sure. He probably doesn't know where I stand."

"Either way, Army popped a couple of Pete's men last night during the shoot-out. Rumor has it that he got a couple more this morning."

"He tracking these motherfuckers?"

Wade shrugged. "That's your man. You know how he thinks."

Titan laughed. "A warrior for sure. But we may have to put a lid on it. This entire thing is tripping me out. Why would Pete go after him in the first place? And why would he try to get at him without getting permission from me?"

Wade laughed, startling Titan. Wade never really laughed. "Are you ready for this shit?"

"What?" Titan gave Wade his full attention.

"I don't know if this is the reason or not, but Pete's girl was up in Armand's spot last night."

"What you mean *his* girl?" Titan sat straight up.

"His daughter. Monica or some shit?"

"You're shitting me?" Titan coughed.

"I shit you not. I was sitting up in there, man. We had just finished the count. We was sitting back chillin' and she strolled up in there like new money. Came with Army. Fine as hell. Checked me out."

"Somebody is always checking you out. Forever using them crazy, glowing eyes of yours to lure these ma's in."

They both laughed.

Titan thought about it then shook his head. "But it couldn't've been. How you know it was her?"

"Can't miss her. She look just like her moms. You know Ms. Rodgers, the teacher. Plus, she had that shield thing on her chain."

"So, Armand is fucking with Pete's daughter." Titan sat still, staring straight out the window. "What is that fool thinking?"

107

Wade laughed. A moment later he became silent again, shaking his head. "I don't know if Armand know who she be. But he cleared us all out of there."

"What?"

"Yep, he told everyone to get out."

"Then all hell broke loose?" Titan narrowed his eyes, an incredulous expression overtook his face.

Wade nodded his head up and down as if he were bouncing it to some beat. "They was behind closed doors, but the groaning was loud and clear, partner. Then, he cleared out his protection. We bounced. They came blasting."

"A setup then?"

"No doubt," Wade said quietly.

"Pete can't go at my man without permission, and I damn sure wasn't going to give him permission to clap at Army. This shit is on me, man."

"True that. But you got to give it to Armand, he got balls, son."

"I know. He must've known the risk of messin' with her, especially with her wearing that stupid chain." Titan watched the city streets blow by—his streets.

Wade chuckled, but his face didn't smile. "No way to be in this game and not know it. Plus, I tracked Pete's family a few years back." Wade recalled when he was a guard for the Perez family. "My peeps was thinking about taking out Pete and his whole family. Mr. Perez wanted me to constantly be on that. But I didn't report the daughter, though. I didn't do that shit because of you. Back then, word was that you had Pete's daughter protected. So I let her be. But the other night when I saw her, I remembered, son."

"We got to lay back and see how Pete plays it," Titan said. "Would he really use his daughter for a setup?"

"I don't know. But we got to keep our ears to the streets, too."

"Yeah, and make sure don't no more of ours get got."

"For sure."

"Armand will reach out soon. We'll wait till we get the word," Titan said.

Chapter Eighteen

Wade pulled along side the condominium complex on the lower west side, close to the waterfront.

"Give me about an hour, man," Titan said.

"Smooth. I'll be out here, player."

"Naw. I'll get at you when I'm ready. If Army contacts anyone, though, come get me."

"Cool."

Titan tapped the top of the Escalade and then strolled across the thick grass to the concrete stairwell. He walked up two flights of steps and tapped on an expensive redwood door. It was smart that he'd made sure they reinforced the door when he bought the place. Titan thought about it every time he came here.

"Yeah?" Anji's voice broke through the silence.

"It's me," Titan said, her voice causing a stir in the pit of his stomach.

The door opened and Anji stood there with a calm smile. "My man has returned, huh?"

"Something like that," he said, smiling. Calm spread through him as soon as he looked at her. She was larger than most of his women, thick and comfortable in her own skin. Her eyes reminded him of a lioness: large and gently sloped. Beautiful.

Her auburn locks glistened in the dim sunlight pouring onto the concrete platform as her eyes took him in. More important, her life didn't revolve around him, which allowed him the freedom he needed to focus on his game. Titan had never been in love, that was for sure. Anji was the closest thing to a real *like* he had ever gotten.

Titan admired the space she created. She had painted since he came last. The honey-colored walls had delicate gold leaves painted throughout, accenting her brown leather furniture. Flowing sheer fabric spooled from the windows matching the multicolored pillows filling the seating space. Two large pillows rested on the floor in front of the fireplace. She had redecorated. Again. He glanced at her, smiling slightly.

"You like it, huh?" Enthusiasm spread across her face like sunshine.

"You got talent." He liked it. It made him want to call Wade and take off the entire day, to deal with the Pete situation later. But that was impossible.

"You should have told me you were coming." She paused, staring at him.

Titan's eyes drifted toward the rear bedroom. He glanced back at her. He went for his gun.

"Are you kidding me? Titan, stop tripping. When has there ever been anyone here but you?"

"That's what you say."

She smiled at him and shook her head. "I'm going to ignore that. I was just about to leave. Let me call and cancel." She grabbed the phone and left the room.

Titan didn't ask what she was canceling. He didn't care. The details of her life were separate from his on purpose. He had enough problems.

She returned carrying a Heineken. She placed it on a coaster on the glass table.

"Come here," he whispered, leaning against the wall between the kitchen and the foyer.

Anji raised an eyebrow, smiling. "You just want to get right to it? I haven't seen you in two weeks."

"I missed you."

"No you didn't." She laughed, but she went to him anyway, easily sliding her blouse from her shoulders. She leaned forward and caressed his neck. When her fingertips touched his skin, he exhaled deeply. "But I did miss you."

Her voice was deep with something he hadn't heard before. Need? Want? He couldn't tell. She kissed his shoulder and gently sucked his collarbone.

"What's wrong?" Titan said, surprised that he actually wanted to know.

She shook her head and smiled, but her eyes looked glassy. "Nothing."

What was he missing? Titan pulled her full-figure into his arms. It felt good to have her solid body against him. It took his mind off the situation with Pete and Ricardo and Armand. She was the distraction he needed to release his stress. He needed to be catered to before dealing with the mess Pete had caused.

Her lips felt like soft petals against his rough skin. Titan sighed, leaning against the wall and filling his arms with the fullness of her thick body as she bit him and tugged at his belt buckle.

"You good?" he said.

She never moved this quickly. She normally fed him and rubbed him down before ever considering taking him into her. In fact, they always showered together first. Today, despite her calm exterior, he could feel her tension.

Titan ran his hands through her thick locks and traced a finger from the nape of her neck to the tip of her lips. She opened her mouth and slowly wrapped her lips around his finger, starting at the base and moving slowly back, sucking his finger.

Titan sighed, staring at Anji. Maybe he should make her wifey. She was the best thing he had in his life right now. The game wasn't so satisfying anymore, especially not on days like today when the old heads had torn a hole into his finances without forewarning. For every day Armand's shop was out of business, Titan would lose over two hundred grand in profit. Not to mention the overhead he would incur having to cover men who weren't really working. Some of his people were too good to test by leaving them on the streets without work. They had to be paid. He would have to switch them over to another spot to keep it moving.

And then he had to deal with Armand's rage. The boy couldn't be left uncontrolled. Titan couldn't let Armand run the streets freely. There was no doubt that Armand was probably trying to kill them all, every one of Pete's men. It was hard to make a man swallow the fact that revenge was not allowed to him, not without permission.

From what Titan had heard, Armand had already taken lives that were protected, and the forum wasn't expecting anymore losses. The street bangers, they couldn't control, and they didn't really care. The low levels were so easy to replace, so low on the totem pole, that their deaths didn't even warrant much discussion.

But personal employees were afforded some modicum of protection. Pete's men who had been killed outside of the shoot-out would cost Titan. This was Pete's and Ricardo's fault. Titan had to figure out how to make Pete and Ricardo pay without alienating everyone else, even if they didn't know Titan was the one charging them penance.

An image of Monique popped into his mind. Titan couldn't believe that Pete had used his daughter in the game. Pete must have wanted to get at Titan desperately to stoop that low. Everyone knew how private Pete was. With the exception of Ricardo, his children had nothing to do with the business. Common knowledge was that Pete was doing it like the Italians: living beneath his means and keeping his life completely separate from his dirt.

Titan knew that one of Pete's women lived in his district. How could he not know? Ms. Rodgers had taught him in high school years ago. She was younger then; it was almost weird how much Monique was the spitting image of Ms. Rodgers. He had kept an eye out for Monique. He made sure that she was safe and that the streets knew she was hands off. It wasn't something he discussed with anyone. It was just something he felt he should do for Ms. Rodgers. She was good people. One of the few teachers who believed in him and had expectations for his life. He had disappointed her when he dropped out, but he wouldn't fail her. So he kept her child safe without her knowledge.

Pete knew and assumed it was done because they had a truce worked out. It was one of the few times Titan had seen a different side of Pete. Pete had mentioned that he knew Monique was being protected from afar and would look out for Titan because of it. That was actually how Titan had made it into the forum. To date, he was still the youngest member.

The west side wasn't as big as the east. Most folks knew each other or someone's family. Pete had understood that Monique was visible because Ms. Rodgers had her hands in everyone's education, and he appreciated the unspoken protection Monique was afforded, especially wearing that stupid chain: Pete's family emblem that guaranteed Monique safe passage to those in the know.

But that was just like Pete, though, working so hard to protect Monique that he had overdone it, making his inner circle easily identifiable. It didn't make sense to Titan. Then again, he hadn't really cared either way.

Now Pete had played him. Instead of handling whatever complaint he had like a man, Pete had used that very same girl against Titan. Against his man, Armand. So now all bets were off.

***

"Where are you?" Anji whispered into his ear as she bit his earlobe.

He shook his head slightly, coming back to the here and now, making himself concentrate on the warmth of her body and her soft hands. Her hands circled the waist of his jeans and hesitated on the handle of his gun.

Their eyes met instantly.

He didn't trust her or any other woman with his gun. He wasn't going to get murdered while trying to get some pussy. Titan slowly took the gun out of his waistline and placed it on the kitchen counter.

Anji yanked open the zipper of his jeans; he heard them fall to the ground. Her hands found his hard on and glided gently up and down its length. Titan opened his eyes. He wondered what had gotten into Anji. She went to her knees, pulled him out and tasted the tip of him with her tongue.

He wanted to stop her, to pull her up and make love to her, but he couldn't. Mimicking the motion she had used on his finger, Anji opened her mouth and took in his entire mass. Her tongue pressed against his throbbing shaft. Anji grabbed the base of him and turned her head to the side, taking him deeper. His crown bumped against the back of her throat.

Anji's hand groped his legs, squeezing the back of his thighs. He fought the urge to hold her head and, instead, ran his hands repeatedly though her hair, calling her name softly. He felt himself about to go over the edge. It was Anji. Her atmosphere. Her smell. It was the soft clinginess of her moist skin; the warm vibrant colors of the condo. She could get him there so quickly that it was embarrassing.

113

Titan pulled her back. "Wait." He tucked his hands under her arms and pulled her up.

They stood there looking into each others eyes, mouths parted and lips pressed together, but not moving. Anji began to smile as she felt Titan's fingers slowly inching along the slope of her belly, over the bump of her hips, down the inner flesh of her thighs. He nibbled at her bottom lip as he pushed two fingers between her inner lips.

Despite her flirtatious smile and exaggerated sigh, she was as dry as a pan of flour. Titan leaned back against the wall, his fingers fumbling awkwardly across dry terrain. She closed her eyes and pretended to be in the moment, but he wasn't buying it. He wanted to feel her velvet and taste her desire for him. And, after dropping to her knees and putting on the dramatic show, how could she not be even a little wet? Meaning, she was acting the entire time.

The last thing he needed today was to deal with some shit from her. Not here in this perfect space she had created. He didn't want anything to ruin the peace he found with her and almost prayed for her own sake that she wouldn't say the wrong thing.

"What's up, Anji?" he said in a low grumble.

"You baby."

Titan observed her for a second. She didn't seem like she was gaming him, but something was wrong.

"You want to talk about it?" he said.

She shook her head no.

"But you don't want to do this?"

"I want you," Anji whispered. "My mind is just cloudy."

"I got something for you." Titan gripped her body into him and moved away from the wall. He stepped into the narrow kitchen, guiding her backwards with each step. After a few steps, he hoisted her up on the counter and dropped to his knees. "I can clear your head."

It had been awhile since he had gone down. His hit-offs normally took care of him without any effort on his part, but for Anji he was willing to put in some work. Titan licked his two fingers and gently rubbed her pleasure before plunging his head between her thick thighs. He almost smiled at how quickly her body came alive. Her head shot back; her back arched.

Titan glanced up. His eyes feasted on her wide hips. He loved the way her thick body spread out on the kitchen counter. He felt himself rising harder as he inserted his tongue, tickling and cupping and tasting every inch of her. She grabbed at his head, called his name and screamed as he held on to her, kissing, sucking, and licking her most tender spaces. The velvet he loved came forth, coating every inch of her, but he didn't stop as she clinched her legs around his neck and leaned all the way back.

Her head rested on the ledge of the lookout to the foyer. Titan glanced up the landscape of her body, watching her knead her own breasts, pressing them down and gently rubbing the swollen nipples. As he turned his head sideways to tongue kiss her inner lips, she caught him by surprise when she bent her head down and licked her own nipples. She locked eyes with him as her fingertips crept down between her legs, touching her button as he tongue kissed her sweet inner flesh.

"Work it, Anji," he said, stepping back and watching her clench her thighs and pleasing herself past the point that any other person could.

Her tongue flicked across her nipples whenever she glanced at him. Titan couldn't take it. With one deep and targeted plunge, he was completely consumed by her. His pulsing thickness overwhelmed by her sweet tightness. Her fingers continued to circle her love, and he pulled out quickly and plunged again. Anji locked her legs around his waist, reached her hand just underneath him and tickled the underside of his smooth skin as he plunged into her again. That motion made him lose control. He pumped quickly inside of her as she grasped him and suctioned against him.

Titan's mind went blank. He could hear her releasing, could feel the swirl of liquid gushing onto him. Her wetness caused him to shiver as the walls of her petals tightened around him, locking him and creating so much friction that he couldn't contain it. Titan yelled out and bucked suddenly, twisting his body to pull out, hoping to miss her as he released all that was in him.

Anji giggled as he slumped over her. Their bodies were moist from making love. His finger brushed up against something hard on the counter and he tried to move it without opening his eyes. When his

115

hand pushed it, the thing flew into the sink. They glanced in the direction of the loud noise.

"Just my cell," Anji said, reaching over him.

Titan picked up the phone, glancing at it without meaning to. "Twenty-three voice mail messages?" Titan asked slowly, giving her the phone. He had just gone bareback in her; something he had never done with her before, and already the games and the bullshit were starting. "Who?" The tone of his voice and the look of craziness in his eye let Anji know that he wasn't playing.

"It's nothing," she said dismissively as the phone began to vibrate in her hand.

"Why you got the ringer off?"

"'Cause you're here. I want to focus on you."

Titan moved and stood next to her against the counter. "Anji, be straight with me."

She sighed. "My girl is having an issue with her sister. She needed to borrow my car. I was going to get her when you came."

Titan stared at her to make sure her words were truth. He noticed her eyes were misty again, that distant and sad look. "What?"

"It's nothing. Her little sister just got messed up with some young gun. She was in a shoot-out and whatnot. I'm worried about her."

"She'll be alright," Titan said dismissively, pushing against Anji. He was satisfied that whatever this situation was, it wasn't serious.

"I know, but Michelle just sounds freaked out. And, I ... There is only so much I can do."

"That's right. She ain't blood."

Anji glanced at Titan and rolled her eyes. "How you going to say that? Your boys ain't blood, but you treat them like they're closer to you than me, like they're family. Michelle is my girl from way back."

"My fault."

"You know her. Used to go to East High. The real tiny point guard on the basketball team."

Titan glanced in the air, pretending to look like he cared. He didn't give a damn about some basketball-playing female. He wanted Anji to focus on him and let him get inside her at least one more time. "Yeah. On that team that went to states. I know her." He licked her neck hoping to distract her.

"Well, her sister, Mo, is in college and everything. How she got all twisted up in some street shit, I don't know."

Titan kept licking. He was glad Anji couldn't see his face as his mind raced through that last bit of information. Michelle? Mo's sister? Yep, Michelle on the east side was Pete's daughter. Shit, life was stranger than fiction, that was for damn sure.

"Where you say the sister at?"

"We don't know. Took that little Malibu Michelle always drives. That's why I was going over there, when—"

Titan hugged her tightly and lightly bit her earlobe. "Give me another few minutes, then I promise to let you go. I don't want you all up on the streets, though. You need me to do something?"

"No. I'm just going to give her my car."

Titan nodded, flipping her over as she shouted out laughing protests and kissing the small of her back. He ran his hands over her hips and sucked the back of her neck. Her sighs turned him on, and she gripped the counter when he cupped her breasts from behind, rubbing his hands over her mountains and feeling himself throbbing against her plentiful bottom. Titan slid two fingers between the temple of her legs just as he pushed the full length of himself into her from behind. In that moment, Michelle and Monique left both of their minds, but Titan had logged the information in the forefront of his thoughts, and he would damn sure use it to his benefit.

Chapter Nineteen

The bath Anji had given him overtook his senses. When he awoke, she was pacing at the end of the tub, fully dressed, and mumbling into the phone. Her worried look caught his attention, and he wondered who could have her upset. If he didn't know better, he would have thought she was on the phone with a man. Her motions and gestures seemed to defend herself, to over express her regret.

He moved a little, splashing the water; it was still warm. She must have been pouring in hot water while he slept. The tub was a stand alone with faucets pouring water from two huge, golden lions mouths. Titan remembered raising hell when he had come over and found her wearing a wife-beater T-shirt and a short jean jumper while busting up the tile floor with a huge mallet. Even now he had to fight the urge to burst out laughing, thinking about how he had shouted that she was losing her damn mind. Who would tear up a perfectly good bathroom to install an old-ass, claw-footed tub in the middle of the damn room? That was some white folks' shit.

That's how Anji was, though. The hood didn't define her in any way. She was an artist through and through. She had worked on the bathroom for weeks. It was one of the few times he came over every night. He was fascinated by a woman who would watch an HGTV DVD over and over again and turn a nice bathroom into a sexy paradise. Now the tub had contraptions and a chain release to let water ease out while fresh warm water poured in. With the candles, scented water, and plush rug, Titan felt like a king soaking in a royal vat. Anji was the shit.

Titan leaned back on the bath pillow and kept his eyes on her swaying hips. How many women thought to do that, thought to keep their man's bath warm while he rested? Titan realized that part of the reason he was paranoid was because Anji was a good catch. The thought of her with another man made him feel crazy. It was time to seriously think about her role in his life and how to make her more official.

Titan imagined his mother, Deaconess Anderson, staring at Anji's dyed locks with disdain, eyeing her pierced tongue, and her extra weight in disgust. His mother was the head deaconess at their Baptist church. There was no way Deaconess Anderson was showing Anji off to any of her constituents. He smiled inwardly, thinking of all the hell his mother could bring to Anji's life. Deaconess Anderson was the head hypocrite of them all.

But Titan loved his mother, loved putting money in her hand every week. Still, he never could figure out how all that church dedication, pomp, and circumstance on Sunday didn't amount to much of anything outside of church during the week. He couldn't understand how she didn't mind taking and spending the dirty money he put in her hand each week, knowing full well how he had earned it.

Either way, Anji was the woman for him. His mother would get over it after a while. It was time for them to move forward. Titan sat up, letting the water pour from his smokey brown skin. Anji jumped, glanced over her shoulder, and quickly got off the phone.

"That her?" he said.

"Yeah. Baby, I got to go."

"She ain't got no one else?"

"No. She don't want her father to know."

"Who her peoples?" Titan said, testing Anji. How much did Anji really know and how much in this game was she?

"No one you know. Puerto Rican-looking brother named Ricardo, and their little sister Mo. A whole rack of wild cousins ... oh, you might know them. The Pierces."

Titan interrupted her, laughing. "She related to the wild-ass Pierces?"

"Yup. So you know she can't call none of them." Anji shrugged. "Her daddy is huge. I remember him from our basketball games. But he alright. That's it that I know of."

Titan stood up, the cold air overtaking him.

She reached for a towel and handed it to him. "You stay," she said. "Please. I'll be right back."

"Naw. I got to go too."

"Why, 'cause I do?" Anji's eyes suddenly turned hard.

"No. Why you tripping?"

"I'm not. I just wanted to be with you for the rest of the day. I was going to cook for you." Anji rolled her eyes. "That's tripping?"

Titan smiled, stepping out of the tub. He started to pull her into his wet body, but neither of them had time for another episode. Instead he leaned forward and kissed her cheek, causing her to smile and squirm away from him to avoid getting wet.

"Look, I'll have Wade get her and bring—"

"No!" Anji's voice was two octaves too damn high.

He stared at her.

"She don't know anything about you," Anji said, reading his body language. "And I don't want to have to answer about ... this."

"About what?" Titan patted himself dry.

"About allowing myself to be ... kept like this," she spat out.

"Kept? What the fuck you mean, kept? You ain't kept. You are my woman."

"I know, Titan. I know. But nobody else is tryin' to hear that shit."

"Well, they don't matter," he said stiffly, narrowing his yes. "I should—"

"Baby, I am not about to argue. Not today. I ain't seen you in two weeks. I obviously don't give a damn what people would think or I wouldn't be here, right? And I am. I'm here. So"—she glanced at the vibrating phone—"I got to go."

"Alright, baby girl."

"You're good?" she said, relief releasing itself across her face.

"Yep."

"You're not mad?"

Titan smiled, thinking how cute she was. "Nope."

"I'll see you tonight?" Anji stepped out of the master bath and into the bedroom. She started throwing things in her purse.

"No doubt."

She stopped, stood straight up with her hands on her hips. "I'mma see you tonight, right?"

"Tonight."

Anji nodded and headed for the front door. Titan made his way to his closet and selected a fresh Polo shirt and jeans. It didn't occur to him that she hadn't even kissed him goodbye until he pushed redial to call Wade.

Titan glanced around the large space. It felt empty without her. In fact, he had never been there without her.

Wade answered on the first ring. "Yep?"

"Come get me, player," Titan said.

"Been sitting out here for two hours."

"Why?" Titan shook his head. "I told you to leave."

"Homeboy, you trippin'. Armand got blowed up, folks is acting crazy, and you think I'm going to leave you like that? Fuck out of here."

"My man." Titan stepped into a fresh pair of Air Force Ones. "I'm coming out."

"Good. The meet was set up. I was about to call you anyway."

"Good," Titan said. "Look, while you out there, call Carlos and Chris. The girl that set Armand up is on the move, even her daddy don't know where she is. We got to find her first."

Chapter Twenty

Armand's penthouse was empty. Monique sat on the couch in utter defeat. She didn't have a way to reach him. Normally, someone was here, even if it was just the guys who guarded the doors. Monique turned slowly in the room. There was nothing to indicate that Armand had even been there. She didn't see the jacket he had worn the night before, which he would have thrown over the chair. She wasn't about to start digging through his personal stuff, because there was no telling what she would find that she didn't want to know about.

The place felt so bare without him in it. Monique had never noticed that before. There were no pictures or identifying personal effects. This was just another place where he rested his head. She wondered if he ever bothered to come here when she wasn't around. This was the first time she had been here without giving him advance notice. The first time there hadn't been food, music, his beer, and wine just for her. The first time it hadn't felt like him or smelled like him. It was mostly clean with clothes thrown here or there.

She wondered just how different Armand's life was from what she thought, and just how much she actually fit into it. Staying in his empty place seemed foolish. Monique didn't know what Ricardo may have planned, and she didn't want to be in another ambush. But then again, she hadn't been followed. She was sure of that. Plus, if Ricardo knew about this spot, it would have been demolished by now.

Monique went to Armand's bedroom. She wished she could touch him to make it all alright. She wanted to eliminate her doubt from the last forty-eight hours, from his change in demeanor, from both their uncertainty. This space took her back to late nights when he lovingly raked his fingers across her, massaged her scalp, kissed her neck.

This penthouse reminded her of the safe, silent, confident love that never seemed to judge her before. This space made her miss what she and Armand had been, how she had been so sure that he would be hers forever. Now she wished she could just smell him or could have some guarantee that she would lay eyes on him again. Her hand ran lightly over his bed and she touched his pillow. She lifted the pillow and inhaled it.

His smell was still there. The light scent of cologne lingered on the satin pillowcase. Pillowcases that he had put on for her, to protect her hair. She smiled. That was the type of stuff Armand did; the things that his boys could never know about. He often combed her hair and massaged her scalp as he leaned over and kissed the back of her neck. While she enjoyed the feel of Armand's fingers, she needed to tie her hair down at night to keep its shine. When she finally wrapped her head in a scarf one night, denying his eyes and fingers the pleasure of taking in her shiny tresses, he had removed the scarf and trashed it without saying a word.

Monique remembered how angry she had been at the aggressive gesture, at his unspoken coldness, at his rude rejection. They had remained silent. Armand was oblivious to her anger as he placed phone calls and moved around his space as usual, fumbling around in the kitchen for something to drink. Within an hour the doorbell rang. Soft words floated through the air, the front door closed, and Armand returned with ten sets of satin pillowcases, which he began putting on the pillows. She hadn't wanted to ask, had committed herself to being mad, sitting there with her arms crossed staring at the television. But the transaction was so odd, she had to know.

"What's with the pillowcases?"

"Huh?" Armand turned around and glanced at her, seemingly surprised by her question.

"You bought pillowcases in the middle of the night. Why?"

He grinned then returned to his job of stripping and replacing pillowcases. "For your hair, baby girl. No more scarfs, right? No need."

Monique rocked back onto the bed, turning around and crawling toward him so she could see his face. She couldn't tell if he was serious or not.

"What are you talking about?"

"Satin pillowcases," Armand said. This time he spoke slowly as if she were crazy. "Same as the satin scarf. But now you don't have to cover your hair."

Monique smiled.

"Oh, you done pouting now?"

"I wasn't pouting."

"Yeah, you was." He smiled.

She finished crawling toward him, then rested her hands gently on his chest.

"That was sweet," she whispered.

"Yeah, I know."

They both laughed. After that night, Monique had never brought a night scarf for her hair to his place again. That was typical Armand. Typical her. Typical them. It was the simple things that she missed, that she needed to know she would have again. She needed him to be here, needed him to reach out to her and let her know they would be alright. Monique lay on the bed, spreading her narrow frame across its center, pressing her palms flat down.

Where was Armand? Would she ever see him alive again? The night before had started this crazy whirlwind of events. She was used to Armand saving her, not abandoning her. The fact that he had left her in the apartment still played on her mind in stunning disbelief. It couldn't be true, not after the many times he had saved her.

Just like the night she first gave in to him, when he rescued her from a terrific snowstorm. Armand's kindness and charm had torn away Monique's resolve to stay away from him. Who knows what she had been thinking while trying to plow her way up Genessee Street in a blizzard with fried chicken wings from The Coop tucked under her arm. They felt like lead and were undoubtedly frozen in the styrofoam container.

Her head was lowered in a futile attempt to block the frenzied wind. Her scarf covered most of her face, slightly warming her inhale so that the freezing air didn't capsize her lungs. She still found it incredibly difficult to breathe, gasping loudly for air as she tugged at her heavy bag, cursing the inconvenient chicken wings and her own stupidity. She should have caught the bus, but Pete insisted that she stay off public transportation.

Her hood bobbed up and down, rubbing against her hat. A small part of her forehead was exposed and it burned from the cold. The wind and snowflakes blanketed her. She trudged along slowly. The normal ten minute walk had already extended past thirty minutes.

Her next door neighbor drove past, his eyes squinting through the sheet of snow. Monique didn't have enough energy to wave and couldn't even summon her strength to run alongside the car. As his car eased past her, tears tumbled down Monique's face and desperation began to rear its head.

She wouldn't be one of those people she heard about in the news: lady found dead on the side of the road after record-breaking snowfall melts. She wouldn't. No matter what, she had to get home, even if she were frostbitten by the time she got there.

Determined to deaden her emotions, Monique bit her lip and took a deep breath. The cold bit at her lungs and caused her to double over in a coughing fit. Either way, she had to stop crying. The tears just led to more pain as the water trickled down her burning cheeks, feeling like a nail being scraped against the frozen skin.

Frustrated, Monique had literally stumbled right into Armand, who stood directly in front of her in full-winter wear. The thick hood of his heavy, full-length Northface coat had covered most of his square face. She hadn't been looking forward while trudging along with her head down. Her eyes open but her thoughts absorbed her focus.

No one else was foolish enough to be out on the street. Monique couldn't find any words as she stared at him looking dry and warm in the middle of the white chaos. Her mind registered nothing but gratefulness. Her eyes fell on his lips as they curved into a smile and, despite her near frozen state and the inability to move her cheek muscles into a similar gesture, a wave of warmth surged through her.

"You don't have to be out here in the cold, baby girl," he had said, nodding toward a navy blue Lexus that was left running in the middle of the street with the passenger's door flung wide open.

Other drivers slowly eased their car around Armand's without blowing their horns or hurling out insults. That was due to the respect and power Armand's reputation commanded. The cream interior of the luxury vehicle was so inviting to her, and his lean frame in all that winter wear seemed so comforting that she simply kept her eyes on his lips.

His head relaxed back just slightly as he reached out and pulled a clump of ice from the hair over her forehead. "Damn, girl, it looks like I came right on time."

Monique had been too cold to respond. She closed her eyes for a second. She felt him take her bag and remove the styrofoam container from her grip. He shook the container—made a clicking sound with his tongue—and threw the container onto the mounting pile of snow against the curb.

He brushed her off quickly—clumps of snow falling to the street—and escorted her to his warm car. He placed her bags on the back seat and hopped in the driver's seat. Monique leaned back in the warm seat and closed her eyes, trying to ignore the painful sting of the warm air against her skin. When she finally opened her eyes, her brown skin was flushed and red, and the feeling was painfully returning to her fingers and toes. Then she noticed that they were pulling into a heated garage under his penthouse complex.

Armand had rescued her. Monique hadn't made it back home that night or the next.

***

"Damn." She laughed. Monique missed her man and knew that she needed to get off his bed before her thoughts took over. Monique hadn't realized until that very moment how sprung she was. Smelling the bedding? Shaking her head, she sat on the edge of the bed and laughed at herself.

She heard a sound.

It wasn't a loud sound, more like a muffled shuffling. Monique sat very still. It was stupid of her to not have taken one of Pete's guns with her when she left the house. What would she do if that sound turned into a villainous person?

The shuffling became louder; it was steadily approaching the bedroom. Monique quickly came to her senses and moved behind the door. The door creaked open; its bottom dragging across the plush carpet. Monique knew she was about to die … but not without a fight.

Chapter Twenty-One

"Where the fuck have you been?" Michelle looked like an evil elf sitting on the steps of the porch. A cigarette pinched between her fingers. Locks hanging across her face in chaos. "I tell you my little sister has disappeared and you fucking don't call me back?"

"I called you back," Anji said lightly, refusing to get into an argument with Michelle. She breathed deeply and focused on her tension release mechanisms. Everyone around her was filled with negative energy today. First Titan had invaded her space with his fucked up karma, and now Michelle was coming up on her looking like Satan's sister. She wasn't letting either of them invade her inner peace.

"Don't start that breathing shit, either." Michelle stomped her little self past Anji's window and climbed into the car.

"Michelle, you need to calm down. I got here when I could."

"Fuck that. I told you Mo done got caught up in some shoot 'em-up shit with Armand, and she chasing that motherfucker. My dad left. Ricardo is acting like a madman and won't let me touch any of the cars. You were the only way I could get out, and you stood me the fuck up."

Anji shook her head. It was impossible to keep explaining herself when Michelle was intent on being victimized and feeling sorry for herself. Anji had no doubt that Monique would be alright, she always was. In Anji's opinion, Monique and Armand had a good thing going. Anji understood why Monique would chase him.

Anji had met Armand a couple of times when Titan allowed him to come to the condo. Armand was the only person who Titan had ever allowed to meet with him at Anji's home, and she had been alright with it. Something in Armand's eyes reminded her of a warrior, of a real man. She couldn't blame Monique. If she had Armand, she would hold on to him as well. Armand laid more claim to Monique than Titan had ever laid on Anji. That was a fact she couldn't deny. More power to Monique and whatever that young sister was working with.

Anji remained silent, keeping her thoughts to herself as she drove down the pine-lined street, mindful of the speed limit.

"And you driving like fucking Miss Daisy. Pull over." Michelle rolled her eyes and tapped her fingers against the dashboard.

Anji took another deep breath and hummed loudly, tuning Michelle out.

"Pull the fuck over."

Anji pulled the car over, staring straight ahead.

"You were with him," Michelle said.

Anji continued to look out of the front windshield.

"I can smell him on you."

Anji looked at Michelle with tired eyes. She wasn't going to explain herself. She didn't have to, and Anji refused to lie. It wasn't healthy for the spirit, so she simply sat there.

"You aren't even going to deny it. You had me waiting while you fucked him."

"I love him, Michelle."

"Bitch, you said you love me."

Anji inhaled deeply and counted to five in her head. "But it's different."

"The shit ain't different." Michelle climbed out of the car and walked around to the driver's side.

Anji slowly lifted her plump frame out of the car—rubbing sensually against Michelle—and headed to the passenger's seat.

Michelle closed her eyes for a second, inhaling deeply as Anji passed. Michelle shook her head as she slid into the driver's seat, her eyes watery. "Damn. Now you playing games."

"Of course not." Anji chuckled. "Come on. Let's not do this."

"I am so mad at you. I swear to God." Michelle looked like she wanted to slap Anji. "And who is this mystery man anyway?"

"If I told you, I'd have to kill you." Anji laughed.

"Seriously," Michelle pressed.

"Seriously, Michelle."

Michelle let it drop. "So are you rolling with me?"

"Nope. Not with you acting like this."

Michelle sighed, pushing her locks out of her face and adjusting the collar on her Polo. "You made love to him, then me. Just like that."

"One time. I made that mistake one time because I didn't know he was coming over."

"Do you know how that makes me feel? Running in behind some nasty-ass man."

"I shouldn't have told you," Anji said. "You shouldn't have asked, after the fact, I might add."

"'Cause I could taste him." Michelle draped her arm across her stomach as if she were going to throw up. "Just like I can smell him now."

"Michelle, enough with the drama. You are such a drama queen. You don't smell shit." Anji paused. "And you are bringing up shit from months ago. What we did, had, whatever ... it's over. Why you got to do this now? You just like being miserable."

Michelle shrugged. "I'm not miserable. I just realized today exactly how selfish you are. Or how cold you are. Or something ... something fucked up about you." Michelle's voice cracked.

"I'll be that," Anji said. "But I came. That's what matters. Now you can take me back to my place and bring the car by tomorrow."

They continued to ride in silence. Anji wiped tears from her eyes. Both Titan and Michelle made her feel like shit. Both of them were selfish and demanding in private. Both of them didn't give a damn about her, not really. They were trying to milk her for what they could take. It was like they were in competition to snatch the goodness she fought to keep in and feed it into death's vacuum.

Anji kept her head up. She and Michelle had evolved from friends to lovers to this needy and pouty thing that she despised. She loved Michelle, however, and wouldn't bail on her during this time. Later, though, something would have to change. Dealing with Titan's selfish ass was enough hassle, and Titan paid the bills, financed her artist dreams, and took care of her. Michelle wasn't giving her anything but love, and that wasn't enough to tolerate this negativity.

"I'm sorry," she said as she drove toward Anji's condo.

"I know." Anji shrugged. "But I'm tired of you hurting me."

"I'm hurting, too," Michelle whispered.

"I know. And I am sorry. But we agreed that this was what it would be."

"I can't do it, though," Michelle slammed on the brakes at the red light. "I thought I could, but I can't."

"I'm sorry." Anji couldn't look at Michelle right now. She traced her fingertips along the window, watching her neat hands trace the lining of the window. As more tears fell, Anji stared out the window.

"Ride with me," pleaded Michelle. "I don't want to be alone."

"I can't." Anji shook her head, tears dripping from her cheeks. "I want to go home."

Michelle nodded. They rode in silence for the next ten minutes. Anji stared at the lush trees lining the old city streets. Michelle pulled into Anji's complex and parked near the cement steps.

"Michelle, call me if you find her or hear anything."

"I will."

"Let me know, anything," Anji said. She didn't want to leave it like this.

"I will." Michelle nodded.

As Anji exited the car, Michelle reached across the seat and touched Anji's hand. "I'm sorry. I'm stressed out."

"We all are." Anji picked up Michelle's hand and kissed it, then closed the door behind her.

Michelle sat in the car waiting for Anji to climb the two flights of stairs. When Anji reached her landing, she walked over to the balcony to wave and let Michelle know she was fine. Michelle leaned over into the passenger's seat, glancing up at her. That's when Anji spotted two men—both wearing all black with ski masks—dart out of the bushes on either side of the car.

"No!" Anji screamed from the balcony.

Michelle's face went from calm to panic. She finally noticed the gunmen and reached for her own gun. It was too late, though. The man on the driver's side placed his gun flat against the window and fired.

"No!" Anji screamed again, then froze in fear. She watched gunfire jump out of gun barrels on the inside and outside of the car. One of the gunmen stumbled back a few feet, leaned on a car parked behind her car, held the gaping hole in his stomach, then stumbled back into the dark hedges. The other gunman pointed his gun directly at Anji and fired.

Anji tumbled backwards, falling onto the balcony landing. She frantically crawled forward to her apartment; her palms scraped the gritty cement landing. Her keys were still in her purse by the ledge. Fear kept her frozen for a moment. She didn't have enough time. She could hear the gunman running, coming in her direction.

The basic will to survive suddenly propelled her forward. Anji scrambled to the ledge and grabbed her purse. Her door was too far away. There was no way she could open all those locks and pull open that heavy reinforced door in time. Instead, she hoisted herself up on the rail and climbed over the ledge.

Praying the fall wouldn't cause her to break something, Anji kicked off her high-heeled sandals and released her grip from the wrought iron gate just as the gunman reached the landing. Ducking, she ran as fast as she could back toward her car, toward her Michelle.

Anji couldn't let anything happen to Michelle. She just couldn't. Shots rang out in the air and Anji fought the urge to scream. She glanced back up and realized that the gunman hadn't seen her. The gunman was shooting at her door, trying to break into her condo.

Anji reached her hand through the broken window and unlocked the car door. Michelle moaned, blood flowed from her head, face, and shoulders. Anji stifled another scream. She didn't want to move Michelle, but didn't have a choice in the matter or the time. She quickly lifted Michelle's legs and put them in the passenger's seat, then lifted and moved her small frame over.

The door to her condo finally gave way. She knew that door wasn't worth all the hype. Anji could hear it slamming against the wall as he entered, cursing savagely. He was there to kill her, that much was obvious. Anji climbed in the bloody seat, kicked the gun that laid at her feet, pushed the gear into Drive, and sped out of the complex. Fragments of glass scraped at her feet and embedded in her toes as she drove. She didn't notice the pain or her blood sprinkling on the floor mixing with Michelle's. Breathing frantically, she prayed over Michelle.

"Come on, Michelle, hang in there, baby," Anji whispered. She knew Michelle didn't have a second to lose, but she couldn't risk either of them going to jail either. Anji crossed the Ford Street bridge and swung the car along the construction filled water front that used to be the Gateway projects. She ran under the cover of night, barefoot, tripping over rocks, concrete, gravel, nails, and raw exposed metal. Anji quickly slid the gun into the Genessee River and sprinted back to the car, not noticing the blood pouring from her feet. Her mind was on one thing: Michelle's life.

"Come on, Michelle. Hang on, girl," she said as she jumped back into the seat. She patted Michelle's hand but was sure, deep in her heart, her Michelle was already dead. "Come on, baby. Hold on. Please, Michelle. I love you. Don't do this." Anji cried. "Just hold on."

The drive was a blur. She never stopped at a light, never noticed anything around her. Somehow they made it to Highland Hopsital. Anji pulled her small friend out the car; and, on her bare feet, she carried Michelle into the blinding white emergency room, leaving a trail of mixed blood in their wake.

Chapter Twenty-Two

Without a weapon, Monique was vulnerable. Her heart beat kicked the shit out of her chest. Working on the pure will to survive, she reacted. She used her entire body and all her God-given might to slam the door into whomever was opening it.

"Ah shit!"

The male voice terrified her. She had half hoped it was a female, another groupie wanting to be with Armand. Other women hadn't been an issue before, but she expected it sooner or later. It came with the territory. Some tramp would decide to test the boundaries of their love, jealously try to capitalize on what looked like greener grass. Instead, this was another man that she would have to fight, another man who would link her to Armand and try to kill her just because. This time she didn't have Pete's shield to cause hesitation or grant her an unlikely escape.

Monique swung the door again, even harder this time. She felt it hit the other person with a dull thud. A scraping sound filled her ears; and, instinctively, she dropped to the floor just before bullets sliced through the hollow plywood. Monique scrambled to her hands and knees and crawled toward the bed during the awkward pause. She figured that the person on the other side of the door was listening for evidence of whether or not he had hit his target. But she wasn't quick enough. The door flew open, slamming against the wall. Monique felt a pair of calloused hands grab her hair and jerk her head back.

"Oh shit!"

The nasal sounding voice surprised her; his accent was heavy on his tongue. From the view on her stomach with her head painfully twisted back, she didn't register familiarity with the set of light brown eyes that peered down at her.

"It's you," he said. "Oh shit." He let her go, placed his hands over his nose, and leaned his head back.

133

Monique stood up, adjusting her clothes before glancing at her assailant.

Lopreste sighed and opened his eyes. He ran his finger across the tip of his long nose and checked it for blood. "If I didn't know better, I would think my nose was broken."

Monique didn't respond. As usual, she didn't know what to say. She wondered if the black cop was with him. That would certainly mean trouble. Then again ... being in Armand's penthouse all alone with a white cop was also a no-win situation. Nobody would believe her if they found out. Armand would think that she had turned snitch, which would have explained their escape the night before. Monique didn't need the streets or this cop to add anymore strain to her life. She needed to leave.

"What are you doing here?" he said.

She shrugged, backing away from him. He angled his body with her movements, keeping himself between her and the door.

"What are *you* doing here?" She sucked her teeth, eyes locked on his, giving him attitude.

"Shouldn't I be the one asking questions?" he replied.

"Not unless you got a warrant." Monique sighed. She ran her hands through her hair and slowly rotated her neck. It was sore, and it annoyed her that he had been so rough. "Seriously, why are you here?"

Lopreste shrugged. He pushed his gun into the small of his back and pinched his nose again. He wore street clothes: straight-legged jeans covered by a snug fitting gray T-shirt. Monique noticed that he was in good shape and that he didn't hold himself tight in that arrogant, confrontational way like most cops did. Monique decided to ignore the bulge of muscles that flowed from his neck down across his broad chest tapering into an obvious six-pack. She remembered the look in his eyes when he had walked back to his cruiser the night before, the small smile grazing the corners of his lips before he had departed. Flirting didn't seem like such a great idea anymore, not now that she was alone with him and he was holding a gun. The surge of feminine prowess that had guided her before was shriveled and shrunken.

Lopreste coughed and smiled. She looked back up to his eyes, realizing that she had been slowly taking in every inch of him while thinking to herself of the danger of her predicament. Embarrassed, Monique took a step back and resorted to attitude to break the tension.

"I have a reason to be here. You are just snooping for information."

"Oh, you have a reason to be here?" He laughed. "So says you, Miss Monique Waters. Youngest child and second daughter of Pete Waters. Mother is Miriam Rodgers, public school teacher. You just completed summer school at the university, but still tend to like to slum every now and then. Which leads me to your street-hustling boyfriend, one Armand Smith. Drug distributor. West side. Connected to Titan Anderson."

Monique just stared at him. She refused to show her fear, refused to acknowledge that the information tumbling from his lips terrified her.

"And I would think this is the last place you want to be since it is rumored that your brother, one Ricardo Waters, son of prostitute Lesley Decapri, is behind the latest attempt on Armand's life. Probably over you." His eyes shined and his thin lips extended into a wide smile.

Monique wanted to spit at him, to throw something at him, to harm him somehow. But she knew better. Now she knew why they had escaped the other night. It had nothing to do with her flirting. Raymond had thanked her and praised her for absolutely nothing.

Lopreste had been on to them all along.

"So you memorized a file," Monique said. "And now you think you are doing what exactly? Trespassing? Breaking and entering? 'Cause I know you don't have a warrant to be here."

They stared at each other. His grin dissipated and her fear revealed itself. Something about his eyes lost the cop veneer under which he initially hid as they raked in her curvaceous frame, soft face, and delicate eyes. His eyes rested on her bruised cheek. He took a few steps back, no longer blocking her access to the door. The gesture was a show of good faith, a deliberate offering of a verbal truce, for the moment anyway.

135

He stroked his nose again then ran a hand across his beard stubble, observing her. "You are in deep," he finally said, his eyes returning to her blackened cheek. "I don't think even you know how deep."

"I'm beginning to figure it out." She sighed.

"You need to get out of here. Hide. Disappear for a couple of weeks."

"I can't. I have to find Armand."

"And what do you think he is going to do when he finds you?" Lopreste's voice was soft; it floated across the stuffy air like a deep breathe.

He reminded her of that cop from the movie *Training Day*, the consummate good guy. Lopreste had that same vibe, but he couldn't be that good, because here he was breaking into Armand's apartment. Between the intimate smiles and knowing glances, Monique was sure that he was probably as dirty as the rest.

"You tell me. Are you working for Army?" Monique said.

"No."

Monique doubted she would get a real answer about that anyway. But she pressed anyway, keen on letting him know that she wasn't as gullible as she seemed. "Pete then. You are one of Pete's men."

"No." Lopreste crossed his arms, shifting his weight as he answered.

His body language told Monique more than his words ever would. Another Pete truism that she had remembered: the answer rested in the body language, not the words.

"But as far as you're concerned, Armand can make you disappear," he continued.

She glanced at the thick carpeted floor and the blank walls. It seemed that Armand could disappear in the blink of an eye. He had proven it. He wasn't attached to this space. If anything, the penthouse meant more to her than it did to him. That much was evident in its blankness. It was possible that he could make her disappear. He had taken her to that trap house for a reason. And he had left her, even if he had reconsidered and come back for her. She believed that deep in her heart. When she thought it over and over, there was no explanation for where he had been while she waited for him, none other than the obvious.

She had to believe in Armand. She had to trust that although what they had was flawed it was true. She had to believe that his heart hadn't completely closed against her. She had to believe in his love. After all, it was all she really had. "He wouldn't do that." Monique set her chin and met Lopreste's eyes.

"He wouldn't?"

They stared at each other again. Monique rubbed her arm in the spot that had scratched against the door.

"You look banged up." He breathed easily, changing the atmosphere in the room just like that. Now he was smiling again, flirting a little.

Monique immediately noted the change in direction.

"Thank you, I appreciate that." She didn't miss a beat.

They both smiled.

"So, when you pulled us over last night. That was a setup?"

"No." He smiled. "You remember me, then?"

"Of course," she said coyly.

"No, I looked into you after the fact. Once the situation exploded." Monique doubted that. He had connected too many dots.

"So what role do you play?" Monique placed her hands on either hip.

"I can help you." He admired the area where her hands rested. "I can help you get out."

"In exchange for?" Her eyes began to water.

She wanted out more than he could know. She wanted out of the obligation of being Pete's daughter, of being heir to the Waters legacy, of inheriting death and the dollar as one intricately bound package of vice as well. They were curses that she had inherited, souls that her family would pay for, lives that their pursuit of the dollar had destroyed. The retribution wasn't just based on the theory that what goes around comes around. It was deeper than that, verified by the Bible and based on God. Monique believed that God would punish her, eventually.

Monique's mother was from the South, Baptist born and bred. Monique's curiosity led to her reading the Old Testament during each

137

boring Sunday sermon. So Monique was raised on the Bible. It was the only book she could get her hands on during those few hours of weekly service. She had read about God and His wrath, His vengeance, His punishment.

She had read about how He spared the transgressor but poured redemption upon the heads of the sons, upon the following generations all the way to the fourth seed. Meaning that Pete could be spared for the entire empire he had constructed, but she, Ricardo, and Michelle, down to their great grandchildren, could pay the heavy price.

It was something that she never really discussed with anyone, but she thought about it when her fake friends admired her stupid clothes and paid homage to her endless resources of money. They were so simple, so foolish. They didn't understand the real price that she would eventually have to pay. Monique thought of it often, every single time she saw a junkie geekin' in the street with her children standing by. Monique knew that it was simply another person that she, Ricardo, and Michelle would have to answer for. That someday, somehow, God would make the Waters family pay for its crimes against His children.

That particular reality used to trouble her so much when she was younger, before she had stilled her heart and silenced her spirit by hardening them. Before she had refused to even entertain those thoughts because of how sick they made her feel, she had devoured the biblical stories of David and Solomon, Jezebel and Attalia, Daniel and Cyrus, and Nebuchadnezzar. During middle school, she had finally approached her pastor. She needed some assurance, some relief from the idea that Pete had damned them all before she even had a chance to live her life. Pastor Bennettt was a kind man, but his sermons were inconsistent, and Monique felt lost.

She remembered how he stared at her in confusion as she pointed to the text and asked for clarification.

"No, no, Monique. You are reading the Old Testament," Pastor Bennett had said, looking relieved. "That doesn't apply to us."

"But why?"

"Because we are Baptist. We believe in Jesus Christ. All come to the Father through him."

"I kn-kn-know that." Monique immediately hated that she had ever approached the pastor. His answers were always simple phrases that didn't explore any meaning. "But st-st-still, God still punishes. It's right here in Chronicles."

"Monique, the Old Testament doesn't apply to us."

"But, Pastor, you always say God is the same. That God doesn't change. Always. Even though we go through Christ, if God is the same, then He does the same things. Then He hasn't changed."

"Child, where is your mother?" Pastor Bennett stood up, tapping her on the shoulder and chuckling loudly. "Does she know what a bright mind she has here? Huh? God bless you. I haven't seen a mind like yours in a while. You are too pretty to worry about this. As long as you got Jesus, you're alright." Pastor Bennett placed his hand under her elbow and started walking toward the door. "Here, let me walk you out."

***

Monique remembered how deep it had hurt. Her exposed innocence had felt like an open wound that every person rubbed against. Her eyes were too wide open then, her heart too pure. She struggled daily with right and wrong. She prayed constantly and wanted to be a good believer, a good person.

After speaking to Pastor Bennett, Monique started training herself to hide her heart, close her eyes, guard her mind, and present a different persona. A shield. A cover to the sensitive, insecure little girl who resided beneath. She brought an end to the spiritual dilemma by simply ignoring it.

She knew it existed, though. She knew that one day she would pay. Maybe that's what Armand was. The beginning of the spiritual retribution against her. His love was so magnetic that she couldn't let go, but his mindset was so potentially poisonous that it could lead to her unraveling, possibly her ending. She wanted nothing more than to escape it all, but her freedom couldn't come without a heavy price. So she knew that nothing Lopreste was offering would be free.

Monique gave Lopreste her full attention. "I asked you a question: you can help me get out in exchange for what exactly?"

"Nothing," he said with a blink. The blink exposing the uttered lie.

139

"Whatever. A cop never does anything for free." She noticed that he flinched in response. "Anyway, there is nothing for me to get out of." Monique resealed the part of her soul that had dared to hope for a chance out. "I don't know anything. Not on either side."

He stepped forward and touched her cheek. His touch was tender. She was surprised that she didn't mind his touch, that they felt so familiar so quickly. But for all she knew this could be a setup or a test.

Monique watched as he traced along her jaw line with a fingertip. He ran his finger down her neck and stopped just short of her breasts. Instead, he reached for her hand and placed a business card in it.

"If you feel different, call me. I don't want information from you. I don't need it. But I can help you." He took several steps backward, keeping his eyes on her, then he turned and walked out of the room.

It wasn't until she heard the front door close that she looked at his card. Officer Matt Lopreste. Monique didn't know what to make of him. She tucked the card into her back pocket and sat on the bed again. She sat there for several minutes wondering whether this was the end of the search. She no longer felt safe in the apartment. She just didn't have any other options. She wanted to find Armand. Some part of her was compelling her forward in her search, although her mind was screaming for her to return home or to the dorm.

Either way, Lopreste had come to the apartment for a reason. And he hadn't expected to find her there. Whatever he was looking for Ricardo would probably be looking for it also, or Lopreste was working for Ricardo and would reveal her location. It was time for her to go.

Monique headed for the front door. She rethought her plan of action. Armand had stayed with her at the dorm before, so she didn't want to go on campus and risk bringing this drama there. She couldn't take this chaos back to her mother's house, either. Pete's was obviously out. Monique purposely didn't maintain close friendships, not close enough that she could impose upon them in the middle of the night. It had been her rigorous training that required her to keep her circle small—meaning nonexistent—in order to keep her family secrets private. Armand was all she had and she was out of options.

Monique exited the penthouse through the rear entry. She was glad that she hadn't parked in the lower garage. She would have felt afraid stumbling around down there alone. Her mind was racing.

What was she overlooking? Was Armand somewhere obvious, expecting her to find him? Where else would Armand be? It was stupid of her to leave her phone with Ricardo and Pete. She should have forced the issue and fought for it, even if she had to round off with Pete. Her phone was the only connection she possibly had to anyone and without it, she was alienated and alone.

Chapter Twenty-Three

Monique glanced in the rearview mirror and immediately spotted the tail. She sighed. It irritated the hell out of her that she was being followed. She didn't recognize the car, but it was obviously either Pete's people or Lopreste's. More than likely, it was Lopreste or his folks because the tail was sloppy and obvious. As far as she was concerned, neither Ricardo nor Lopreste posed any real threat to her, and she would ditch them if she got a lead on Armand. She knew that they were both just working for Pete, following her to report her location. Getting rid of them would be simple enough.

Monique turned right onto Clinton Boulevard. Traffic was thick because this was the hangout spot. She hoped against hope that she could find one of Armand's men out here, someone who could give her a clue about his location or could pass a message for her. Driving slowly, Monique kept her eyes focused on the black, Latino, and white men riding back and forth showing off their hydraulically enhanced old-school rides. Armand's crew normally came out here every Sunday evening. Tonight, though, she didn't see any faces she recognized.

The abuse she endured was catching up to Monique. Her head was beginning to hurt and her body ached. Monique felt like she had lived a lifetime in the past thirty-six hours. She gave up and eased Michelle's small car out of the traffic congestion and slowly turned down side streets until she pulled onto Main Street. Her drive across the city was relaxing. The summer sky glittered with stars beyond the city lights, and the air was warm and inviting. Monique was returning to the dorm. She would lay low, take a hot shower, wrap in her thick terry cloth robe, soak her feet, and let sleep come to her. She was mentally shutting it all down and leaving it all behind.

That was the beauty in having gone to college after all. In hindsight, she should have gone somewhere out of state. She had stayed local for her mother, for Pete, for Armand. The campus could still be an easy reprieve. She would be surrounded by folks content to let the world spin and wonder how much knowledge they could take in with each turn, how they could leave their thumbprint on the universe.

The student's pursuits were so much higher than the crumpled, filthy money and the grimy burn of the streets. Students' problems were so much easier to solve, the consequences not resulting in someone's murder or being killed.

It was an option that Monique had. The option that had placed a small, unspoken wedge between she and Armand in the first place. It was the place that was melting her iced-over heart, causing her to reread, restudy, rethink without being shunned or disregarded or ridiculed. She had purposely taken a theology course this summer, having obtained special permission from the department head to participate.

There was no laughter or begrudging amusement when she explained that she had read the entire Bible two complete times and had began an intense discussion with Chairwoman Myrieckes of the History Department about the relevance of the Old Testament to the understanding of the New Testament. Within fifteen minutes she had received her approval. At the end of the course she had also received another meeting with Chairwoman Myrieckes, this time to be offered a partial scholarship by the History Department. For once, Monique felt like she had found home.

So home was where she was returning. Her new home, free from the Waters's rigors. It was metaphoric, in some sense, that she was being tailed, being followed by her past life as she made the decision to submerge herself into her new life. It offered some comfort that they were back there escorting her without realizing it to the decision that she had made without realizing it. By returning to campus, she was choosing to actually be there, to stay there, to remove herself from the game in every way. It was a decision that felt right.

Humming to herself, Monique turned down the dark strip of Mount Hope. She took in the huge oak trees lining the old road. She should have kept her prayer promise yesterday and left Armand after they managed to escape from the cops. Imagine that. If she had, she would never have been in this mess and wouldn't have suffered the physical or emotional scars.

This time she was getting it right.

Leaving Armand would hurt, but it was simply another hurt she would seal in her heart. Plus, she wasn't leaving him. He had left her. He had disappeared, and she had searched for him, had been diligent in her loyalty. Now that she couldn't find him, there seemed to be something liberating in his absence, something right about her decision to move on. Monique knew that she would miss him, that her heart would surely break before it was all over. For tonight, though, all she could do was celebrate that she was, in fact, making a positive move forward.

She veered right onto Wilson Avenue, approaching the main campus from the rear. She could just make out the campus guard house in the distance. The gate was closed, and she didn't have her student ID on her. She hoped that the guard was there to let her in. Monique peeked in the rearview mirror at her tail. It was obvious where she was going now, obvious that her finding Armand was no longer an option. They couldn't get past security at night anyway. She wondered whether they would turn back or follow for the next several minutes until she was at the gate.

She glanced back out of habit and saw that they had turned off their headlights. A thin trail of fear raced up Monique's spine. They weren't Pete's people. She had taken for granted that they were. Pete's folks would never turn out the lights and ride under the cover of dark. Lopreste could have done whatever he wanted to her in the apartment, so it didn't make sense for it to be him or his people. Monique sped up, hoping that her internal panic was a mere false alarm. Who else would tail her so openly and then turn off their lights toward the end of her journey?

The first smack from the wide grill behind her made Monique's body fly forward as her neck snapped. Screaming, she grabbed the wheel and floored it. Someone was trying to kill her. They rear ended her again, slamming their large truck into Michelle's small Malibu. Monique's forehead hit the steering wheel. She was spinning. Her hands gripped the steering wheel. Pure terror made her unable to react. The side of her car slammed into one of the large oak trees.

Her head bumped against the steering wheel again, bringing a temporary end to consciousness.

***

Monique bolted upright in the car. Her door was open. A set of rough hands reached across her body, unbuckled her seat belt, and pulled her from the car. For a second, fear jump-started her body. She swung her arms and legs wildly; the person pinned her flat against his wide chest. She felt like she was a rag doll being hugged by a polar bear. Afraid that he might suffocate her, and aware that he was much stronger than she could ever imagine, Monique stopped fighting. She knew that she needed to stop the dizziness before she vomited all over this big bear of man and got her ass kicked for that, too.

The man literally threw her into the back seat of the SUV, bumping her head on the center console. Monique curled herself into a tight ball, whimpering in fear.

"Goddamn, Carlos! You damn near killed her," Chris, the passenger, said. His loud voice made Monique's head throb, and she covered her ears with her hands.

"Sick of driving around this damn city behind her. Shit."

Carlos' soft and raspy voice sickened her. The voice didn't match the huge man, and it made him seem freakishly terrifying.

"Yeah, but now the truck's fucked up." Chris knew there would be consequences for this. He shook his head, hoping the consequences didn't fall on his shoulders too.

"Fuck it, Chris. Get this bitch where she got to go, so I can have the rest of my night back." Carlos exhaled. "Dump the truck later."

"That's word. I got some shit waiting for me tonight, too. Let's get to it, man."

Monique wouldn't open her eyes. She was terrified of what they would do to her if the waves of nausea resulted in vomit splattered across the back of the truck. Monique heard the tone of numbers being pressed into a cell phone.

"Tell Titan we got her," Carlos said. "Yeah. It's her. She was up in Armand's spot. I know, man, she a stupid bitch. Who knows why she was up there. These hoes always be scheming, though. It's all good. Twenty minutes."

Monique groaned, tears poured down her face as she finally admitted to herself that she was in real trouble.

Chapter Twenty-Four

He watched her slender fingers move along the ridge of the Glock. She slid the barrel and checked the chamber. The seventeen-shot cartridge rested on the narrow table in front of her. She loaded the gun, cocked it back, and then aimed at the window. Her eye peered through its sight. Pete figured he better make himself known before he got shot.

"Miriam, it's me." Pete stood just outside the side door with his back to the house.

Miriam opened the door with a bag in one hand and her gun in the other. He had passed two cars on his way here, stationed at the end of the street. They had to be Titan's men. As he pulled onto the quiet street they turned on their bright lights, momentarily blinding him. He drove slowly and they nodded at him, turning the lights off. Pete knew they wouldn't recognize him, and he drove past with ease. None of the young cats knew him, not many older ones either. Getting Miriam out of there without being followed and possibly attacked would be another thing altogether.

Miriam didn't look directly at him and didn't open her mouth to speak. It was the first time they had seen each other since Monique's graduation from high school. After Monique graduated, there had been no need—no time really—for their worlds to cross. But he missed her. Deeply. Heartbreakingly so. It was a pain he suffered silently, though. She had made her choice years ago and stuck to it. He wasn't a man to beg or plead.

"You got everything? Enough to be gone for ..." He hesitated and glanced around the yard to make sure nobody was lurking.

"You said you would be here three hours ago." She quickly walked to his Cadillac, threw the door open, and climbed in.

"Miriam, I got here as quick as I could." He stopped outside of her car door. "You got to lock the house up."

She tossed the keys through the window and then sat back and

He wondered whether the fools would flood his car with light again as they left. The tint on his windows was deep. The most they would see would be shadows with the windows rolled up. He pressed the buttons, rolling his windows up. Somehow Miriam's stayed down. Pete glanced at her hands. One rested on her lap, the other lay along the arm panel, pressing down the window.

"What are you doing?" Pete said.

"I need the air." She cut her eyes at him.

"No," Pete said, his voice soft.

There was no explaining that henchmen sat at the corner waiting for the opportunity to hurt her, the opportunity to go after Monique. How had he and Ricardo thought they were going to teach Titan a lesson and not remember to get Miriam and Monique clear? Especially since he knew Titan had been keeping Monique safe for years, making sure his men didn't try to lure her into the game.

Pete pressed the button for the window to go up.

"Leave my fucking window down!" Miriam shouted.

Pete gripped the steering wheel, numbing his heart to her tongue. The only tongue in the world that could still hurt him.

"No."

Miriam moved her hand in surrender, and he rolled her window up.

"Bastard."

She was pushing her luck now. But, then again, the Glock in her lap was fully loaded.

Pete chuckled. He realized that she probably didn't have a fear of him or anybody else. Not with her baby girl missing.

They eased toward the end of the street. The old cars still sat there, old junkers that could be easily ditched after a hit. Titan was sitting on his family. Titan and Armand. The thought alone enraged him. This thing had to end.

Pete rode past. The young guns must have recognized his car from earlier because they barely paid him any attention. It was obvious they were waiting for a certain person or a certain car. What if they had gotten Miriam? How would he have been able to live with that? She would have to move out of the neighborhood whether she wanted to or not. The hood was too dangerous, and Titan knew too much.

"Anthony's little brother," Miriam whispered, staring intently at the young man sitting in the old junker. "Rodney Taylor, I believe is his name. His grandmother is a member of my church. Who does he think he is waiting on?"

Pete didn't have to answer that question. The fact that Miriam had scoped him out and identified him proved that she was already alert and fully aware.

"What the hell did you get Monique in?"

"What did I get her in?" Pete's jawbone throbbed from clenching his teeth and anger filled his mouth like glue. "She dipped herself into this mess."

"I doubt it."

"How long she been with this Armand cat?"

Miriam arched an eyebrow. "For damn near a year, Pete. You're the easy parent, letting them run the streets and do only God knows what. Why don't you know that?"

"A year?"

"Probably longer." Miriam breathed. "Why?"

"Monique was with him when some business went down. We got her out of it, had her at the house, then she left."

"Why did you allow her to leave?"

"I didn't, dammit." Pete clenched his fist.

They rode in silence for a few seconds.

"Why do you have her phone?" Miriam said. "If she just up and left, she would have taken her phone with her."

Pete didn't answer.

"So you tried to hold her in the house and keep her phone and she just walked out, huh? What is the truth, Pete? Don't bullshit me about my only child."

He glanced at her. Pete didn't like being questioned, but Miriam wasn't one to play with, not when it came to Monique.

"I gave it to you straight. She was at the house, but Armand tried to contact her. And she can't have any contact with him. Not now. I took her phone. She left."

"So my baby is running the street looking for him. I called the dorm. Her roommate said she hasn't been back."

"No, she ain't going to no dorm. She trying to find him."

Miriam laughed. "Well, he's trying to find her, too. So what's the problem? And why do I have to leave my home?"

Pete clutched the steering wheel, head bowed, chin set. There was nothing left for him to say.

"Answer me, Pete. If Monique and Armand are looking for each other, why the hell does that involve us?"

Sometimes people didn't need to know the information they sought. It was a rule that Pete lived by. Miriam didn't need to know anymore. The rest would expose him too much, would make him liable should something happen. If she knew that Pete had put a hit on Armand and he was retaliating by killing Pete's men, and somehow Monique was killed too, Miriam would turn his ass over to the police quicker than a blink. Pete knew that for sure.

True, Miriam was part of his inner circle. She knew all the secrets. She had faithfully kept them and shielded him when she could for over twenty years, but Monique was the guarantee. Her daughter's safety had been all Miriam needed to continue with one foot in this life and one foot above board.

The reality was that Pete doubted Monique would make it through this alive. If Armand were the type of man Pete had been at that age, she was already dead. The only hope he had was that the streets would spit her out first. He was hoping that a snitch would clue them in. Pete had to damn near break Ricardo's neck when he tried to put a price on Monique's head. That would only lead to more chaos. Every lowlife would want to get in on the payout. And Monique was a woman, he couldn't have just anybody searching to return her. Sometime, Pete swore Ricardo didn't have any common sense.

Instead, Pete put the reward on Armand's head—100K, dead or alive. No questions asked. If the girl was with him, she had to be returned alive to Pete's print shop on Park Ave.

No one knew that Monique was his daughter, so they couldn't put the amount any higher than that without raising suspicion and having every lowlife in the city vying to capture and kidnap her and request more money. Pete had contacted his police hookup. He arranged for them to comb the streets looking for Michelle's car or someone who fit Monique's description.

Once he hid Miriam, he and Ricardo were taking to the streets with a small crew, too. While he was driving to get Miriam, their guard, Deondre, had gotten sprayed standing outside a storefront on the east side. He was hit in the neck and the ear. Whoever shot him was aiming high, shooting to kill. Within minutes the streets were humming. The streets attributed the shooting to Armand and the hunt that everyone now knew about. That was five of his men down and his daughter missing. All the casualties were on his side to the best of his knowledge, and all whispered belief of his might was simply swirling down the drain.

Pete glanced at the clock. It was just after 11:00 pm. Plenty of time under the dark of the night to do dirt and easily hide it. Plenty of time to wipe Armand and Titan off the face of the earth forever for even considering crossing him, or involving his baby girl in anyway.

Plenty of time.

"Where are we going?" Miriam said when Pete changed gears and sped onto the highway.

"My spots are all hot. If he is with Monique, I don't know whether she told him where the safe houses are. I am putting you up in the 'burbs."

"No. Monique won't know where to find me."

"Miriam." Pete's patience was wearing thin. "Monique ain't looking for you or me, and she obviously don't know the streets as well as she thinks. I am putting you and Michelle out in Victor. In a townhouse out there. It's safe. A gated community with guards. No one, not even Ricardo knows about it."

"None of your men?"

"No." He shook his head. "Can't trust anybody right now."

Miriam sighed and nodded.

***

Ricardo glanced at his phone again. His thoughts were torn between the delicious chocolate woman standing in front of him with seduction on her mind and his hardheaded sisters who were intent on ruining his life. Michelle and Monique were blowing his mind. Where the hell had Michelle gone? She'd just up and left without telling him

151

and after he had told her to stay her ass put. This night felt so crazy, so wild. Only bad things happened on nights like this, when the normal limits of life didn't kick in.

He had experienced this before. The insecurity of the future; the risk of sudden death. When he finally decided to live with his mother was when he had given in to the fear, when he realized that his life was damned. Who else would protect his sisters from the men rolling in and out of the house, drugging up his mother and laying their heads in his home at night? The home his grandmother had left for him.

Even now Ricardo felt like throwing up thinking about it. Thinking about the cold taste of metal against his tongue, the drool choking him, the heavy metal making him gag around sobs. Lesley Decapri, his mother, had sat there. She balled herself into a knot and watched them jam the gun down his throat. Oblivious to it. No fear on her face, no worry in her eyes.

Pete saved him. It was Pete's fault, though. So Pete had only saved him from the hell of which he had created. Pete had been Lesley's first pimp. The first one to completely turn her out, keeping her trapped under his eye by feeding her hits of the drugs she had come to rely on. Living with Pete...wanting Pete...breathing Pete.

Ricardo could remember, although he knew that Pete didn't realize it. He doubted that Pete even cared. Ricardo remembered his mother being sweet and gentle up until Pete yelled at her to put Ricardo to bed and come to him. He would force her to sit at the table and divide up the blow, count it out thinner and thinner. Ricardo had watched his mother with the scales and the baking soda when Pete didn't have money for the chemicals down at the art and chemical store.

Eventually, the fumes got to her. Ricardo remembered when Pete found her snorting. How he had stripped her in front of everybody, even the other strange men that were sitting around bagging. Ricardo remembered Pete taking off his belt and whipping her like she was a child. Ricardo had screamed, wrapped his arms around his poor mother, around his thin angel. Pete had pulled him away, looking murderous.

Ricardo remembered. He remembered when Pete put them out, called Lesley a trick and put them on the streets. What else was his mother to do? So tricks she turned, living in a tiny apartment on the east side with a house full of other women. Pete knew. Ricardo would see him. Pete would take him for days at a time, then drop him back off at the house of whores.

Ricardo leaned back and inhaled marijuana smoke as he watched the naked woman in front of him gently caress her breasts as she rolled her body to the deep bass filling the room. Clear as day. It still made him feel sick to his stomach. Lesley had been beautiful. His mother looked white. She wasn't, but she definitely looked it with her blue eyes and blondish brown hair. Very thin and always a perfect smile.

Lesley didn't have any other family after her mother had died. Ricardo had no idea where she was originally from or who his people were. Pete had eventually played Ricardo's savior, leaving his mother and his baby sisters to rot.

Ricardo hit the blunt again and glanced at his phone, thinking of calling them. This time the marijuana smoke choked him. He would never abandon them. His mother was a shadow of her former self, but he took care of her and his sisters and, now, his sisters' children. "More fatherless children in the world," he thought. It made sense; it wasn't his sisters' fault that no one knew who their babies' daddies were. They were just lying in the bed that Lesley had made.

His sisters thought he was lucky to have a daddy that cared enough to take him away. Ricardo would never tell them the truth. He would never tell them that Pete was the same bastard who ruined all of their lives. Instead, whatever money he had, separate and apart from Pete, went to them. Whatever he had went to alleviate the hell Pete had created and then left three innocent women to wallow in.

The naked, butter brown woman in front of him danced slowly to a hypnotic old song by the Art of Noise called *Moments in Love*. At that moment he loved her. It was a fleeting feeling, though, one that would leave him as soon as he released himself into her, which would somehow make her no different from every other woman. But while he was here staring at her naked hips swinging softly from side to side, staring at her heavy breasts bouncing slightly as she churned her body while he had her hypnotized to the sexy beat, his heart skipped a bit.

Tandra was everything his mother wasn't. Everything his sisters from his mother weren't. All of his women were like this, dark brown, thick, voluptuous ass, and big eyes. Michelle teased that all his women looked like her and Monique, that he wanted queens like them. He would just nod and shrug. The truth was he wanted the exact opposite of his mother. Opposite the woman whose pathetic life tormented him night and day.

Tandra leaned over, her behind high in the air, her hands around her ankles. "You like that, Ricardo?"

He didn't respond, pressing his lips together and letting the smoke seep slowly from them. Her thick hair bounced up and down; its medium length was in choppy sharp edges around her face. She was a hairdresser by profession and a ride or die chick by trade. She had more hustle in her than Pete and Ricardo together. Thus making her willing to perform, willing to do what Ricardo needed to get what she needed. It was mutual use, and he didn't give a damn.

Tandra had two little boys that he saw sometimes when he went to her place. She was careful, though, and didn't let many men around her children, didn't expose them to too much drama. Ricardo respected that, and actually respected her for that. A little more respect than most, at least.

"Come here," he said.

Tandra gave him a full smile and licked her lips a little. Ricardo wondered for a moment whether she had ever stripped for a living, but then decided that he didn't want to know. He didn't want to learn how low she had to stoop to get her business started. He didn't need any more family horror stories on his mind tonight. Let her business just be her business, he thought.

Tandra sat on his lap and leaned forward to kiss him. Ricardo didn't kiss on the mouth. EVER. The taste of another person's tongue reminded him of that gun pressed against his cheeks. Plus, he didn't trust Tandra enough to break his habits for her.

She kissed him anyway, planting her soft lips on his forehead, lightly licking the tip of his nose. Her fingers gently caressed his scalp. He glanced up at her, watching her face as she played in his hair. He had to chuckle; she loved his hair. Sometimes she got off track, like now, forgetting about lovemaking and admired his silky black waves instead.

"I would think you would be sick of hair." Ricardo laughed.

"I love your hair," she said. "You know that."

"Yeah." *Women always do.* "I got hair in other places too, you know."

She sucked her teeth at him, pretending to be annoyed. She took the hint, though, and moved her naked frame down his body, lap dancing for him until all the memories of his mother, father, and sisters disappeared from his mind, and only her chocolate ebony held his attention.

Just as Ricardo leaned his head back and experienced the full pleasure of Tandra's deep throat, his phone vibrated.

"Yeah," he said, tapping his earpiece.

"Where you?" Pete said, sounding annoyed.

"The spot." Ricardo palmed the back of Tandra's head, pushing her down harder.

"Good. Who else?"

"Crew is here. Deondre didn't make it." Ricardo's voice cracked when he said it.

Tandra sucked more. She grabbed the base of his erection and held on.

"I'm on my way. I can't reach Michelle."

"She ain't answering?"

Pete didn't respond and Ricardo sighed. It was a stupid question. He pushed Tandra's head back, hoping she would stop. He needed a minute. She stood up and continued dancing to the deep beat of *Moments in Love*, which seemed to go on forever.

"She ain't at home."

"Why?" Pete's voice got deeper.

"I told her not to leave. When I came downstairs, she was gone. Probably with her friend. The one she used to hoop with."

"You got her number?"

"Who ... Anji? Naw, I don't have it." Ricardo shook his head. *Why in the hell would I have Anji's number?*

"Get it. Find Michelle." The phone disconnected, but the fury in Pete's voice terrified him. At that moment he hated Pete, hated the fear he inspired. But what could Ricardo do? He only had one father, one real parent.

Tandra returned to his lap. She straddled him and played in his hair again. Ricardo buried his head between her large breasts and inhaled deeply. He licked them as she laughed in delight.

"I got to go," he said, wishing he could stay.

"What?" The pleasure turned into attitude in a split second. "Why?"

"I just do." Ricardo leaned back and studied her, focusing his hazel-brown eyes on her. "Some business..."

"Well, you got business here to take care of." She moaned as she rubbed her body against him, proving her point.

"Move," Ricardo said, his voice cold and his patience apparently gone. He didn't have time to play, not when it came to Pete.
Tandra stared at him a second, then backed up and stood up.

Once again, he couldn't help but stare at the thick thighs and legs mounted on high strappy heels. "You can wait for me here."

"In a storefront full of men? I don't think so," Tandra said, moving around the room picking her clothes from the floor.

"Don't go. I just got to find my sister and her friend."

"Who, Anji?"

Ricardo stared at her.

"I heard you just say," she answered the unspoken question.

"You know her?"

"Of course. She does nails in my shop sometimes. It's just a hobby for her, though. She don't never really need money. We went to school together."

"What's her number?" Ricardo said.

Chapter Twenty-Five

The cold, flat tip of the blade pressed against Monique's lips. Her eyes narrowed with anger. She looked around the garage and lost all hopes of escaping.

"Call me a punk again," Carlos dared Monique, squinting his eyes and grinning slightly at her. "And I'll cut the pretty off your face."

He pressed the blade harder against her lips. She had been silent during the car ride, needing time to collect her thoughts. She recognized her kidnappers. They had that west side flavor. She didn't really know the huge one, Carlos, but the thinner one, Chris, she had definitely seen around the way before. Monique was sure they were after Armand, that they had something to do with the terrible mistake that would make Ricardo go after Armand.

Monique pushed air through her nostrils. If she was going to die, it wasn't going to be like this, not handcuffed to the back of a chair in the corner of a filthy car garage. "Fuck you, pussy motherfucker." She spat on him.

Chris stood next to her and laughed while Carlos wiped his face. He slowly retracted the blade, keeping his eyes on the floor as he took a step away. He turned suddenly, stepping back toward her and power slapped her with an open hand. His hand was so rough and callous it felt like a claw as her head whipped on her shoulders. He hauled off and slapped her a second time across the same cheek. *First my father. Now this look-alike brute asshole.* Monique pursed her lips. She tried to ignore the pain as tears rolled down her bruised cheek.

"Say it again, bitch. I dare you," he said, turning to walk away.

Monique didn't know what was happening in her mind, why she suddenly had the weird giddiness of a good laugh or a drink-inspired buzz. Either way, worry and fear had oozed from her and nothing really mattered anymore. Monique accepted the reality that she was going to die. Why else would two grown black men kidnap her? The fact that she could get Carlos worked up—despite her impending doom—gave her some undefined euphoric buzz, some fake sense of power, which forced her to push the boundaries when she should have stayed quiet.

Maybe she was going crazy. Finally, a blessing in the midst of chaos that allowed her to release her capacities and free her mind, *crazy*! That was the only way someone survived this much chaos without it forever marking their soul or tormenting them.

Her uncle had done it. Pete told them how her uncle had snapped, how he entered into another realm and charged two men with guns. He injured both before a third gunman finally killed him. Uncle Jon went out with a blaze, with pride. Whenever Pete mentioned him, it was with a rare type of respect that Monique knew came from the way her Uncle Jon had died.

She sighed, hoping that this strange desire to make Carlos flip out was a sign that crazy was upon her, ready to be released to whatever her fate would be without fear. The bastard could have killed her ramming into Michelle's car like that. Then he had talked shit the entire ride to this piss-poor garage. She hated him, hated his big hands, and the stupid tight-fitted shirt he wore.

Pete would kill him soon as he look at her. Monique could envision it, although it wouldn't happen. The truth was that her father would never know why she had disappeared. They probably would never see her body again.

Even that thought didn't inspire any sadness. Monique no longer cared about life or death, pain or hurt, or anything logical. Her mother was the only thought that made her sad. Her mother had no one else. Losing Monique like this would devastate Miriam; even that thought wasn't enough to sober Monique.

"Look at you." Monique laughed awkwardly, spitting blood from her busted lip. "Your big ass must be some kind of faggot. Slapping the shit out of me, then switching your nasty ass across the room." Monique giggled, shaking her head. "I ain't scared of you, 'bama."

"Shut the fuck up," Carlos screamed at her, leaning close to her face.

She moved back, scrunching up her nose at the smell of his hot breath.

Carlos had his knife out again. "I'm about to do your ass."

"Fuck you," Monique said. "You ain't gonna do shit."
He took a step toward her, hate seeping from his eyes.

"Chill." Chris stepped in. "You know the drill."

"Yeah, I know that shit." Carlos reached for the duct tape. "But I ought to kill this bitch and worry about the consequences later. She got my man Mike killed. They said his head was blown off, all because of her and her peeps. We could easily just make her disappear."

Monique didn't say anything. She kept her eyes closed. She tried to dull the pain that was shooting up the side of her face. She felt blood pouring from her lip but couldn't do anything about it. There was no use wiping it away with her other hand, it was filthy. She was filthy.

The cop. She should have listened to the cop. Even if Lopreste was a setup, she would have been in a better position. Finding Armand seemed irrelevant now. Why the hell wasn't Armand looking for her anyway? Michelle was right: Monique had been playing the fool. Another girl's life ruined over running around behind some drug-dealing loser. She had always thought she was too good to be like the girls she saw growing up or read about in the paper. Yet, here she was.

Monique giggled, thinking about Armand's face when he watched her with Lopreste. Yep, Armand was just another loser. He was willing to turn his back on her over stupid jealousy.

"Open your eyes," Chris said.

She ignored him. His grip on her face made her cheeks feel like they were on fire. Her eyelids popped open.

"You got my mans' and 'em killed. You gonna get yours eventually. Until then, shut the fuck up until I tell you to speak."

Something in his narrow eyes reached through Monique's adrenaline rush, ending her desired crazy. She knew that he would be the one to snap her neck and take the blame for it later. Coming face to face with real crazy made her illusory bubble pop. She still wanted to live and Carlos would be the one to kill her. Monique closed her eyes as more tears ran down her face. She clamped her mouth shut.

"Call them man," Carlos said. "I don't want to be with this chick all night. I got to get to my peeps."

"No need." Chris pointed toward the nearest garage window. "They're here."

Monique began to shiver. Whoever these men were waiting on was obviously someone in power, someone who had told them to kidnap her. Her anger was replaced with sadness. This wasn't the life she wanted. She had wanted to get her degree and start a career, establish herself until she got a law degree that she parlayed into some real paper. She wanted to take care of her mother. She hadn't hugged Michelle in the longest of time or told Ricardo that she loved him. She hadn't told Ricardo how proud she was of his decisions to love and protect. In her opinion, Ricardo was the definition of sincere love. And Pete, she didn't owe Pete anything, but her death would rock him and kill his legacy. However, she didn't want to do that either.

"Stop whimpering," Chris said.

Monique hadn't realized she was making a sound. She quickly became quiet.

"They both here," Chris said, unenthusiastically.

"Alright." Carlos stood up. "We about to get the fuck up outta here."

"Hopefully." Chris looked at Monique.

Monique used her free hand to wipe at her wet face a little, ignoring the feeling of stickiness that met her raw skin. She smeared tears and blood onto her linen pants as she wiped her hands against them. It was no use. There was no need to worry about her appearance anyway, no reason to care about being appealing. Her only care was survival. She wouldn't be using any flirting to get out of this situation, that was for sure.

Monique blinked, her eye was sore. She couldn't remember what had caused it at first. Within seconds, the image of her head slamming against the steering wheel reminded her. Her forehead ached from bumping against the center console when Carlos had thrown her into the back seat. She probably looked like a black and blue blowup of some crash dummy.

Monique kept her eyes on the garage door, expecting it to slide up. Instead, the small side door she had been brought through earlier swung open. Her mouth fell open as Carlos reached out and slapped hands with a handsome brother with magnetic brown eyes. Wade, the same man who had winked at her the night before in Armand's trap house.

Monique shook her head. What the hell was going on? Who was he and why was he there? He was Armand's man. Could Armand be behind her kidnapping?

Another brother walked in. *Titan*. There was no way to miss him. Everyone on the west side knew him and all the women wanted to be with him. Monique had felt him watching her a few times as she walked past or as he drove by, but he had never said anything to her.

So Wade works for Titan? Did they set up the shoot out on Army. The two slapped hands with her captors and stepped fully into the garage. They stopped short as their eyes landed on her. They both stared at her as if she were monstrous. The cigarette fell from Wade's lips and Titan took a step back, his fist covering his mouth in surprise. Wade and Titan stared at each for a second, and then Wade quickly turned and headed right back out the door. Monique wondered how bad she actually looked.

"What the fuck did y'all do?" Titan screamed.

"Nothing," Carlos mumbled.

Monique laughed a little. She coughed and more blood tumbled from her lips.

"Are you fucking kidding me?" Titan shouted. "Why does she look like this? Shit!" His eyes were on Chris, the leader of the two, the responsible one.

Chris shrugged. "I had to run her off the road to get her. Half of that was already done to her when we got her." Chris pointed to the dirty bandages on her hands and cheek. "Other than that, I don't know."

Titan kneeled in front of her, squinting as if trying to find her eyes through a sea of scars. "What happened?" The reflection of her swollen face bounced from the surface of his glassy eyes.

"I just told you," Chris said softly.

"You're a liar." Monique smiled and looked past Titan at Chris. She still had some of the power in her hands. That Titan cared about her appearance at all let her know that she was to be kept alive, that she had to look a certain way for a reason, at least for now.

161

"T, this bitch will drive you crazy," Carlos spoke up.

"You ran her off the road? Off the goddamn road?" Titan stood back up, his back to Monique and squaring off with the captors. "You stupid assholes left evidence of a car wreck for the police. Her mother's a goddamn teacher; her daddy owns the damn cops. There will be a missing person's report, you fucking idiots." Titan clenched both hands.

Monique shook her head, wondering which one of the two, Carlos or Chris, would suffer the consequences.

It was Chris. Titan took him down with one punch. Chris landed square on his back.

"This is your man," Titan said calmly pointing at Carlos, his voice barely audible. "You brought him to the game. You are supposed to control him. I tell you to get Pete's daughter. Pete Waters. I trust you with that. You know what the fuck that means? And you leave a fucking trail, a banged up car, blood, no doubt tire tracks, and she sitting here a bloody fucking mess?"

Titan kicked Chris in the head. Carlos took a step toward him, and Titan's gun was pointed at Carlos's chest quicker than he could blink.

"Boy, unless you want some of this here," Titan whispered, "don't you ever walk up on me while I am handling shit. Ya heard?"

Carlos shook his head, threw his hands up in surrender, and took a few steps back.

Titan lowered his gun, staring at the far wall of the garage. Monique knew he was thinking, going through the options. She hoped he wouldn't decide to kill her now that the job had been so badly botched up and the trail led back to them.

He finally snapped out of it, glaring down at the Chris. Titan kicked him again for good measure. "Get your ass up."

Monique overheard talking by the door, two deep voices, muffled but interchanging. Titan moved back in front of her, blocking sight of her from the door. She peeked around him. She hadn't heard the voices before, but now it sounded like a low rumble of conversation growing louder with each exchange. Then, the one voice she had desperately wanted to hear until that very moment, drifted toward her and dread filled her heart.

"Wade, what the fuck you mean that I can't go in? Why the hell would T set it up if he don't want to talk to me? Get the fuck outta my way."

There was pushing and scuffling. Then there was a strong thud against the door. Monique, at that moment, knew Wade had been thrown against the wall of the garage.

***

Armand stepped through the door, slowly taking in the scene, his eyes questioning Titan, his pistol in his hand. "You good?" Armand clearly suspected mutiny. "It's some shit poppin' off up in here?"

Armand hadn't noticed Monique yet, couldn't notice her. Titan was standing directly in front of her. Chris scrambled to his feet and both captors eyed Armand suspiciously.

"I'm good, man." Titan smiled, shaking his head. "My crew just fucked up is all. You 'bout to come in here and do them all, huh? My man." Titan laughed. "Where is Wade?"

"Shit, Dut and Chew got him pinned up outside." Armand stepped farther into the room. He kept his back against the wall and Chris and Carlos in his sight. Obviously he was not yet convinced that the situation was safe. Armand's eyes rested on Titan's gun.

Titan moved slowly, exaggerating his motion so Armand could see him replacing the gun in the small of his back. Armand's eyes continued to scan the room slowly, looking around the garage. "Wade was talking crazy, talking about I can't come in."

"Naw, baby, it's all good." Titan nodded. "Tell them to come in and bring Wade."

Armand didn't move, his eyes never left Titan's. Monique could see Armand's perfect lips as they curved sharply and let out a low, short whistle. There was some more scuffling and Wade stumbled into the garage with Dut and Chew in his wake.

Wade eyed Armand. Wade's glowing brown eyes blazed fire.

Armand gave Wade a quick once-over and turned to Titan. "He's alright."

At the same time Titan nodded at Wade, a quiet signal for Wade to keep calm. "Just a misunderstanding, y'all. It's all good."

"Who that behind you, T?"

Monique recognized the voice from a deep place in her soul. Something about Chew's voice made her feel panic. Frantic. It was a tone she couldn't place, and it reminded her of fear.

Titan was standing so close to Monique that she could smell his cologne. So close that her one free hand could touch him. Armand was here. He had done this to her. He had her kidnapped. Something inside her broke, and it hurt worse than her cheek, her lips, her head, her eye. Her heart ached. She eyed the gun in front of her. The gun in the small of Titan's back. Titan hadn't even pulled his shirt down over it.

Chapter Twenty-Six

Armand still hadn't noticed Monique. She could tell by the way he shifted his stance in response to Chew's question.

"Who the fuck is behind you, T?" Armand pointed his Beretta straight at Titan.

"Put that gun down," Titan said, taking a small step to the side to offer Armand a better glimpse of Monique. "Don't ever point a gun at me, son."

"Who is that?" Chew said.

His voice still shocked Monique. Monique shuddered again, wondering why the voice had that affect on her.

"That look like—"

With the last bit of strength she could muster, Monique leapt from the chair and wrapped her hand around the gun handle protruding from Titan's waist.

"What the—" Titan pushed her away but it was too late.

She already had the gun in one hand while her other wrist remained handcuffed to the metal chair that hung awkwardly scraping the floor.

"Ain't this about a bitch." Titan chuckled as Monique aimed the gun at his throat.

She wanted to point the gun at Armand but Titan was too close to her, his menacing eyes locked on her.

Wade and her two captors had drawn their guns, all pointing at her. She wanted to laugh out loud. *Damn.* She hadn't thought about all the firepower in the room, she probably should have reconsidered. But then again, her gun was trained on the right person. The main person whose business ran them all: Titan.

"Army, you asshole," Monique shouted, taking a step back and dragging the chair so she could look at Armand without taking her eyes off Titan. "You had me fucking kidnapped?"

"Mo?" a thin voice said.

They all looked at him for a second, including Monique.

In that second, she knew that she hadn't imagined his voice. "Chew," she whispered.

"Mo, what the fuck happened to you?" Chew pressed.

"Motherfucker, how she here?" Armand stepped forward, his gun switching to Titan. "You working with that Ricardo cat?"

Wade changed positions, focusing his gun on Armand.

"Shit," Dut said, training his gun on Wade.

Chew took a step back, locking his sights on the two kidnappers.

"What?" Titan laughed incredulously. "This bitch got a gun on me and you questioning me?"

"You set me up?" Armand's chest rose and fell with anger.

Monique flinched. She had never seen Armand like this before.

"You led them to my spot?" Armand said.

"Army, I don't know what the fuck you are talking about," Titan said, his eyes wide in amazement.

"You need to put the gun down," Wade said, focusing on Monique. "I would hate to have to kill you, sweetheart."

Armand turned his gun on Wade. "Bitch, you ain't about to kill no damn body."

"I left the safety of my home to come looking for you, and you had them run me off the road? You left me in that fucking shoot-out, then had my car crashed?" Monique's voice trembled as the gun shook in her hands. "What, Army, you planned on killing me?"

"Somebody shoot this bitch," Titan screamed.

Monique took the safety off Titan's gun. She did it slow and deliberate, demonstrating that she knew how to work the gun. She steadied her shaking hand with the other—the chair hanging—keeping the gun leveled on Titan. "Shut the fuck up," she said to Titan.

"Army, this skank set you up and you letting her get at me?" Titan laughed. "I can't believe this."

"Wade, you was in this, too?" Armand said. "You was in my spot right before they came. You knew he gave me up to them?"

"You know it ain't like that, Army. Think on that, man," Wade said, shaking his head in disbelief.

"Mo, put the gun down." Chew took a careful step toward her.

"No," Monique said. "I hate you, Army. You hear me. I hate your ass. You think I'm going to just sit here and get popped."

"Chris, you better shoot her," Titan screamed. "Shoot her."

"Don't do it," Armand repeated. "Wade, don't do it."

"Put that fucking gun down, Mo. Please." Chew's quiet voice seemed like a whisper in the wind to Monique. She barely heard him.

"Baby girl," Armand finally spoke directly to her, his black eyes blazing, his lips twisted. "I don't even know what you're talking about."

"Do you know who this bitch is?" Titan shouted at Armand.

"Don't matter now," Wade said, looking forward to pulling the trigger.

"Mo, just put the gun down, girl," Chew whispered.

Monique shook her head as tears rolled down her face and Armand stared at her.

"This is Pete Waters' daughter." Titan jabbed a finger in the air at Monique with each syllable.

"Who?" Armand said. His brow raised in confusion.

"Ricardo is her brother, fool," Titan said. His voice was harsh and loud. "He didn't have her kidnapped, that's her peeps."

Armand stared at Monique as Titan continued: "Her father, Pete, put the hit on you. And Pete's the main connect."

Armand's eyes expanded, his mouth hung slack. "Your father is ..." He fell into thought.

Monique stared at him, wondering how to shoot both Armand and Titan with one hit.

"So you the reason why they shot up my spot. Your pops was after me over you?"

Monique shook her head. None of this made any sense. Plus, she didn't want to talk about them, she wanted Armand to feel what she was feeling. Pain. "How could I have set you up, Army, and I ain't even know that spot existed? I had never been there before. I didn't know we were going there and you didn't either. Change of plans, remember? What my father look like trying to take you down with me up in there? You think my daddy wants me shot?"

Monique accepted that she was going to die. They were talking in circles and none of it was relevant to her pain. Armand had

167

abandoned her. Twice. She watched Titan's mouth move and felt like spitting.

Titan's voice was irritating her; Armand's questioning glare was killing her; and Chew's voice was making her sad.

Titan shouted, "One of you niggahs better—"

Monique pulled the trigger. The blast tore a hole through Titan's leg.

"Shut. The. Fuck. Up," Monique said slow and clear. "Or the next shot is to the head, bitch. Now tell another motherfucker to shoot me."

Titan moaned loudly in pain, clutching his leg in disbelief. Monique didn't care. If she was going out, she was taking Armand and Titan with her. She owed Pete that much. She owed her family that much. For the first time she understood what Pete and Ricardo had been trying to tell her, and she had walked away from them for a conniving bastard. Armand would pay for her mistake. He would pay for the pain her death would cause her mother.

In the second that it took for them to register that she had shot Titan, Monique pointed the gun directly at Armand and screamed.

Wade fired a shot. "Mother—"

Monique didn't flinch. She had no idea where the bullet went, but when his body fell limp, Monique looked at Chew and Dut. It was Chew who had blasted Wade in the back of the head.

Shots fired out from Chris's gun. Dut fired back while Chew ducked behind a car. Monique didn't think to duck. Someone's fingers grabbed a hold of her ankle, and she felt herself being pulled down. Screaming, Monique stomped on Titan's hand, kicking awkwardly for him to release her.

She stumbled a few steps and heard Dut yell out in pain as she fell into an air pump. Regaining her balance, Monique aimed her gun at Armand and watched him shoot at her captors. Chris lay dead. Dut was shot. Chew had his gun on Carlos.

Armand looked up to find her waiting on him, waiting for his full attention before she pulled the trigger.

"You gonna shoot me?" Armand said. A slight smile formed on his perfect lips.

"Mo. Please, baby, put the gun down." Chew locked gazes with her.

"I'mma about to do this bitch." Dut's deep voice shocked her. "I swear, I done had enough of her shit."

"Be cool, Dut. Just be cool, man," Armand said.

"Army, kill her." Titan pressed his fists into the bloody hole in his leg. "You better kill this bitch or your ass is marked."

"Monique, you gonna kill me?" Armand said again, his smile growing wider, his eyes warming.

Her hand faltered just a bit. There was no turning back now, though. "Fuck you," she said. The gun trembled again. She gripped it with her other hand. Her arms were tired. The gun was heavy, and the chair was heavier. Her head was throbbing and her chest hurt.

"Monique."

She met his gaze.

"Monique, you set me up?"

"What do you think, Armand? Would I have thrown myself through a glass window if I set you up? Would I be standing here now if I set you up?"

Armand lowered his gun. "Then put the gun down."

"No, Army. You left me to die. That man had a rifle to my head and you had left me."

"Who had a rifle to your head?" Chew said.

"Tell this bitch to put that gun down, Army," Dut said.

Armand took another step toward her. "I went by your mom's."

She didn't know how much longer she could hold the chair and the gun up. "Why?"

"Looking for you." He stepped closer. "Tell her, Chew."

"We went by your mom's for real, Mo. My lil' brother is still waiting on your street in case you show up."

"Army, Pete's coming for you. You got his daughter, the whole city going after your head. You got to kill her," Titan mumbled through clenched teeth, anguish causing him to sweat.

Carlos took a step toward Titan.

"Don't move." Chew cocked his gun for effect.

"Army, how are you going to do this? I'm Mike's people. We fam'," Carlos said.

Monique wondered what had happened to Carlos's gun.

Armand shrugged, his facial expression never changing. It was hard to imagine that Armand even knew Carlos, much less considered him family. Armand kept his eyes on Monique.

"Army, you can't do this," Carlos pleaded.

"It's already done, son," Armand said quietly. He gave Monique his full attention. "Who did that to your face?"

She pointed at Carlos.

"What else he do?"

Monique shrugged, tears rolling down her face.

Armand stepped closer to her. His eyes were kind in a way only she could see. She needed to do it, to shoot him now before he got close enough to knock the gun out of her hands.

"Mo, I didn't leave you," he whispered.

"Army, move, man," Dut said. "I got her."

"Dut, dammit, be cool." Armand took another step. "Monique. Monique."

She should shoot him. She had to do it now. She couldn't. She wouldn't. She needed him to be in attack mode, defensive and hateful, so pulling the trigger would feel good. Instead, she felt confused and frustrated with herself. Why hadn't she just pulled the trigger yet? Why hadn't she just accepted her fate? Was something in her so small and weak that even now she needed Armand's love, needed to know that he cared about her?

That wasn't the type of woman she thought she was. But she couldn't do it. Couldn't stare into those deep eyes and prepare for death. Couldn't take in the outline of those perfect lips and not feel her heart flutter. Monique shook her head, fighting the inner turmoil.

Fuck him.

The barrel of that shotgun pointing down at her face filled her mind; those never-ending minutes of silence while she waited terrified in that apartment came back to her. She loved him more than she loved herself, Pete, or Ricardo. With Armand she felt safe because he held her in his arms for hours, inhaling her and muttering how much she meant to him. She felt safe with him because their lovemaking had taken her to spiritual places she never before knew existed. He could make her orgasm so deep that she cried like a baby.

Armand was part of her soul, and he would exit this world with her.

Her eyes met his. Somehow she knew that he knew the decision had been made. She steadied her hand on the gun and swallowed. Armand ran and dived at her. He moved so suddenly that surprise made her stall for a second, just enough time for him to tackle her like a football player. The gun fired as they hit the cement floor, her head bouncing wildly on the concrete. Pain and a weird warmth shot through her neck and down her spine.

The leg of the metal chair landed heavily on her hip. Shots rang out. Monique saw Titan squirming away from her. Her vision blurred. Armand rolled off her, snatched the gun from her hands.

This was it.

She watched him look down at her for a second and smile at her as if she were the loveliest thing in the world. A loud pop rang through the air. Monique closed her eyes and waited to feel the pain. All she felt was the pressure released from her wrist as the chair fell away.

Monique moaned and tried to push herself back onto her elbows and wriggle backward. Armand had his gun in Carlos's ear. Armand's mouth moved, just barely. He pointed his finger at her and made Carlos look at her. She couldn't focus on them and couldn't gauge what was happening. Another explosion made her jump. Carlos slumped over.

She had never seen Armand kill before, not that she ever wanted to. She didn't know that he could be so blank and unemotional. Like Pete. Armand had executed the man just like she knew Pete would do. Would Armand kill her just as easily?

Dut held his arm, complaining as blood poured from it.

Chew moved to Monique and bent down. "Mo? Mo, you alright?"

She couldn't focus, blinking her eyes furiously. She knew she needed to stay awake. If she lost consciousness, she might never snap out of it. Survival kicked in and Monique shook her head as hard as she could. She was glad she could move her neck, despite that terrifying feeling of warmth crawling down her spine.

"Don't touch her," Armand yelled out.

Chew ignored him. "Mo, I don't think you're hit. Try to stand up."

The motion of standing made her nauseas. Chew jerked back as she gagged.

Two more gun shots filled the air. Monique and Chew jumped. Armand stood over Titan with two smoking guns.

"Damn," Dut said, his voice barely above a whisper, still moaning and gripping his arm. "Why the fuck did you do that? The whole west side is going to come after us."

"That motherfucker shouldn't have never laid hands on what is mine."

All three of them looked at Monique. Twisted relief washed over her just before blackness overtook her mind.

Chapter Twenty-Seven

Chew drove the Accord just under the speed limit as he thought of all that had transpired. The car was quiet as each of its passengers swam in a pool of drowning reflection.

"That was a mistake," Dut said.

Monique's limp body lay against Armand in the back seat. They rode in the early morning hours—when the city seemed harmless and tired, its building leaning like battled warriors in a never-ending brawl. They slowly passed a street cleaning truck.

"We don't have the resources to go against Titan's people." Dut looked over his shoulder at Armand.

Armand nodded. It was a point he couldn't disagree with, but what other options did he have? Monique had stood before him like a battered doll, black and blue marks spotting her face, her lips swollen, her eye half closed.

The moment he saw her, his heart knew she hadn't set him up. One look at her made it clear that she had been fighting to get back to him. Those fools hadn't busted in and tried to save her before blasting up his trap house, either. She didn't know she would be there, either. They were going to kill everyone up in the spot, and Monique would have been dead as well. There was no way her father could have known she was in there.

He fingered the delicate necklace in his hand and glanced at her. She had lied. Maybe not lied, but she knew more about him and his lifestyle than she ever let on. How could she be the person he thought he knew when she hadn't even told him about her family or her life? Her brother, most of all, her father? He would have left her the hell alone had he known.

Now Armand had her and the main connect for the entire city and his son wanted Armand dead.

"Armand," Dut pressed, "we are fucked, man."

"Naw we ain't," Armand said. "I ain't never let you down before. Why are you trippin'?"

"Because I ain't never seen you put a bitch over the game before, that's why." Dut paused to let his words sink in. "My cousin caught a bullet for the game. We running these streets, hustling and dying for the game, and you just threw away everything for this bitch."

"Don't call her a bitch again," Chew said through clenched teeth.

"And you. You acting like she with you. What the fuck?" Dut aimed his stare at Chew, his voice loud with exasperation.

Armand waited for an answer to Dut's question. Armand was curious. Chew did seem to be connected to Monique in a way Armand hadn't realized before. It was one thing that they knew each other from school, another thing for her mother to know Chew like that, and something entirely different for Chew to be the first to Monique's side.

"She was like my sister, man, back in the day." Chew shrugged.

"Well, now your sister got us all marked."

"Enough, Dut," Armand said.

"Naw. Hear me out. I ain't saying they was right. Or that they shoulda been allowed to kill her. But poppin' Titan like that in cold blood?" Dut shook his head. "When that gets out, the higher-ups are going to get involved."

"It's the higher-ups that came blastin' us yesterday. The higher-ups was making Titan pay tithes with our lives." Armand leaned forward in the seat. "Don't you get it? Titan did some shit that made them come after us."

Chew nodded his head.

"Bitch, stop nodding your fucking head," Dut said.

"Then he kidnapped the main man's daughter. For what? Give her to us? Make it look like we killed her. Change the focus from him to us. So whatever they was pissed about would change to huntin' us down for kidnapping one of their daughters." Armand shook his head. "Dut, you got to think sometimes. Think ahead of the day to day. That motherfucker Titan was about to do us in. I could see it in his eyes."

"Maybe." Dut shrugged. "But she ain't who you thought, neither. You got to think of that."

"No. She ain't." Armand sat back and pushed Monique's hair away from her face.

"And when word gets back about Titan, we are through, I'm telling you."

"How is word going to get back?" Armand was starting to get pissed off. "The only people who know what went down tonight are in this car. She already proved she keeps her mouth shut. You plan on spreading the word?"

It was a direct challenge. Dut looked at Armand, some of his bravado fading. There was no doubt that Armand was capable of putting the gun to his head on the spot. Both Dut and Chew realized it.

"I didn't mean it like that, Army."

"Then how you meant it? If we the only ones walked out of there, and the garage is burning as we speak, how the streets gonna hear anything different than what we say?"

Dut shrugged. "I guess they won't."

"No, they won't. We tell the streets what to report. Ya heard?"

"Yeah. But the streets know this girl is in the mix."

"She ain't got nothing to do with none of this," Chew said as he snapped out of his trance.

Dut and Armand glanced at each other, then Armand leaned back on his seat, lost in thought.

They rode in silence.

***

The print shop was uncomfortably lit, or maybe it was just Ricardo's nerves getting the best of him. Pete's unblinking stare felt like it was penetrating his skull.

"I can't find her," Ricardo admitted, staring up at his father's solid frame. "I have looked everywhere, but Michelle ain't answering. She probably pissed off at me about Mo."

"You call her mother?"

"Yeah. Just asked to speak to her, didn't tell her it was me. Her moms say she wasn't there, said she was staying at her dads. Here."

"And you ain't heard from Mo yet?" Pete drummed his fingertips against the table.

"No. Mo ain't called or nothing."

"What about the boy?"

"Nothing on him or Titan. No word. First crew is looking for them."

"Where at?"

"Down in the west side, but they can't go too deep in daylight. And morning is here now, so they on their way back." Ricardo shrugged.

"What about our in?" Pete shifted his wide frame in the small chair.

"No word from him yet. Last message he sent was they were looking for Mo just like us."

"For?"

"Just to find her. Said they were on the search, too." Ricardo paused, meeting his father's eyes. "If he gets to her, she will be safe no matter what. He will protect her."

"I don't want my daughter caught up in this shit," Pete said.

Ricardo glanced at the office door. There were other men sitting around the shop. They were checking their phones and calling folks. A couple of them even looked like they were strategizing.

Ricardo knew he had to come clean. "Uh, I got someone up in here. She know the girl Michelle probably left with."

Pete eyed the office door. "You just now telling me."

"Yeah." There was no explanation, and he didn't want to waste words that would make Pete lose his patience. "The girl ain't answering, so Tandra going to take me by her spot."

"Who is the girl Mikki is with?"

"Anji. From the basketball team."

"How she know her?" Pete gestured toward the office.

Ricardo swallowed. "My girl is a hairdresser. She know everybody that think they on the come up."

"Your girl, huh?" Pete exhaled thick smoke from the cigar wedged between his lips. "Your sisters are missing and you telling me you got some pussy up in here?"

"It wasn't like that."

"The hell it weren't. You better find Mikki. She was on you."

Ricardo nodded. It was always on him. His mother. His other sisters. Monique. Now Michelle. Somehow, by mere birth, he had become the dustpan for all of Pete's bullshit. He shook his head. The feeling he had for Pete at times like this wasn't anything close to love.

The front door was opened just as Ricardo reached the office door. They weren't expecting anybody else. The muscle was here but the crews were out. Pete's hand rested on the sawed-off under the counter. Ricardo pulled out a Glock that had rested in the front of his pants.

Two bulky men stepped in and nodded at Pete. They did a sweep of the room with their eyes and nodded to someone through the glass door. Within minutes two old school players strolled in. Pete's age. But unlike Pete, they seemed to gleam: fresh, expensive casual suits over button-down, open-collar shirts. They were men of power, and they were the last people Ricardo wanted to lay eyes on. Pete glanced at his men, who quickly stood up around the tight space as the men walked forward.

"Pete, what's up?"

"Nawly. Nothin' happenin'." Pete stepped forward and gave both men an old school hug.

Ricardo hoped Tandra would stay her ass in the office. If she walked out and spotted these old men, uncomfortable decisions would have to be made.

"What's good?" Pete said.

Nawly, the shorter of the two, motioned to the table. Pete nodded in affirmation and all three men sat down. Ricardo lingered behind Pete.

"We hearing that a lot is happening, Pete," Nawly said, leaning back in the chair. "Lot going down on the west side."

"Is that a fact?" Pete asked blankly.

"That's the word," the other one named Butch said.

"Well, we haven't heard the word up here, Butch. Why don't you tell us?" Pete's eyes narrowed.

"We know you tried to handle Titan. Without the forum. No need to take this kind of attitude, Pete," Nawly said.

"Didn't need the forum's permission. Titan killed my man Lyons. That action calls for a response, with or without the forum."

"What example you setting, Pete, if you presiding over the forum and don't use it for these types of decisions? How that affect the

177

power of this here thing?" Butch questioned, his dark skin shining brightly in the early morning light.

Ricardo's cell vibrated. He turned his body away from the men and looked at his phone. Flipping open the screen, he quickly read the text message; it filled him with relief. *Got Mo, She safe*, it read.

One down, one more to go. Ricardo felt a weight lift from his chest. Monique was the one in danger, the one acting like a fool to get back to Armand. It's a good thing he and Pete had people in unforeseen places. But it was going to cost him dearly.

Ricardo met Pete's eyes and nodded to let him know that Monique was contained. Ricardo noticed that the pulsing vein near Pete's temple relaxed just a bit.

Pete continued talking, "I ain't understanding what y'all are asking. Be straight."

"Any straighter and I would have a metal rod up my ass, Pete. You wrong."

"Alright." Pete shrugged. "Maybe I was wrong, but that bastard ain't gonna be killing up old heads."

"Maybe." Nawly's hands were held together like he was about to pray. "But the problem is with your approach, Pete. You ain't bother to clue in Lyons's people. What, you thought they wasn't going to retaliate?"

Pete's closed lips protruded as he ran his tongue across his teeth. Ricardo lowered his head. They hadn't thought about Lyons's people. Titan had become a nuisance, and Lyons's death was the excuse they needed to do something about it.

"Once it's handled, they don't have to worry about it. I'll put that on my head; I'll pay the price." Pete wondered where Mikki was. This was no time for her to be out of pocket.

"Oh, you paying the price. No doubt. Shit, you owe because we all paying more for muscle now that damn boy of Titan's is on the prowl. He getting at anyone got anything to do with you."

Nawly said, "Hell yeah. Between the shit you caused and Lyons's folks firing up the city looking for Titan too, I had to muscle up all my spots."

"They got at him yet?" Ricardo interrupted.

All three looked up at him.

"Lyons's folks? They got Titan yet?

"Naw, boy," Butch said, staring at Ricardo as if he were stupid. "They ain't got shit but a couple of females. You motherfuckers ain't listenin'."

"That's one less motherfucker I'mma be, you keep disrespecting me." Pete drilled his narrow gaze through Butch.

Butch waved his hand. "Pete, put that pride shit away. Lyons's people are going guerilla style. Heard they jumped out the bushes on these two females. Lyons's people had followed Titan to the females spot earlier. They shot them females all up. Then, they hit Pootchie's spot over by the harbor, killed two of Titan's workers. And you know Titan's car garage over near the warehouse district? That shit is ablaze as we speak. All this in the last twenty-four hours."

"Yesterday, Titan requested a meet," Nawly said. "I'm granting it."

"You can't grant shit," Pete yelled. "It's my damn forum."

"I'm calling the meeting, Pete. Already talked to the other families. Just like I am stopping to tell you. Some limits have to be put on this ... this firestorm you and this young gun here started. I ain't losing or spending no more money on this shit here."

"And that's my word," Butch added.

Pete stared at them. He felt breathless. Ricardo knew this was exactly what Pete wanted to avoid: his authority being compromised, his decisions being questioned.

"Since when can Titan—"

"Ain't Titan." Nawly stood up. "It's me, Pete. It's all of us. This thing is burning resources, and you did it around us. Titan got a right to be heard. And without Lyons around, someone got to come up with a way to get control over his people."

Butch rose too. "Sorry, Pete. It is what it is, and them folks for Lyons better pay funeral expenses for Titan's girl, too. I ain't contributing to that shit."

"Naw," Nawly said, "as usual, Butch, you got the damn story backward. Wasn't his girl got shot up. It was her friend who was borrowing her car for something. They shot her up, thinking she was Anji."

Ricardo didn't hear anything else but the loud thumping of his heart. In that instant, he knew Michelle was dead. It was the rhythm of his life. The give and take. The ebb and flow. There was never any peace without intense grief, never any payment without unbelievable loss. The sister he was the closest with would surely be the one to die.

There could be other Anji's, but Ricardo's heart told him the truth. He couldn't keep the ones he loved. That much had been proven in the last twenty-four hours, if never before. And if he did love them, then they were cursed. They were bound to suffer and to be degraded. It made sense. That was the only way Michelle wouldn't have answered her phone on a night like last night when he and her had felt terrified for Monique.

Pete didn't miss a beat. He watched the old heads walk out then stood up suddenly. "Same Anji?"

"I don't know," Ricardo said.

"I'mma call the hospitals. You go to Anji's place. Make sure my baby wasn't with her."

Chapter Twenty-Eight

Monique felt cold water against her face, pressed gently against her burning skin. She felt so thirsty but didn't have the strength to ask for any water to drink. She slowly opened her eyes. The room seemed strange and foreign. A plain room with basic furniture. Where was she?

"Mo, how you feel?"

The whispered voice wasn't Armand's. That's the first thing she knew without having to look. Her head turned slowly because her neck felt so sore.

"Chew," Monique whispered. "Where are we?"

"Safe house, baby girl," he said. "You want something to drink?"

She nodded. She wished that she had just said *yes* instead. He leaned over the bed and helped her pull herself up. Something cold fell against her neck. Monique slowly traced a path across her chest until her fingertips pressed something very familiar to the touch.

Her chain.

"You gave me back my chain?" Monique touched it again. "How?"

"No. Armand cleaned it up and put it on you before he left."

"Where did he go?" Monique felt her heart seize. She didn't want to be left with Armand's people by herself. Not even Chew. Especially not Chew.

"Meeting." Chew shrugged.

"Thank you for ... earlier." Monique remembered Chew's concern.

"I ain't do nothing."

"You were the only one who gave a damn about me. More than Army."

They didn't say anything as she sipped the water.

He took the cup from her. "Army is just different, Mo. You can't expect that type of cat to touch emotion and run the streets. That's just not him."

181

"I know." She wiped her mouth with the back of a hand. "You know you and I used to be tight back in the day."

"Yep." Chew sat on the bed.

"Then you left."

"Started hustling."

"But ..." Monique pursed her lips trying to figure out how to express herself. "We were friends. Then it was like you didn't know me."

Chew shook his head slowly. "Started hustling," he said again.

They glanced at each other and smiled.

"What's that necklace mean anyway?" Chew pointed at her chain.

Monique glanced down, her fingers grazing the chain. "My father had a rough time in Vietnam. Said that if he ever made it back here he would establish his family, treat it like gold. Before I was born, of course. So, when he got back here from the war there were no jobs for vets. Black vets, it was even worse."

"Yeah," Chew muttered. "My uncle fought in Vietnam, too. Wasn't shit when he got back, crazy acting. I only met him a couple of times. He's in the pen now." He shrugged.

Monique gazed into Chew's eyes. There was always so much going on behind the friendly exterior, always so much pain. Chew had been her friend during the years she worked so hard to be cool, during the years she cared so much about what everyone else thought. She remembered how she would hang in the hallway with her home girls, flirting with the boys or gossiping about other girls. When the bell rang, she would slowly saunter away until she was out of sight, then she would sprint up the three flights of stairs and down the hall to join the other honors students in their nerd quadrant. Pathetic. Monique had to admit that on so many levels she was simply pathetic.

The things she had done to fit in, to hide who she really was. After being ostracized for being the only black girl in the "white" classes, Monique had mastered the chill-and-sprint strategy so that no one but her best friends ever really knew what courses she was taking. She even moved her books around in the morning, leaving them in the back of each class so that she looked like her friends when she joined them: book free and worry free.

It was Chew who had convinced her that all the work was unnecessary. He had been watching her. He was the only person paying attention to how she conveniently disappeared. He had bumped into her while she was running down the hall as if the school was on fire. She remembered how he had grabbed both her arms in concern.

"Mo, what are you doin'?" he had said.

"Nothing." She took a deep breath, frantic that she wasn't going to make it to the class by the second bell.

"Mo, I know you don't come running down this hall every day?"

"Where are you coming from?" Monique said, using her tried and true method of avoiding a question by asking another question.

"Counselor." He shrugged. "Where are you going? You still hiding that you are in the honors section."

Monique shrugged, listening to the shrill second bell in defeat.

"Mo, you got to be you. You're fine, girl. You should know that."

Monique hadn't believed Chew, but she appreciated the kindness in his eyes, the understanding in his tone. From that day forward, Chew was the only person she confided in, the only person who she always felt herself around. Eventually that led to their first quick hug, their first lingering embrace, their first meaningful kiss.

Chew was the first person who had taken her breath away. She had never told Armand, and she had hoped that Chew had the good sense not to mention it either. They had been so young messing around during her freshmen year in high school. Chew had dropped out the next year and she saw him less and less after that. Compared to what she and Armand had, she and Chew had only experienced puppy love.

She and Chew had a special friendship, one that would last a lifetime. She knew he would always be on the fringes of her life, always somewhere in the background. There was a change in him that she suspected but couldn't quite put her finger on it. She had to know the truth, though.

"When Pete couldn't work, he had to hustle," Monique said, coming back to the here and now. "And as he got better, he grew the family name, I guess. Decided he would make a family armor like those white families do, you know, in the South, like a family shield to

183

remind us of our family at all times. So me, Michelle, and Ricardo will always have us, will always have the family. Even if we don't see each other for months, I know that my family is out there. That they got me no matter what." Monique's lips quivered, but she forced the words through anyway. "I know that I am protected."

"That's what's up."

"Yep." Monique stroked her necklace. "This saved my life the other day. The guy yanked it off my neck instead of shooting me. Army must have fixed the clasp."

"Hmm." Chew stood up and gathered the towel and cup. "But what's the TW2? What it mean?"

Monique smiled. They both knew that was something else she wasn't telling.

She shrugged her shoulders. "Folks who work for my father long enough, they recognize it sometimes. And his muscle. They all know. But for the most part, since me and Michelle aren't part of the game, we are the only ones who know what it is around our friends."

"Don't side talk me, Mo, feeding me bullshit instead of the real. I know better." Chew nodded his head at the necklace. "What it mean?"

Monique grimaced, knowing that Chew was right. The words were stuck in her throat. She was so conditioned to keep secrets, so thoroughly trained to hide the truth, that sometimes it was impossible to simply push words through her lips. "Uhm." Monique fingered the necklace.

"Mo, tell me."

She nodded her head, more to herself than Chew. She could trust him and she knew it. She just had to reprogram her mind to let the words ooze out.

"Mo."

"Troubled Waters, the second generation." She spit the words out, her eyes watering as she struggled through the feeling of betrayal. The words hadn't been spoken out loud in years; it was a private code to all things reserved for her, Michelle, and Ricardo. "We are the Troubled Waters. Me, Michelle, Ricardo."

Chew stared at her.

"You don't get it? Folks wade in the water waiting for God, but they got to deal with us instead. We are the Troubled Waters. The second generation."

Chew shook his head, a blank look on his face.

"Damn, Chew." His ignorance angered Monique. Her voice rose as the last of her patience evaporated. She spoke slowly as if she were talking to a child. "It's a play on the gospel song Wade in the Water. Damn."

"Whatever."

Chew's eyes hardened and Monique knew that she had offended him, but she felt irritated. Monique had broken down her own walls to share a secret that Chew seemed too simple to fully appreciate. Where was the intuitive man who used to understand her without spoken words? Who was the simple creature sitting with her now who couldn't read in between the lines?

"I forgot, we ain't all on your level." His lips curled and his eyes narrowed.

The typical look of jealous weakness. Monique had seen it a million times before on the faces and tongues of so called friends or Michelle's cousins. The hateful flippant comment that suggested Monique thought she was better than them. It was something Monique despised more than anything, something she never forgot or forgave.

"I guess not." She should leave it alone, but some tiny part of her couldn't. Monique swung her legs over the side of the bed and leaned forward as Chew headed for the door. "You know," Monique said, stopping him in his tracks, "the shooter with the shotgun up in Army's trap house? He knew it."

"Yeah, you said already." Chew turned to look at her, his expression questioning.

"It was weird because he didn't believe I was who I said I was. But he knew the symbol." Monique tried to stand up. Her legs felt too weak. "He, no doubt, worked for my father. He knew to look out for the symbol, even if he didn't know me. Someone must have specifically told him."

Chew leaned against the door, shaking his head slowly. His eyes were pleading with her to be quiet. He didn't want her to put words to the heavy insinuation.

"When I was hiding in that apartment, I heard a voice. Kind of familiar, but I hadn't heard it in such a long time. I think I was too scared to really notice. But the voice stuck with me—yelling out orders, telling the man who almost killed me to look for us, to make sure we got got. The way he was giving orders he definitely worked for my father."

"Mo."

"Chew." Mo shook her head as her eyes filled with tears. "How long have you been down with my dad? Or Ricardo? Why you straddling the fence?"

"Mo, you're confused. Them lumps got you twisted up. Go back to sleep." He tried to leave again but her voice stopped him.

"Chew, I know your voice. I know you. It didn't hit me until later … in the garage. I know it. Why were you there? Why were you leading them against Army?"

Chew stared at her blankly.

"Chew, say something."

"Why did you have to say anything at all, Mo?" Chew sighed. "Even if you put it together, why didn't you just leave it alone?"

"I want to know. Why are you in the middle of something that doesn't have anything to do with you?"

"Because, Mo, I got to feed my family. My hustle is the only way for me to survive." He grabbed the doorknob.

"But you was directing them to kill Army. You wanted him dead."

"Fuck Army." Chew scowled, walking back into the room and shutting the door behind him.

Monique sat as straight as she could to appear more able than her body actually felt. She didn't think Chew would hurt her but there was no telling.

"What the fuck were you doing there, Mo?"

"I don't even know."

"So you shouldn't have shit to say. You know I didn't know you was up in there. You know I wouldn't have sent Desmond after you."

"But you're playing traitor."

"I ain't playin' shit. I told Army to leave my little brother out of the game. Where he at? Sellin' over on Jefferson. I ain't got voice over my own brother? My people? Army ain't my god, and he don't get to decide my brother's fate ... or mine."

Monique nodded slightly to look as if she agreed. She didn't. Chew wouldn't be rewarded from either camp. "You know Ricardo and Pete, they don't trust someone they think is a traitor, Chew. No way you're going to get something good out of this."

"They don't think I'm a traitor. They know where my heart stands. They know where I am loyal."

"But you don't even know the east side."

"Ain't got to. Who they trusted with keeping up with you when you ran off after this fool here? Me. I am part of the family you spoke of and you know it. So if you tell Armand, you burning the circle, baby. Your own family. Then again, from how you acting lately, you kind of a traitor, too."

"I wouldn't have told Armand either way, Chew." Monique sighed.

Pete considered her a traitor. That much she already knew. Chew saying it out loud hurt her. Especially after she had just told him about TW2. "You think I'm a traitor now, too?"

"I don't know why you're questioning me," Chew said. "What I ever do to you, Mo, that I wasn't good enough?"

"What are you talking about?"

"Me. Why wasn't I good enough?"

"We were baby boyfriend and girlfriend. What are you talking about? You disappeared. Stopped coming to school. Didn't go to any more parties. You stopped calling me. You didn't have to disappear." She shook her head. "That was years ago anyway."

"Yeah, but look at where being with Army got you."

"That's low, Chew. You're hitting below the belt, and for what?"

"I'm just saying. If I am traitor, so are you." His voice sounded like it had in the trap house: high-pitched and muffled.

It made her sad that she could no longer respect him, but she simply nodded. "Yeah. I guess I am a traitor, but I'm not kissing Army's ass like you, playing the friend role. I'm not trying to kill someone one day and driving him around the next. You are heartless."

"I'll be that, baby girl," Chew said, putting his finger under her chin and forcing her to look at him. "I'll be heartless if, in the end, you are all good. But you need to leave Army's ass alone."

"Chew, Army and I are good."

"You think you the only one, Mo? Shit, the night of the shoot-out some chick was at his place crying about him and some baby bullshit."

Monique had no idea of what he was talking about. She cringed, not wanting to think about Armand and some other woman with a baby.

"Don't trust him."

Chew stared at her until she leaned back and moved her head until his finger was no longer under her chin. He dropped his hand, his eyes searching hers.

There was a hungry look to him that she hadn't noticed before, almost like he was neglected and needy. She gave him a small smile, but her nerves were mounting. Chew's neediness was dangerous; it was a thin step above resentfulness.

The floorboard creaked.

Suddenly, Chew's head turned to the door; his mouth fell open. Monique followed his eyes. In her heart she knew that Armand filled the doorway before a word was uttered. In that instant, she could feel his anger bouncing off the walls like static. How could she and Chew have been so careless, so caught up in each other that they never heard the door open?

The blast was so loud and sudden that Monique shrieked and threw herself on the floor where Chew had thrown himself. Chew had already pulled out his small gun.

"Army, put that piece down. Use a silencer at least," Dut shouted, knocking Armand's arm down and pushing him back into the hall. "It's a safe house, dammit! You want the neighbors to call the cops?"

"This shit just gets better and better." Armand pulled out his second gun.

Dut's head appeared in the doorframe. "Put that gun down, Chew. I got you."

"Mo, tell my brother I love him," Chew whispered then shot toward the door at Dut.

"This motherfucker here," Dut said, his screaming voice betraying his surprise. "Chew! I know you didn't just shoot at me. I'mma kick your ass when I get in there. You better put that fucking gun down." Dut's words bounced around the large room.

Monique instantly knew what Chew was planning to do. "No, Chew, please. Don't do this. Just blast through."

"Mo, these fools will shoot you tryin' to get to me. Trust me. Army ain't got no love for nobody else."

"Chew, please." Monique crawled closer to him, her hands trembling as tears flooded her face. "Don't consider it. Chew, listen to me."

"Get back, Mo," Chew said, pointing the gun at her.

She stopped crawling, but kept sobbing.

"They will kill you, Mo. Get away from me. Get back."

Monique turned and headed in the opposite direction, quickly crawling back toward the dresser, her knees and hands slapping the wood surface with her back to Chew.

Monique glanced back. He stuck the gun in his mouth.

The explosion rattled her essence.

Chew's brains splattered across the floor. The ugly sight blinded her for a second, everything went white. There was only so much death one person could take, only so many gun battles and mini-explosions anyone who was used to a calm reality could stomach. Monique screamed, turning her head too late. The image of him pulling the trigger with his eyes closed was forever burned into her psyche. Monique had lost her old friend and long-ago boyfriend.

She had caused his death. She should have left it alone. Had anyone else questioned him, he wouldn't have responded. And he definitely wouldn't have told the truth. Since she was the one doing the asking, he responded. Monique and Chew were family in some strange inexplicable way. Deeper than she and Armand could ever be because they had history. Chew and Monique had a past together before the game transformed him into a bitter man wearing a lighthearted exterior. Now he was dead.

"Chew! Yo, Chew." Dut's voice sounded miles away.

Monique barely heard him through her screams.

"Damn," Dut said.

Armand stepped past him and walked directly to Chew's dead body, which still convulsed as blood and nerves continued to pump through it.

"Fuckin' fool did himself," Armand said to Dut.

Dut nodded, his eyes unreadable, but locked on Monique.

"I can't believe this shit. My man Chew? My man Chew was the hit man at the trap house. The one who dipped out?" Armand said. "Dut, you knew?"

"Who the fuck you askin'?" Dut frowned.

"Mo, you knew. Again, you knew. And you wasn't going to say shit, huh?" Armand looked at Monique as if she were the cruddiest bitch on earth.

Monique couldn't answer him. She was still crying, still trying to piece together some resemblance of reality. Dut's cold eyes judged her, but she didn't care. Chew was under the banner of Pete's armor, so Monique would have never told. That much truth she knew without thinking about it. Even Chew had known it.

Armand didn't reach out to hug her. His black eyes stared back and forth between Monique and Chew, and finally his eyes met Dut's. Monique noticed the long, silent glance between them. It was filled with a million words and a million questions, but she didn't care anymore. She watched Armand finally stare at Chew's dead body. With a long sigh, Armand bent down to his knees and closed Chew's eyes. Armand remained there with his eyes closed, squatting by Chew's body, his head hung down, listening to Monique's pain.

It was Dut's vibrating phone that angrily broke through the tension and shattered the silence. "Army, this spot is blown. We got to wrap it up."

"Son of a bitch," Armand said. "Your father is a dead man." He pointed his finger at Monique as he spoke. "If that's where your loyalties lie, I understand. But I'm telling you, all bets are off."

Monique didn't answer. She wiped her tears away and crawled back up on the bed slowly. Neither Dut nor Armand offered her a hand.

"You know what? Fuck this! They wanna play? Let's play," Armand continued. He talked to himself and paced the room blindly. He left a trail of blood in his path. He flipped open a cell phone Monique didn't recognize. "Mo, what's your number?"

She didn't answer him. There was nothing she could think of to say. Chew was right, the real one that seemed heartless was Armand. He had chosen her over Titan but then again, Monique knew enough to understand that Titan had caused the entire mess in the first place. Now Armand was pulling the trump card. Calling her father and making threats? Using her for bait? Now he was doing the unthinkable.

Chapter Twenty-Nine

Armand's world was collapsing. He thrust his phone toward Monique. "Number," he said, ignoring her sobs.

Chew was his man, second only to Raymond and Dut, really, in the scheme of things. Armand didn't know what he would have done to Chew had he lived, but he never expected the brother to swallow a bullet. To actually kill himself. A sinful solution, really. *Wasn't it true that people who committed suicide were stuck in purgatory or some shit like that?* Armand hoped that Chew wasn't stuck.

The thoughts that were entering his head were crazy. He needed sleep. That was why he had come right back after getting Dut taped up at the doctor's spot instead of tracking Ricardo. He had simply wanted to hold Monique and feel her warm body against his, to kiss away all of the black and blue marks and her swollen eye, to release all that pain penned inside of him by rocking inside of her body and taking them both to ecstasy. That's all his mind could think of.

Doing Titan was more difficult than it seemed. Armand had to appear heartless. That was the way to keep order and minimize backlash. Titan had been his mentor, though, the one who saw something special in him. Titan hadn't actually done shit but overstep his boundaries by kidnapping Monique, and even that wasn't a huge deal in the overall scheme of things. Armand could tell that Titan was wavering, though. The solution was easy for Titan: turn over Armand and his crew in order to make peace with the other families in the game. Armand refused to be the ticket price for that bill of sale.

It was ultimately instinct that told him to take out Titan. Armand knew without reason that Titan would forever remember the mess that night had transformed into and would somehow make them pay. Shit, once they pulled guns out on Titan and Wade, it was over with anyway. Those spiteful two would never forgive that act of betrayal. Armand knew that for a fact.

So it was Monique that he chose in the end. She wasn't going to die because Titan and his men were one-track minded, and he was mad as hell about how she looked. Carlos shouldn't have laid a finger on her. He knew better. Armand's temper had interceded, there was no doubt about that. Unchecked, he could have killed everyone in there without so much as a second thought.

But Dut had a point. Armand didn't really know Monique. Armand had felt sure they could work past her not disclosing who her peoples were. A sign of loyalty in a woman was a good thing, even if it was for her family over him, but his entire idea of her had faded as well. How much more of this game did she know to ascertain that Chew was a mole? Plus, Armand didn't like Dut knowing that he knew so little about her. The eye contact and the unspoken vibe between he and Dut felt thick. Armand knew that Dut would soon gain a false sense of bravado that could turn into mutiny, relying on the idea that Armand had undermined them all for some pussy. It was something Armand wanted to avoid at all cost. He needed Dut just like he had needed Raymond. Family. He needed some sense of family around him. Monique, the devious secret keeper, wasn't worth sacrificing what little family he had left.

"You heard me, ma, what's the number?" Armand's heart broke each time he looked at the damage they had done to Monique's pretty face, but his resolve to stay gangster overruled.

"You know my number, Armand." Monique rolled her eyes. "Probably better than me."

Armand took a few steps over to her and stopped at her knees. She was so badly bruised that he wondered whether he should take her to the hospital. A trip to the hospital would mean questions and information. Possibly police. The last thing he needed today.

"Mo, you wanna try me next?" His heart ached when she looked at him through shielded hate.

"You threatening me now?" Monique folded her arms across her breasts.

He clasped her face, his fingers closing in around her jaw. Armand saw Dut smile slightly and it turned his stomach. What type of ass was he being by putting on a show for his man?

"Dut, get the fuck out," Armand said, his voice smooth and steady.

193

Dut's head jerked up, a questioning expression overtaking the previous pleased smirk. "What up?"

"This is my bis' right here. Get out."

"My bad." Dut walked out of the room and shut the door behind him. "Y'all want to stay in there with a corpse, be my guest."

Those words made them both stare at Chew's body. Armand stood up and pulled Monique off the bed. They slowly walked through the hallway and into the room across the hall. The room was completely empty. The old hardwood floor was slightly dusty.

"What is wrong with you?" Armand said to Monique.

"Me? What is wrong with you? With this? Why did you put me in this shit? I didn't want to know."

"Why ain't you tell me about your pops?"

"What was there to tell? I wasn't in your world like that. You and my pops have no reason to connect on anything. What you wanted me to say?"

"Something like 'by the way, you fuckin' with the main connect's daughter. So if some shit go down with me, the entire city is going to be blowin' you up'."

"Stop being dramatic." Monique felt irritated. "I don't even know what you mean by the main connect. My daddy ain't no different from anyone elses."

Armand thought he was going to choke on his tongue. "Mo, the entire game goes through your dad. All vice, baby, all of this shit here is cleared by the main man. The one with the pipeline to the stuff. Your daddy."

"So?" Monique sunk to the floor and lay flat on her back. Her thin body arched. Her breasts and nipples protruded into the air as she stretched and covered her eyes with a hand. "What's that got to do with you and me?"

"Shit, fucking with you can cost a brotha his life, that's what."

She didn't look up, so he continued:

"And you weren't going to tell me about Chew, huh?"

"I don't know. That depended."

"On what?"

"On whether I thought he was trying to do you in again. I would have told you, eventually. Or at least I would have made sure you found out if you needed to know."

"If I needed to know? Ain't that some shit."

He plopped down on the floor next to her and lightly ran his hand under her tank top to caress the warm flesh of her stomach. "Mo, this—"

She removed his hands and looked at him. For a second he almost swallowed the words and leaned down to kiss her instead. He didn't want to hurt her face, though.

"This thing has to come to an end."

Monique smiled. "That's what you were going to say. I thought you were about to end it between us."

Armand shook his head. He was considering ending it, but something deep within him—his instinct as usual—told him not to. "You don't want to end it yet?"

Monique shook her head no. "I hate you right now, but I still love you."

"Why you hate me?"

"You treat me like shit in front of everyone. You shot in the room at Chew with me sitting right there, Army. He thought you would shoot me to get at him. Your ass don't care shit about me or anyone else when you got a vendetta. And I know you left me in that damn apartment, don't deny it."

Armand shook his head. She didn't understand the millions of thoughts he had to weave through with each move he made. Emotion and love and heart had to take second place, even if he thought of them first. He had fucked up, and he wasn't going to deny it. "I do care, Mo. I just do shit fucked up sometimes."

"Yeah, and your fucked up shit leaves me where? In a garage handcuffed to a damn chair?"

"No. You can't put that on me. Why you hit the streets? Why didn't you stay with your peeps?"

"I was looking for you, bastard." Monique felt anger swelling again. "Titan's folks trailed me leaving your apartment. I went to your place. What the fuck was I thinking?"

Armand lightly kissed the back of her neck. His hand moved up the smooth skin under her tank top. "You was thinking that you love me, that's what," he whispered in her ear.

She pushed his hand away, sucking her teeth.

He smiled, resting his hand on her hip. "Say you love me."

Monique shook her head no.

"Say it, Mo."

"No," Monique said, her tone sharp. "You say it. You never say it. I want to hear it or I'm out."

"You're out? Where you gonna to go?"

"Fine, Army." Monique sat up. The fast motion caused her to lose her breath, but her adrenaline propelled her forward. She pushed herself off the floor. "And you know what? Fuck you. And fuck Dut, that nosy down-low bastard."

Armand laughed, catching her by the waist. "Mo, I love you. There. I said it. I love you."

"That's not how I want to hear it. Not with all the shit I've seen over the last seventy-two hours. You can keep that shitty-ass *I love you* to yourself."

"Monique. I love you and I need you. We gotta finish this thing. I'm tired now."

"Oh, you're tired?"

"Mo, please call your peeps and set up a meet."

"No." Monique scooted her knees to her chest and wrapped her arms around herself. "No, Pete won't meet with you. Not now."

"Then I have to pretend I have you against your will and force a meet."

"You'll die for sure if you pull that shit." Monique shook her head.

"Either way, the call is being made. This shit has to end."

"You need someone to broker it for you. Someone on Titan's level or better."

"No, I don't. Not if I got you."

Monique sighed. "Alright. But I want to get the hell out of this house with Chew lying dead in the next room."

"No doubt." Armand handed her the cell phone. "You make the call."

Chapter Thirty

Pete blew through a red light as if it were green. Ricardo sat in the passenger's seat with a discomforting worry etched into his posture.

Ricardo never left to go to Anji's because Pete rethought his game plan. There was no reason for either him or Ricardo to run around in circles. Nawly and Butch wouldn't have that effect on him or his life. Pete sighed and set back in the driver's seat of his truck.

Four tours of duty in Vietnam, all major shipments to the city through him, and Nawly and Butch wanted to overtake his power. If it wasn't so ridiculous, he might have been pissed off. Worry for Mikki had momentarily distracted him, but Pete always had people in the right places, all the ducks lined up in a row. This thing would work out in his favor no matter what. He had already played all the odds.

One phone call to his boy in blue had yielded him the name of both victims in the west side shoot-out and their attackers. One had been apprehended. They found him shot and laying in the bushes. He was confirmed as a Lyons's worker bee. Michelle had been shot, but both she and Anji were alive. Michelle was in critical condition, but alive.

That she wasn't dead was enough for Pete. The armed services had shown him death in every variation and form. Life was finite and it wasn't guaranteed. He lived every day fully aware of that, always expecting each day to be his last. How could people hold on to life like it were a partner, like it were a friend that would always be there? They shouldn't have such nerve. He didn't have such nerve, and he wasn't afraid of death.

Not for himself.

Michelle hadn't had a shot, hadn't had a chance to figure out what life was yet. Thinking of that made the lump form in his throat. The game had always been a risk. The only solidarity was in family. The only comfort was in family. Monique had torn a hole in that when she left home yesterday. Her exit brought chaos into his home, something

197

he had never allowed before. The streets could hum all they wanted to, but at the end of the day, death's drama very rarely crossed the threshold of his house.

Monique had brought it home. She had lured it into their lives when she left, creating a scenario where Michelle would have to go look for her. Pete had spent their time together training his children to look out for one another, to fight one another's battles, to be one another's best friends. It was ingrained in Michelle to seek Monique out. Monique should have known better.

In the end, though, he would gladly give his life for Michelle's. And, even though he knew she wasn't owed another minute, he would do a deal with the devil himself to spare her life if he could.

"Right there." Ricardo pointed to the visitor's parking lot as they approached the hospital.

"I see it, son." *Son*. Pete rarely said it. He couldn't express emotion well, except anger. But he loved his son. He glanced across the seat at the smaller version of himself.

"She'll be good," Ricardo said with certainty.

Pete wondered how Ricardo could still have hope or faith after all the shit he had been through. How could Ricardo think that Michelle might not die just to pay karma for all the hell his family business had reaped on the city? They owed someone for the peace they'd had, for their prosperity. It was obvious that was all coming to an end. Pete decided not to correct Ricardo.

The two men quickly entered the hospital. They tracked down Michelle's room information then headed for the elevator. Pete kept his eyes peeled for anyone who looked like the game. Hospitals were the perfect spot for ambush; word had to be out about Michelle by now. The only saving grace was that most people thought she was actually dead, so anyone with a vendetta might not show up there. But he had to be careful. Always had to be careful.

The moment the elevator doors opened, Pete's heart fell. Michelle's entire family was there performing and carrying on. The nurses were forcing them into the family waiting room against their will. Rebe saw Pete and headed his way, tears running down her face.

"I thought she was dead." Rebe cried and collapsed against Pete. "Oh thank God she ain't dead."

Pete caught her in his arms as she embraced him. He wanted to shake her off and make her stop all the drama, but what could he say? Michelle was Rebe's oldest daughter and she was entitled to her pain, to her drama.

"Ricardo," Rebe said when she noticed him. "Hi, handsome."

Pete had to give it to them. Rebe and Miriam always treated Ricardo and the opposite daughter like their own. Good hearted women.

"What they saying?" Pete said.

"Already had one surgery. They had to go in and open her up to get to the internal damage. Saying it might be a couple of more surgeries."

"But she'll make it?" Ricardo put his eyes on her.

"Lord willing. Where lil' Mo at?" Rebe said, looking behind Pete and Ricardo. "I wanted Michelle to hear her voice. They only letting in immediate family, but I let the nurse know you and Ricardo and Mo would be here."

Pete leaned down and kissed her on the cheek. She was what he needed right now, a reminder of what family was. Regardless of who the mother's were, they were family. Ricardo's man had confirmed that Monique was all right; so, until this moment, Pete felt nothing but anger at her. Now images of Michelle and Monique running around family as little girls chasing each other through the sea of Michelle's cousins as Rebe prepared plates of food for Monique to take home to Miriam entered his mind. The picture of his two girls, both smiling from ear to ear with matching pigtails, summer dresses, and sandals that Miriam had bought for the annual parade invaded his memory. His girls.

Pete needed Monique to be here, to put an end to the foolishness and come support Michelle. Of course she would if she knew what had happened. He had no doubt about that.

He needed to contact Miriam. She would want to be here. Pete took out his cell phone and dialed her number. There was no telling if he would have the presence of mind to contact her once he laid eyes on Michelle.

"Monique? Is she?" Miriam sounded breathless.

Pete could imagine her pacing in small circles, her arms moving in the air as she thought out every unthinkable disaster and reacted to it. The first time she had done that was when he and his best friend Monty had stashed marijuana in her attic and she found it. He remembered how she had stormed in the house, arms waving and muttering to herself. Pete had thought she was crazy and loved her even more, but he moved the stash before she put him out with it.

"Pete, is Monique—"

"She is fine. I wanted you to know. We found her and she's all right. We have someone with her," Pete said calmly, more than he actually felt.

"Thank God." Miriam breathed, the sound of her pain releasing.

"But Mikki got into a situation."

"Dear God, what now?"

"Meet me at Highland Hospital." Pete coughed. Hearing Miriam's voice made him want to comfort her and feel her pain. This time the pain was his, and it hurt so deep that her voice was the gate to an avalanche of hurt. "Mikki was shot."

"Pete." Miriam remained silent.

They didn't say anything, he just held the phone listening to her silence for several minutes.

"Pete, this isn't your fault."

"Of course it is," Pete said. "A lifetime of death wouldn't make up for the shit I've done."

"It doesn't work that way, Pete, and you know it," Miriam said, her strength pushing through the phone. "I'm coming down. Where are the keys? How do I—"

"There are keys to the black Cadillac in the drawer next to the fridge. Press the button behind the fridge for the garage. The remote for the garage door is on the visor in the car."

"It's clean?"

"Everything I buy with you in mind is clean, Miriam."

She didn't say anything for a second. It was the closest to expressing his emotion for her that Pete had ever come. His code for saying "I love you." His expression for thanking her for all those years of support and raising Monique into a fine lady, for leaving him and saving herself and loving their daughter enough to choose them instead of him. The townhouse, the car, anything else she wanted was hers.

"I know, Pete," Miriam whispered. "I know."

They remained silent for a few more minutes. He heard her opening the drawer and withdrawing the keys, heard the side door open to the garage. She kept the phone on and next to her so that Pete could hear her. He stood in the hospital lobby trying to steady himself for the sight of Michelle.

"I'm on my way," Miriam said, her words tumbling out from a soft spot in her heart.

Pete nodded, aware that she couldn't see him, but knowing that she understood.

***

Pete patted Ricardo on the back as they entered Michelle's room. "Get in touch with your man in a minute or two. Make sure Mo knows about Mikki."

Ricardo nodded.

A large young lady sat in the chair next to Michelle. She wore a hospital gown and the matching cheap robe. Her feet were taped, and she sat with them up on a small stool. The long, auburn locks that flowed from her head reminded Pete of his daughter, and her healthy skin had an ethereal glow to it.

Ricardo approached her, rested his fingertips on her shoulder and grabbed her as she turned into him to cry. Pete had to admit, the boy had a way with women. They both looked over at Pete and Anji motioned to him to come over.

"Dad, this is Anji."

"I remember you. From our games. I am so sorry, Mr. Waters. I was just letting her borrow my car. I didn't know we were going to an ambush. I swear I should have just rode with her." Tears streaked her full face.

Pete shook his head. "Sweetheart, life is life. That simple. No one to blame." He reached down and awkwardly hugged her.

Ricardo remained next to Anji as Pete got closer to his daughter. The forum didn't matter. Titan didn't matter. Lyons didn't matter. Armand damn sure didn't matter. All of Pete's theories about life and death went out the window. This was his daughter. The most perfect thing he had created was his children, and the streets he created had brought her to this state of tubes and needles and IVs and machines. Pete kneeled over and began to hyperventilate. For a second he was sure it was a heart attack. He couldn't lose his daughter. Not now. Not this way.

Immediately, Ricardo was by his side. Ricardo. A father couldn't ask for more. Pete had shown some weakness, and he wondered whether Ricardo would look at him the same. But Ricardo kept it moving, touching his sister's hand and speaking quietly in her ear.

Pete sat in the chair next to Anji. He took out his cell phone again. It was over. This entire thing was over. His anger was gone. His confusion had dissipated. He just wanted his daughter back here and his family together. He needed Michelle to live and their strength around her as she recovered.

Pete flipped open his cell phone to call his contact in blue and to get Monique an escort to the hospital. The games were over. His man answered immediately and agreed immediately. The safe house was easily identified, and they had a man sitting on it. Monique would be delivered to him within the half hour.

As he tucked the phone back into his pocket, the other phone rang. Monique's phone. Irritated, Pete pulled it out and glanced at the caller ID. He didn't recognize the number. He tucked her phone back into his pocket then pulled out his phone and called back the sergeant.

"On second thought, I want my daughter and that fool that she with. Yeah, Armand. Bring them both and keep it clean. Meaning, whatever's in the house was there before they got there. I don't want no shit with my daughter involved."

Pete slapped the phone closed and leaned forward. His hands were clasped and his eyes were closed. He hadn't prayed in over a decade, but now seemed as good a time as any to reconnect.

Chapter Thirty-One

"No answer." Monique threw the telephone on the bed. Relief flooded through her body. What did Armand expect her to say? *Hi, Daddy, I am here with the boy you want dead. We need to talk.* She shook her head and thought about Chew. This nightmare had to end. All of it. Life's colonic was cleansing them all away one by one. She slowly made her way to the hall and stood there staring at the door.

She didn't want to see the bits of Chew's brain scattered about the room or the mess of blood, but she felt so guilty for leaving him here in this old house alone. Rodney, Chew's brother, wouldn't have wanted that. Hell, Chew wouldn't have wanted it. She was a traitor to her family. Now to Chew. And what was any of it worth anyway?

"I am leaving." Monique used her hands to steady herself as she walked down the long hallway. Her entire body ached. She imagined that this was what being old felt like: when your mind was very clear about its destination, but the body seemed unwilling to assist it. That's how she felt.

"Mo." Armand was right behind her.

She wanted him to move away from her, to leave her alone. She couldn't say it, and what she wanted didn't really matter to him after all.

"Where you going?"

Dut came running up the steps. "Army, man, just got word. The streets say Lyons's people gunned down Titan. Jose and Ezra just came by to tell us. Said they are trying to nail down exactly who did what, so we can retaliate against them." Dut's smile covered his entire face.

Monique stared at him in disgust before pushing past, not bothering to look at Armand for a reaction.

"What?" Armand laughed. "We finally catch a break."

"Yep. And without Wade, Ezra said folks is looking at you for some answers on what to do next."

Armand nodded his head up and down, then he and Dut clapped hands. Had it played the other way—the streets knowing the truth—they would have been hunted by every family Titan was connected to. Now Armand could keep his operation, could step forward and claim a piece of the west side throne. Monique pushed forward to the stairwell. Holding the rail with both hands, she slowly walked down it.

"Dammit, Mo, you leaving prints all over the damn place," Armand said, walking behind her dragging his white T-shirt down the staircase to remove her prints.

"We got to go anyway," Dut said. A look of disgust overcame his face. "Chew is bleeding right through the floor. It's leaking from the ceiling, man."

"Yuck." Monique frowned. She managed the narrow hallway on the lower level and pushed her way to the back door. She didn't know who was looking for them, so she wasn't walking out the front.

Dut and Armand talked behind her. Monique ignored them, pressing toward the sunlight. She had to leave this house, leave this place, leave the shadow of death that hung around Armand like a thick blanket. Monique loved the comfort of her mother's clean house, the quiet place where she lost herself in books or cooked to her heart's content.

Pete's world, Armand's world, was a space in which she didn't really belong. Armand scared her now, just like Pete. She knew too much and, unlike Armand, knew what he would become. She wouldn't be with another Pete. There was no future in him. No future in anyone surrounded by so much death, capable of causing so much death. There was no future in someone who kept fools close and traitors closer and good people at bay.

Suddenly, Monique understood Miriam. All those years of thinking of her mother as a prude made her feel foolish. This was what Miriam had tried to save her from: a life of pushing past dead bodies and warped values, a life where the dollar was God and goodness was weakness.

Enough. Monique had enough. She was going home.

"Wait up, Mo," Dut called from behind her as she used both hands to push through the heavy screen door.

Monique stumbled into the sunlight as she stepped down the back porch steps onto the patio. Armand was just behind her; Dut still in the shadow of the house.

Shielding her eyes from the sun, Monique stood still for a moment. She gave her eyes time to adjust to the brilliant rays of light. Her heart fell when she noticed him sitting on the trunk of the car. He had a gun pointed straight at her. She began to laugh. Guns no longer scared her, which was terrifying in and of itself. At this point, another gun pointed at her induced no more fear.

"You should have come with me, Monique," Lopreste said, his voice husky and thick. "You would have been treated better."

"You're right," Monique answered, holding her hands to her head.

Armand noticed the badge on Lopreste's hip and did the same.

"Tell the other one to come out," Lopreste said. "My partner already has the front of the house covered. If I got to go in there, he dies."

Armand gave a low whistle. "Dut, you got to come out," he said evenly. "It's the po po."

"I told you," Lopreste said, studying Monique's bruises. "I told you I was your safer bet."

Dut walked out with his arms raised.

"Yep." Monique nodded. "You told me."

"Let me guess," Armand said, then spit through clenched teeth at the ground, "you know this dude, too."

Monique glanced at the flem that landed inches from her feet. Then she raised her eyes to meet Armand's, to confirm that he had just spat at her. They stared at each other coldly, his black eyes radiating spite, unflinchingly hateful.

Monique wasn't even going to try to explain herself. Not anymore. The truth was that she was who she was and Armand was who he was, and neither was going to change. Monique no longer wanted to be a part of Armand's world.

Lopreste patted down Armand and Dut. He admired both of Armand's guns in the sun, nodding his head up and down appreciatively before placing them in the patrol car. He didn't touch Monique.

"You got a destination," Lopreste spoke directly to Monique.

"Is that right?" Monique flinched. "Can I put my arms down?"

"Yes." Lopreste looked through squinted eyes at Armand. "From what I hear, you are one lucky bastard."

Armand smiled. "Did my luck just run out?"

"I actually don't know," he said. "Get in the car."

"Shit. I ain't getting in an unmarked cop car. You can do anything to me."

"I can do anything to you regardless." Lopreste put his gun in his holster. "Danny," he called. "They came out back."

Another white man turned the corner of the house, eyed them and shook his head. "Let's get this over with."

"Where to?" Monique said.

"Your sister was shot. We are taking you to Highland Hospital," Lopreste said.

"What?" Monique cried out. "Is she dead? Who shot her?"

Danny shrugged. "She is alive. We are trying to identify both shooters."

Monique lowered her head. "Take me there." She climbed into the car without hesitation.

"Looks like you need to go there anyway," Lopreste joked, although no one laughed. Lopreste cleared his throat. "Armand, you in the car too."

"Hell no," Armand whispered.

"You climb in or I do your friend here," Lopreste said blankly. "Then I shoot you and throw your ass in anyway."

Armand stared at Dut. "Why?"

"The big man wants to see you. Talk to you, I guess."

Armand nodded at Dut, then he climbed into the car next to Monique.

"You just got a freebie, kid," Lopreste said to Dut, smiling, as he and Danny lowered themselves into the car. "If you are here when we raid this place in thirty minutes, then you are ours." Lopreste winked at Dut as they pulled away.

Monique leaned her head against the warm rear window and cried.

Chapter Thirty-Two

The ride to the hospital was the longest ride of Monique's life. She was embarrassed more than anything else. It was one thing to live on pride and return vindicated, but it was downright embarrassing to storm out and return battered and bruised, life having stamped its painful imprint across her tired body.

She had search for Armand and gotten her ass kicked in the process. She had searched for Armand and found a shell of the man she thought she loved. She had searched for Armand and never actually found him because the Armand she loved didn't exist. She had thought he was her protector. He had barely been a cover. She had thought him quiet and moral, a leader of wolves. The alpha male. The truth was that he was weak. He was able to kill without a blink but unable to love her, unable to not put on a show for his friends.

Growing up with Pete for a father had ruined her. Monique was sure of that. Pete was the quintessential warrior. She hadn't wanted a warrior for a daddy; Pete scared the shit out of her. She wanted the warrior type for her lover. For her man. And the one man that she thought was her protector had spat at her feet.

Armand spat at her feet.

Maybe she was wrong, but she didn't give a damn. Maybe it was her father who had come after him, but she still didn't care. It no longer mattered that he had left her in the apartment alone. Her father had taught her how to handle it. It was irrelevant that he never came to her when he thought she was with Ricardo. She had freed herself. It was insignificant that he had stood there word battling with Titan without ever noticing her when Chew had noticed her on the spot.

It was all irrelevant now. Her sister had been shot. Michelle. Her lifeline. Her sister. While Monique had been bouncing from one disaster to the next, her sister had been fighting for her life without her.

"You still have my card?" Lopreste said.

Monique glanced at him for a long moment. "I asked you if you worked for Pete and you said no."

"I don't. I work for the police department."

"So how are you doing this?"

"I am here on orders of the police department."

Monique waited.

"I was closest to the scene?" Lopreste tried again, chuckling with Danny.

"Or Pete is the damn police department," Armand muttered.

"What does it matter?" Lopreste watched them through the rearview mirror.

"It doesn't." Monique held Lopreste's gaze.

They drove onto the emergency ramp. Danny climbed out of his seat and opened the back door for Monique. He pulled at her small frame, helping her to climb out of the car awkwardly. She immediately spotted Ricardo standing by the door. Monique smiled as Ricardo put out his cigar and moved toward her, his forehead scrunched in concern.

"What the fuck happened to you?" he said.

"Nothing," she said. "I am just so glad to see you." Monique tried not to breakdown, but the sight of Ricardo relieved her to her core.

"Did he do this to you?" Ricardo aimed his hatred at Armand.

"Of course not."

Ricardo wrapped his arms around his little sister, holding her tight. "Mo, don't ever do no shit like this again. You hear me?"

She nodded.

"Mo, Michelle went looking for you. I talked to Anji. She was borrowing her car."

Monique nodded.

"I ain't saying it's your fault, but we are all we got. She shot up over this bullshit."

"I know, Ricardo." Monique reached up and kissed his cheek. "I'm sorry."

"Monique?" her mother's high-pitched voice carried across the waiting room lobby and outside to the bay doors where they stood. "Monique, what happened to you?"

"Mom." She sighed again. This time relief released all the fears and manifested into sobs.

"Monique, what were you thinking?" Miriam pulled Monique into her embrace.

"I don't know."

Pete's presence filled the space behind her mother. Monique was afraid to look at him.

As usual Pete was Pete, noncommittal and distant, but he reached out a hand and touched her face.

"Did he do this to you?" Pete looked over Monique's head and glared at Armand in the back seat of the police car.

Monique shook her head.

"Mo, tell me the truth."

"No, Titan's people did."

"Your sister's upstairs," Pete said. "Go see her."

Monique nodded.

"I'm glad you're back, baby girl," Pete said directly. He stared in her eyes.

Monique paused. Normally she tried to avoid his unblinking stare. But today she withstood it and looked back into it. She had traveled miles in the last few days. Her spirit was changed, permanently affected. Damaged. She had seen a glimpse of the low parts of his life and it was too much for her. There was nothing left to say. She was wrong. She had made a mistake. She had paid a price. Innocence had been lost, had disappeared. It wasn't Armand's fault. It wasn't anyone's fault. It was life.

She couldn't try to be something she wasn't to fit into Armand's world, either. The price had been paid for her life; Pete carried the scars. She had a spiritual covering that Armand didn't have. She wasn't going to join him in that struggle and link herself to his realm of chaos. It was a generation away from her. She wasn't going back.

Monique smiled. She was glad to be with her mother and father. As she walked into the hospital, her instincts sounded an alarm. Monique turned suddenly, wondering where Ricardo had gone.

Monique watched Ricardo take a step toward the police car as he eyed Steelo who was leaning against the disabled rails. Steelo moved down the ramp and quickly followed Ricardo. As Monique hugged her mother, she watched Ricardo walk up on one side of the car and Steelo approach the other.

"Ricardo, he didn't do this to me. Titan's people did," Monique said.

Pete looked at her strangely.

She didn't say it out of love. She said it out of obligation. Regardless of how she felt, Armand had saved her life. "Titan was going to kill me," Monique said to her father. "Armand saved me."

"How?" Pete glanced at her in disbelief.

"It wasn't Lyons's people who took out Titan. It was Armand."

"How you know?" Pete's voice never changed, his expression never shifted.

"I watched him put two guns to his head and pull the trigger."

Miriam whimpered, holding her head down. Although Monique no longer wanted to be with him, it was clear what was about to happen. She owed Armand enough to say the truth, didn't she?

Pete nodded his head. "It's all good, Mo. Don't worry."

"Daddy," Monique said. The innocence of her voice belied the mature women she had become. "I am not bullshitting. I watched him kill Titan instead of letting Titan do me. Titan kidnapped me and told Army to kill me."

"Titan kidnapped you?"

"Daddy, we owe him. I went after him. He didn't ask me to come. That was my fault, but when they tried to kill me, he saved me."

Miriam stared at her with a knowing glance.

Pete sighed as he and Monique watched Ricardo and Steelo say a few words to Danny and all three quickly entered the car. Ricardo and Steelo squeezed on either side of Armand. Armand didn't even blink. He stared at Monique out of the rear window as they pulled away. His eyes black and blank. She stared back; hers just as blank, just as emotionless. She still loved him, but she could never be with him.

"Daddy, Michelle's shooting is already on my head. I can't live with another one. Not when he saved my life. Daddy, please."

Pete ran his hand over his bald head. "Miriam, tell Rebe I'll be right back." He whipped out his cell phone as he headed to his car.

Monique and her mother went into the hospital, walking slowly to the elevators. When they exited the elevators, there was a flurry of commotion as they hugged and kissed and stepped around people and tripped over children. But when Monique entered Michelle's room, all of her inner turmoil and physical pain disappeared. Her mind went blank. Her only sister lay on the bed with tubes and IVs flowing from her veins.

Monique's decisions had endangered lives tonight. Her own. Michelle's. Chew's. Anji's. Even Armand's. If Pete and Ricardo did what she suspected they were going to do, all of this had happened because she reacted on emotion. She could never ever let that happen again.

Chapter Thirty-Three

"You strapped?" Pete said. He sat opposite Armand at a small table in the back of an empty restaurant.

Armand wanted to laugh and tell him to go to hell. Instead, Armand simply stared at him.

"I know they patted you down. But I know you got heat hid. Produce it."

Armand glanced at Ricardo. Armand wondered how their paths had never crossed before. The city was too small for that, but for some reason Ricardo's face brought up no memories.

Ricardo stared back with an ice grill.

Armand chuckled.

"Do it now!" Pete rapped the table with his knuckles. "Or the meet ends now."

Armand bent over slowly and pushed the inner side of his Timberland's. A small gun was strapped to the inside of his boot against his ankle.

He unstrapped it and placed it directly on the table. "Why am I here?"

"What happened to my daughter's face?"

"When I found her, she was like that."

"When did you find her?"

"I set up a meeting with Titan." Armand shrugged.

"No doubt Titan would have told you at that meeting that you can't just go around killing my men."

"We never got that far. He had Mo. Monique. The entire meet fell apart." Armand shrugged again.

Ricardo and Pete both stared at him for a long moment.

Armand returned Pete's stare.

He had nothing to hide. "Y'all plan on killing me?" He wanted to know. If this was the end, he could decide how he wanted to go out. It wasn't going to be sitting at some neat restaurant table catching a bullet in the back of the head. He had purposely sat with his head against the wall. Whether or not his guns were on the table, he could still get to them in time enough to blast someone if he had to.

Pete stared at him. "You're a pain in the ass."

"I've been told that." Armand couldn't read Pete.

"But you are a warrior."

Armand nodded his head. It was a compliment and he respected it. That was the closest thing to an acknowledgement anyone on the streets would ever receive.

"My daughter. You also saved her."

"No. I saved my woman." Armand didn't care what Monique thought, she was still his. She was the love of his life. He had done some wrongs but so had she. How she expected him to keep learning about her secrets—one after the other, like repeated jabs from a shank at the lowest moments of his life—was beyond his comprehension. In a few days day she had gone from innocent college student to street savvy cop manipulator to the daughter of the game.

How could he wrap his mind around so much in such a short period of time? For her to have also known the cop was more than he could bear, but he loved her. His heart was true, and he hadn't flinched in that. So he would let her have her time apart, let her tend to her sister and mend her family hurt. He would remove himself while she overcame Chew and forgave him for his actions, but Monique was still his whether she knew it yet or not.

Armand leaned forward and looked at Pete. "Whether she was your daughter or not, she is my woman. Titan had no business putting his people on her."

"Either way," Pete said, "Monique matters most. And you did that."

"Me and Chew," Armand said, testing.

Ricardo leaned forward. "Where is Chew?"

"Did himself." Armand refused to look at Ricardo now that business was being discussed. There was no reason to acklowledge a lesser man. He kept his eyes on Pete. "Through the mouth. Monique asked if he was working both sides. I overheard."

"You killed my man Chew?" Ricardo said.

Armand didn't answer him.

"Committed suicide, huh?" Pete eyed Ricardo.

With that question, Armand knew that Pete thought Chew was weak. Armand was still hurt by Chew, still hurt by his death, but he didn't want Pete smearing Chew's memory. In the street, that type of reputation would stick around forever; it would mark Chew's little brother, Rodney, and any children that Chew had. Armand wasn't letting Chew's memory go down like that.

"He got put in a bad situation," Armand said. "He made the wrong decision."

"You got to pay some restitution for my men you took." Pete pushed Armand's guns back to him.

"Shit." Armand picked up the piece from the table. "Seems to me you owe me the same. Whatever happened between you and Titan wasn't justification for killing Mike or Raymond."

They stared at each other in silence.

"You gonna work for me," Pete said.

Armand returned his gun to the boot holster. "Don't have to. I'm taking over Titan's territory."

"Not without backing you ain't. I operate invisible. Silently. But I can put you over all the west side."

"What's the price?" Armand leaned back against the chair.

"You got to be in or out."

Armand thought about it. The price seemed obvious. No doubt they would tell him to leave Monique alone and pay some ridiculous overhead fee to them. And he could swing the price for a little while. On the other hand, if he didn't pair up with Pete, then he would have to fight him or fight whoever Pete set in place to trump him. Pete could make things difficult.

"I need legitimate resources for muscle," Armand said.

"Boy, please."

"What's the split?"

"Sixty-forty, what else?"

That was better than Armand had expected. Much better. "I'm in. So what's the catch?"

"The catch is I'm taking down the forum."

Armand's brow raised. "The forum?"

"The coalition of families. I'm destroying it. I am taking over not only the west side, but both the northwest and the southeast. I already got the east."

"So y'all the ones got that preppy white dollar locked. I been trying to find out," Armand said.

"You got a lot to learn," Ricardo said.

Pete and Armand ignored him. Pete chuckled. "Yeah, I got it locked. Something like that. But for the rest, who just been buying from me but overseeing their own distribution, I'm ready to eliminate the middleman. Those areas are going to come directly under me and my men now."

Armand pressed. "What about the Upper Falls quadrant: Clinton, Joseph, Hudson?"

"The Perezes? Naw, they aren't on my radar. El has the Hispanic population sewed up, gets respect from everyone over there. I make out better the way things are now. The Perez family has operated their own dominion for over a decade. Honestly, that's a fight I don't want."

"They go hard." Ricardo was once again ignored.

"But Nawly, Butch and Lyons's people," Pete continued, "and all those thinking we on equal footing, when I been more than gracious, they about to see a shift. Understand?"

"South quadrant?" Armand leaned forward, soaking in all of Pete's direction. This was the man with the power. It was plain to see. Armand wanted to learn everything from him that he could.

"Already mine." Pete blew smoke from his cigar. "With the exception of the Perezes, it's all already mine. I am simply reclaiming, terminating some leases. You feel me, young gun?"

Armand nodded and actually smiled for the first time. "I guess that's why they call you the main connect."

"Damn straight."

"Then that's what's up." Pete stubbed out the cigar with his finger tips and leaned it against the ashtray. "And you and yours have to roll with me. Loyalty."

"You can't buy loyalty," Ricardo said, taking his place beside Pete.

Armand didn't acknowledge him. The burning desire to slit Ricardo's neck surged forward every time Armand heard his voice or looked in his face. Ricardo's relationship to Pete gave him an advantage by forcing Armand to release the life he had sought to end over the last seventy-two hours. Armand had more to gain by making the deal with Pete and ignoring Ricardo than satisfying the deep hunger that would be satiated by Ricardo's death. But Armand gritted his teeth whenever Ricardo spoke.

"He's right, you know." Pete nodded. "My son is right. But I ain't buying it, 'cause you already got it. You just have to decide to apply it to me."

"You set me up on the west side, Mr. Waters, and the west side is behind you."

"My man," Pete said, standing up.

They shook hands on the deal while Ricardo watched, skepticism etched across his face. Armand was relieved Ricardo didn't try to touch him. He would have shot him in the head, deal be damned. Armand nodded, glad that Pete was giving him this opportunity, although it still felt unreal. The change from pursuing to joining made Armand feel unbalanced. He needed to leave and collect his thoughts, weigh out all that had happened.

Pete watched Armand walk out. Shaking his head, Pete sat down to think as Ricardo followed Armand out of the restaurant. There was no more time for playing and relaxing. Michelle had reminded Pete that time was short. He needed to stockpile some cash to make sure he could retire comfortably. He needed enough money to set up Ricardo, Michelle, and Monique for life, to make sure the TW2 lived on in infinity. Butch and Nawly had sounded the trumpet, but he was issuing the battle cry. And it was time for the Waters family to reclaim its throne.

***

"Yo, hold up a sec," Ricardo called to Armand, stepping onto the stoop behind him.

Armand turned to look at him, his eyes blazing with anger. "What up?"

Ricardo shook his head. He couldn't figure out what the hell was going on. Pete had never in his lifetime brought an enemy into the fold. Once a person was on the other side, Pete never considered them again. Chew was Ricardo's inside man and the only reason Pete

216

had made some sort of exception for Chew was because he had been close to Monique. Ricardo knew Pete was forever suspicious of Chew and, eventually, he would have been cast out. The only thing Pete hated worse than an enemy was a traitor, and he would have always viewed Chew as a traitor.

But this time Ricardo could tell that Pete was changing the rules again. Ricardo couldn't understand why he would choose Armand of all people. He would be damned if Armand had it easy and refused to let Armand simply ease under the Waters family banner after having killed some of his men. Good men. And Armand had killed them in cold blood. Pete's new plan didn't seem to take that into consideration.

"How long you been with my little sister?"

Armand shrugged.

"That's over. For this deal to go through, you stay the fuck away from Mo."

Armand pulled a cigarette out of his pants pocket and lit it slowly. Squinting at the street light he inhaled lightly. "The terms don't get announced out here on the stoop," Armand said. "You had something to say it should have been said at the table."

"I'm telling you now," Ricardo said, ignoring the truth of Armand's statement.

"And I am telling you now. You ain't in a position to lay down rules, son."

"You think I don't have my father's ear? You want to test it?"

Armand held Ricardo's gaze. Unwavering. "The deal I just entered into don't include you, don't got nothing to do with you. I don't answer to you. Get that straight now."

They stared at each other. Armand puffed on the cigarette and exhaled slowly, letting the smoke ooze from his lips.

"Another thing," Armand said, his calm irritating Ricardo. "Chew. That's my man. His memory don't suffer no tarnish."

"If he went the way you say. If he didn't, then you and I have a problem."

Armand stepped off the stoop, dropped his cigarette to the ground, and stubbed it out. "How you sound? You and I have a problem." He laughed. "Ain't no problem. You ain't no problem for me. I been tracking you for the past two days. You were slated to die, son."

"You issuing threats? You couldn't have found me unless I wanted to be found."

"I don't issue empty threats. You should know that by now. But you sound like a fool talking at me about Mo after you almost got her killed."

"Had I known—"

"That's the problem, you should have known." Armand jabbed his finger in the air while taking a step closer to Ricardo. The façade was gone and pure hate radiated from Armand's eyes. "You claiming your sister like you protecting her, but you don't even know the man in her life. You don't know who she spending all her time with for the past year? But you her guard? You need to back up off me with that bullshit."

"Mo said it's over. So stay the fuck away from her."

Ignoring Ricardo, Armand continued: "Now me, on the other hand, when I need to know something, I focus all my attention on that shit. You think I couldn't have found you, huh? Maybe not. But turns out that there is this house off Portland Ave. with three women living up in there. Two fine-ass chicks with a white momma. Bunch of rugrats, though. It's too bad." Armand shrugged, shaking his head as if they were ruined. "Wouldn't you know a Puerto Rican-looking brother be spotted coming and going from there on the regular?"

Ricardo stared at Armand in disbelief.

"I am not to be fucked with, son. You don't know?" Armand said. His teeth clenched. His lips did not move when he spoke. "Let me be clear, you don't communicate directly with me after this. Only because of Mo and for Chew am I even talking to you right now. But understand, Mo is my woman. That ain't going to change. And I answer to the head man. Not his boy. You need to get at me or you got a message you been sent to deliver then you filter it through my lieutenant, Dut. You don't open your mouth directly to me. Not about business. Not about Mo."

Armand walked away.

Chapter Thirty-Four

When Monique stepped into the room, Anji gasped. Monique was used to it by now. Every one of Michelle's family members had something to say about Monique's bruises. They weren't cool about it either, staring at her as if she had two heads. Michelle's uncle had flat out asked who had whipped her ass and if the person was selling it in cans. Even in her state of distress, Monique had laughed out loud at that. She loved honest people, even when they were rude as hell.

"Damn, Mo, what happened?" Anji said, holding her arms up for a hug.

Monique smiled and leaned in to kiss Anji on her cheek. She knew about Anji and Michelle, knew how heart broken Michelle was. Monique also realized she was the only person who probably knew the entire truth, the only person who knew and would never mention it. It was another bag strapped to her back, another secret hung around her neck. Monique, the secret keeper. What did all these secrets get her? What was it all worth?

Nothing. Being loyal and being a traitor got her to the same place. There was no glory in loyalty, no shame in being a traitor. At the end of the day, her ass was still whipped beyond recognition. Chew was still dead. Armand had still spat at her feet. Titan had still had his head blown off. Michelle was still laying here in a coma.

There was nothing to be gained by any of it.

"Mo, what happened to you?" Anji said again.

"You wouldn't believe me if I told you." Monique looked at her sister's small body. She tore her eyes away and glanced down at Anji's feet. "I didn't know you were injured, too. They shot your feet?"

"Naw." Anji moved the chair that her feet rested on. "I was running barefoot, gravel, cement, glass, mulch. It all got embedded in my feet."

"What happened to Mikki?"

"She was borrowing my car. Looking for you. She dropped me off at home and they were waiting for us there."

"Who?"

"I don't know."

"Why would they wait at your house? Who has beef against you?"

Anji shrugged.

Monique studied her carefully. Something didn't make sense. There were gaps in the story and holes in her explanation. Anji's house should have been the last place that anyone would have been to ambush a member of her family. Anji didn't want the world to know she was bisexual, so Monique was sure no one knew Michelle was in love with her.

She knew better than to keep questioning Anji. Monique knew that the truth lay in the unspoken words that couldn't be pried from a person's soul until they were ready to release them.

"How many?"

"Two men that I saw."

"I don't mean this how it's going to sound," Monique said, hesitating for a second before looking directly at Anji. "But how she did she get shot up like this and you didn't get shot at all?"

"I wondered who was going to ask the question. None of your peeps asked me directly, but I could tell they were thinking it." Anji shrugged. "We were arguing, Mo. I had her waiting while I was with my friend, so when I finally picked her up she was pissed. I had climbed out of the car and was going in my place when they opened fire. She was alone in the car. She shot one of them, I think. The other one came after me. I managed to get back to the car and drove her to the hospital." Anji shrugged.

"Damn."

"Yeah."

They sat in silence. The sobs that Monique had been swallowing since Chew died filled her chest. She bent over and cried. The wailing sound coming from her mouth was unrecognizable. She needed to release it, though, needed to release the pain. She could see it as if it were happening in front of her. She could imagine them shooting up the car and Michelle trying to fire back, but trapped. There was nothing Monique could do about it. There was nothing she could change. She couldn't fix it or make it right.

Monique stared at Michelle. Her face was covered with bandages. The huge tube taped to her mouth made her skin barely visible. Monique was afraid to touch her. She was afraid of what Michelle was probably experiencing, afraid of the pain she had caused her. Monique just sat there and stared at her sister.

Monique wanted to make things right. She didn't want to leave Michelle's side, but she also wanted to check on Armand. Was he dead or alive? Had Pete listened to her, or was there another body count to add to this experience, another regret to tag to her soul?

"Did you ever find Armand?"

The question came out of nowhere and tore across Monique's thoughts. She looked at Anji, unsure of how to answer.

"What?"

"Michelle said you were looking for Armand. I figured you must not have found him because he wouldn't have let you get hurt. Not like how you look now."

"I didn't know you knew Armand."

Obviously, Michelle had been talking much more than she should. Michelle had always been more open than Monique. She was more open than any of them.

"Don't really know him. But he came by my place a couple of times."

Monique looked straight ahead at her sister. She was trying to seem calm and nonchalant. She knew that body language could give her away and if she moved suddenly or reacted, Anji would remember herself and stop talking. Monique couldn't risk that. "Did he?"

Monique wondered if Anji was sleeping with Armand. If she was the other woman Chew had mentioned just before he had died. She could feel the anger rising in her chest, irrationally sweeping across her mind. Why in the hell would Armand be at Anji's place? And why in the hell would people wait to ambush them at Anji's place?

"Yeah, business stuff with T, really. I only saw him for a few minutes both times. But did you ever find him?"

Monique didn't answer at first. The information stunned her and she didn't know what to do with it.

"T? Who, Titan?"

Anji glanced at Monique, seeming to catch herself at the mention of his name. Monique didn't waiver. She stared intently at Anji. She wasn't letting Anji off the hook that easy. The cat was out of the bag and Monique intended to milk it like a cow.

"You live with Titan?"

"No, it's not like that, Mo."

"But hold up, Army met with Titan at your place?"

"Just a couple of times …"

"So the folks that shot my sister, they were sitting on Titan's place?"

Anji closed her eyes and began to breathe deeply. Monique didn't know what the hell she was doing and she wasn't sure whether Anji was preparing to haul off with some jujitsu or karate or some other worldly stuff. Anji had always been a different type of person. Monique stood suddenly and took a step back. She would whip Anji's ass in this hospital room if she had to.

Anji opened her eyes when she heard Monique stand. She raised her hands gently. "Mo, it wasn't like that."

"Anji, the folks who shot up Michelle, were they sitting on Titan's place?"

"I guess."

"Shit!" Monique stared at Anji in disbelief. Had Pete's people shot up Michelle by accident, trying to get at Titan after they had attacked Armand? Was this Ricardo and Pete's mistake, like she would have been dead had they been successful in Armand's trap house? And if Pete knew that Anji was Titan's woman, would she be a target? "Anji, did you tell Pete that? Did you tell my father?"

"Tell him what? I told him what happened just like I told you."

"Yeah, but you didn't mention nothing about Titan to him."

"Titan is irrelevant."

"No, my sister is laying up here in a coma solely because of him and you still protecting your paycheck, telling that bullshit story without mentioning him."

"Damn, Mo. You know it ain't like that."

"Where Titan at now, Anji?" Monique stared at her. "How you know he won't come up here looking for you? How you know them men that was after him won't come up here to finish the job?"

"Mo, I wasn't thinking about any of that. Michelle doesn't have anything to do with that. Those men aren't coming up here. I think they fired at us just because Titan wasn't there."

"Shit, Anji. Girl, you can't be this blind. You and Michelle could have been killed over Titan's bullshit."

As soon as the words tumbled from her lips, she felt like the biggest hypocrite. Anji was doing for Titan what she had done for Armand. Faithfully believing in him, completely trusting, counting on his love to prove her right. It was the reason so many women were in jail right now, the reason so many girls did time for their men, leaving their children motherless. There was no difference. Monique remembered how Michelle had tried to warn her. Here Anji was sitting with Pete's daughter, who had been shot up instead of Titan, and she was clueless to what it all meant, to what the links were. Instead, she trusted in Titan to a fault.

Monique wasn't going to tell her about Titan. It wasn't her place to burst Anji's bubble. The kidnapping, the shoot-out, and Titan's death weren't going to tumble from her mouth, whether she was anguished or not. "Anji, don't tell my father about you and Titan. Ever."

Anji nodded.

"Anji, look at me," Monique said, her voice quiet, her tear stained face focused. "Don't ever mention Titan to anyone in this family, not even Michelle. Ever."

"I hear you, Mo. I normally don't talk about him. I just, I'm just caught up."

"Shit," Monique said, her voice a tight whisper. "Anji, I'll be right back."

"Mo, I'm sorry. I didn't expect my connection to Titan to touch anyone I love."

"Anji, we are in the same boat. My stupid self running behind Armand is what led Michelle to you."

***

223

Monique stood in the small memorial chapel that was set aside for praying. She wasn't there to pray. Instead, she sat in the empty chair while fingering the business card. She didn't want to call him, but she didn't have a choice. She had to make sure that Armand was still alive, that Pete and Ricardo hadn't done him in. She had to know. Anji reminded her so much of herself. She wondered what Anji would do when she finally found out Titan was dead. Monique wondered how she would be affected on the day that Armand finally took his last breath.

Love didn't release its chokehold just because the mind took over. Love didn't relax its ferocious grip even when separating from the loved one was the only way to stay alive. She and Armand were finished, but she loved him just the same, if not more. And it hurt. She needed to know that he was alright, that her father hadn't done the unthinkable, even if only to release the vice grip of guilt on her chest.

Monique dialed the numbers into Miriam's cell phone.

"Lopreste." His voice sounded clear and relaxed. A person with a clean conscious and an easy life.

Suddenly, Monique found that she didn't have anything to say.

"Lopreste," he said, not seeming irritated that he had been bother.

"Uhm, this is Monique. Monique Waters."

"Monique. Seed of the throne."

"I guess."

They both remained silent.

"I need to speak with you," Monique said.

"About?"

She hadn't expected that. She didn't really have it clearly worked out in her mind. It seemed stupid to ask the questions that she wanted to ask over the phone. Plus, she could call Armand directly, or at least Ricardo. She didn't have to ask Lopreste. And the reality was that Lopreste wouldn't incriminate himself in any of it anyway. It wasn't a conversation for over the phone.

"You still there?" he said, his words fast and choppy.

"Yeah. Uh, this was a mistake. I'm sorry I bothered you." Monique lowered the phone but heard his voice call out to her through the air.

"Monique, no, wait."

"Huh?"

"Let's meet."

"I can't be seen meeting with you." Monique shook her head wondering whether he was really crazy.

"We won't be seen. Let's meet for a few minutes. In an hour?"

"Where?"

"There is a bookstore in Forestville mall called The Literary Joint Bookstore down the street from the hospital. They have a small café in the back, can you get there?"

"I'll find a way."

"One hour."

"Ok."

Monique hung up. She felt a little better. But only a little. She still had a more pressing issue to follow up on. She keyed in Ricardo's number.

"Hello?"

Monique assumed he had answered politely because it was Miriam's phone. He was still mad at her, and would be for a long time. Everyone knew that Michelle was his favorite person in the world, so every day that her life was at risk Ricardo probably would barely talk to her. But Monique knew that Ricardo loved her, and that love would force him to deal with her, even while he was furious at her.

"Ricardo, it's me."

"Oh," he said.

The disappointment in his voice hurt Monique's feelings, but she pushed forward. She had to know. She needed to make sure Armand was alright.

"What up?" he said.

"You with Daddy?"

"Yep."

"Who else?" She could tell by the way he was speaking that he wasn't alone. The short choppy answers and the deeper voice always gave him away. He didn't lose his words so quickly under pressure in front of people he was uncomfortable with.

"Armand just left."

Monique felt air seep back into her chest.

"He did?"

"Yeah."

"Daddy reconsidered?"

"Yeah, unfortunately."

"Good."

"Good, huh? What if you were Michelle? Would you like this outcome?"

"It's not like that."

"That's why you calling me, to check on him?"

"No. I wanted to talk to you."

"Bullshit. But you better stay away from his ass. And, Mo, I ain't giving you an option."

"Ricardo, Anji was with Titan."

The line was silent. She thought he had hung up, but then she could hear his breathing.

"I know," he finally said.

"Was it you? Were you sitting on her place?"

"Hell no. It's deeper than that, Mo. But no, I didn't get Michelle in that hospital bed. That's solely on you."

"But had it been me killed when you hit Armand's spot, it would have been solely on you. Not that you would have cared as much, that much is obvious. Either way, we are both fuck ups." Monique was losing patience. She felt bad enough. Ricardo and Pete had started this, she wasn't going to keep eating shit from Ricardo.

"Yo, whatever, man. You got want you want. As usual. And that's all that matters to you, right?"

"Ricardo, what—" The line went silent.

He had hung up.

She started to call him back but decided not to. It wasn't worth it. She would let him have his anger … for now.

Monique stood slowly. She had to find Miriam and try to use her car. She wanted to escape, to disappear for a few days like she often did with Armand. But that option wasn't available to her. Instead, she had to find a way to meet Lopreste. For what, she wasn't even sure. She just wanted to see him, hear what he had to say.

Chapter Thirty-Five

The Literary-Joint Bookstore was a comfort to Monique. Its soft blue colors were soothing to the soul. She loved this store although she hadn't been here in a long time. She didn't know where to wait, Lopreste hadn't named a specific section of the store, other than the café. She decided in the lounge area that was arranged like a living room. She was so nervous about being spotted. The whole thing seemed to be dying down, the last thing she needed was to be seen talking to Lopreste. The thought of Lopreste reminded her of Armand spitting at her feet, though, and she felt sad all over again.

Monique moved to the new lounge area in the cafe, away from the windows. She observed the hardcover books, her hands running across the bound novels. There was always something comforting about a novel. Maybe she should actually look for one, find something to read during the time she would be sitting in the hospital. *The Loudest Silence* by Kai caught her eye. She picked it up and read the cover blurb.

Large hands picked up the book next to her, brushing slightly against her.

Lopreste.

"You found me," Monique said, sighing.

"Of course."

They stared at each other for a few seconds, his eyes penetrating into her. If she weren't so bruised, she probably would have been confident enough to flirt, to play with him a little. But she didn't.

Lopreste ran a finger along her chin again. "The hospital didn't admit you, huh?"

"I didn't give them a chance," she said.

They both chuckled.

"At some point, Monique, you are going to have to sit down somewhere and rest. Recuperate."

She nodded. "I plan to. In my sister's hospital room."

"So, you had something on your mind."

"Well, when I called you, it was stupid—"

"You don't have to have a reason to call me," Lopreste said, interrupting Monique.

Monique wondered whether Lopreste was gaming or not. She needed to feel the arms of a man around her. She wanted to escape all of it, not think about any residue of her life. But Lopreste was part of all of it, too. He was under Pete's authority. So turning to him was just staying on the same merry-go-round.

"I appreciate that." Monique paused, trying to formulate her thoughts. "I didn't know if Armand was dead. I didn't know if your offer to hide me still stood. I wanted to know what the terms of going away for a little while would be."

"Really?"

"Really. I need to weigh all of my options."

"Armand is still alive. Intel says that he was recruited and is now under the authority of Pete Waters."

"What?"

"Yep. That changes things. I can't move you in an official capacity. Only unofficially."

"Unofficially?"

"Yep."

"What is unofficially? Me staying with you?"

Lopreste laughed. Monique smiled. She wasn't going down this path. No need to jump out of one fire to another, although he was a cutie.

"Unofficially is unofficially."

"I'll think about it."

"But if you need something, anything, call me."

Monique smiled again. "Thank you."

"Come on, let's get out of here." Lopreste pulled out a couple of twenty dollar bills and put them on the counter, pointing at Monique's book to calm the clerk, as they walked out. "Go home and get some rest. Alone. Promise."

"I promise," Monique said.

"The next time I see you, I want you to look like your gorgeous self again."

"Gorgeous?"

"Yeah, gorgeous. That's how I want to see you."

"Deal."

She and Lopreste walked through the store doors out into the sun.

"Where did you park?"

She pointed to the Cadillac Miriam had given her without explanation. Monique didn't want to know if the car was from Pete or not. Her parents' bullshit wasn't something she could add to her plate just yet. Lopreste walked her to the car. Again, he ran his hand across her jawline and caressed her cheek.

"Take care of yourself," Lopreste said. "Time to start taking care of yourself."

"I will."

A car pulled into the lot.

Monique paid it no attention, her eyes closed as she leaned her head against Lopreste's open hand. Lopreste yanked his hand away. Monique opened her eyes, wondering if her gesture had been too intimate. She searched his face. Lopreste turned away from her, his eyes locked on the car. Confused, Monique followed the direction of Lopreste's glare, her eyes resting on the car as it approached. Monique felt her heart stop.

Armand and Dut slowly rolled by. Dut was driving and Armand was staring at them through the open car window. At the sight of them, Monique stepped forward, her instinct to run and join him overtaking her common sense. A smile had covered her face unknowingly. Her body and soul were excited to see him, the equivalent of home rolling in front of them.

It was Armand's eyes that stopped her in mid-step. His facial expression didn't change, but his eyes roamed between she and Lopreste. His anger felt like electric charges zapping through the air. He ignored Lopreste, who moved slightly and pulled at Monique's arm, keeping her from running forward, protecting her. But there was no protection Lopreste could offer. Not really.

Monique unflinchingly met Armand's eyes, determined to stand up for herself. She didn't have to answer to him. She couldn't help whatever conclusion he came to. He no longer had her. And, if he was going to stare at her like she was trash, then they were better off apart anyway.

She yanked her arm from Lopreste's grip and took another step forward. Armand shook his head slowly from side to side. In that instant, her bravado faded. Armand's quiet "no" said it all. Monique had messed up. She was standing there with Lopreste. Not the cute college looking white boy, but a cop. The same cop who had stopped them a few days ago, who had met her at Armand's penthouse, who had picked her up from the safe house and was now standing here, tugging at her arm.

It occurred to Monique that she looked like a snitch, working in concert with the cops. With Lopreste.

"Shit," Monique muttered as Dut and Armand passed by.

"Go home," Lopreste said, his voice quiet but urgent. "Not the hospital, not the dorm, but home. Pete's home. Understand?"

Monique nodded. She climbed into the car and Lopreste shut the door.

With tears in her eyes, Monique maneuvered the vehicle out of the parking lot towards Pete's dominion, back to Pete's protection.

I'm releasing you
moving on
checking the time wasted
shaking my head in shame
but no more looking back
dismissing you and all
this pain

Naw, I'm releasing this,
this magnetic thing
this animal attraction
so simply mis-termed love
got me stuck in an emotional rut
a bottomless pit
while lust disguises itself
hides the price of my soul
bartered out in pieces for
the mere association to you

Yeah, I'm releasing,
stepping forward into the sun
dusting off the coat of neglect
brushing away the lint of rejection
recognizing that my life has meaning

Despite my flaws,
within lies an inner beauty
an eternal pureness
I'm rebuilding my center
reconstructing my very core
pushing forward with my
eyes locked upward
finally realizing a future
Of my own

Finally, I'm releasing
leaving you and all your dirty
in the dark folds
of my past...

The Wrong He's Done
A Novel by
Nathan Gadsden

Greatness is only a step away for Damon Masters. Partnership at his firm is within his grasp, all Damon has to do is prove to the firm that he can handle its main client. His wife, Priscilla, has found entreprenuerial success at her boutique. The only speed bump in life is his annoying mother-in-law, Queen, whose jealous ways wreak havoc on his marriage. When the firms client turns out to be Frank Vanetti, mob boss and racketeer, Damon has to decide whether his life is worth risking for the idea of greatness. In the meantime, Queen has managed to split his household, leaving him to pick up the peices of his fractured marriage. With the help of his best friend, Antoine, Damon goes on a road trip to meet past loves and reevaluate where life went wrong. But walking away from Vanetti does not mean that Damon is safe from the mob. And best friend Antoine's schemes and manipulations seek to sabotage Damon's trip and further destroy what is left of his marriage. When ex-loves remind Damon of what he had, and all the drama and chaos of his current life become overwhelming, he must decide whether his current life is worth fighting for.

COMING SEPTEMBER 2010

Deceitfully **WICKED**

COMING WINTER 2010

The beauty in a nightmare became very real...

COMING 2011

PUBLICATIONS PRESENTS...

EVIL roots

A Novel By

M. McCall

COMING 2011

Publications Presents...

I'll Never Tell

Karmyn

COMING 2011